PASTURES NEW

Margaret Thornton

severn
House

This first world edition published 2017
in Great Britain and the USA by
SEVERN HOUSE PUBLISHERS LTD of
Eardley House, 4 Uxbridge Street, London W8 7SY.
Trade paperback edition first published
in Great Britain and the USA 2019 by
SEVERN HOUSE PUBLISHERS LTD.

British Library Cataloguing in Publication Data
A CIP catalogue record for this title is available from the British Library.

ISBN-13: 978-0-7278-8716-0 (cased)
ISBN-13: 978-1-84751-823-1 (trade paper)
ISBN-13: 978-1-78010-887-2 (e-book)

All Severn House titles are printed on acid-free paper.

Severn House Publishers support the Forest Stewardship Council™ [FSC™],
the leading international forest certification organisation.
All our titles that are printed on FSC certified paper carry the FSC logo.

Typeset by Palimpsest Book Production Ltd.,
Falkirk, Stirlingshire, Scotland.
Printed and bound in Great Britain by
TJ International, Padstow, Cornwall.

ONE

'What did I tell you? I knew they would rue the day they adopted that child. But would they listen? Oh, no! Mind you, I think it was Valerie that was keen on the idea and Samuel just went along with it.' Beatrice Walker was in high dudgeon, but her husband, Joshua, was used to her ways, knowing she was always determined to be proved right.

'Leave it alone, Beatrice,' he replied. 'I don't suppose the little lad is worse than any other child of his age. Damn it all! He's only just two years old. He's got plenty of time to improve. He's just a bit jealous, like, with the new baby coming along. Thinks his nose is being pushed out; it's only natural.'

'Yes, and that's another thing . . .' Beatrice would not be stopped. 'They didn't need to have adopted a child so soon. They'd only been married two years; no time at all, but Valerie was so determined to go ahead with it.'

'She'd had a miscarriage and one or two disappointments, though, hadn't she?'

'Yes, I know that, but no sooner had they adopted the child she finds she's pregnant again.'

'Well, she wasn't to know that, was she? I've heard that often happens and we were delighted about it, especially when she came through it all right this time. And she's a jolly good mother to both of them – you know that, Beattie.'

Beatrice bridled, as she always did when her husband used the name she had tried so hard to forget, the name she had been called when she was a girl. She had been known as Beattie Halliwell before she had married Joshua Walker, the mill owner's son, and taken a step up the social ladder. She had been an employee at a rival mill at the other side of town but had tried to forget her humble beginnings.

'I know she's a good mother, Joshua,' she replied. 'I've become fond of Valerie; she's a good wife to our Samuel as well.'

Beatrice had objected strongly at first when their younger son, Samuel, usually known as Sam, had told them that he intended to marry a young woman called Valerie Horrocks who was employed in the mill office. Sam's brother, Jonathan, had shown his displeasure, too, but he had changed his opinion since then and now agreed that Val was a most suitable wife for Sam. Beatrice, also, had been forced to eat her words when she was reminded that she, too, had married a mill owner's son and gone up in the world.

This conversation was taking place one evening in the September of 1960, at the home of Joshua and Beatrice in Queensbury, the rather select residential area of Halifax, at the top of the hill which rose from the town at the bottom of the valley. It was a substantial detached grey-stone house in its own grounds, and had been the home of the mill owners for three generations. When his father, Jacob, had retired, Joshua had taken over as the mill's manager and had gone to live at the family home. His parents, now in their late eighties, lived nearby, as did their two sons, Jonathan and Samuel, with their wives and children.

During the spring of the previous year, Val and Sam had adopted a little boy, Russell James, then seven months old. He was a local child who had been tragically orphaned when his young parents, only recently married, had been killed in a car crash. The people of the town had been saddened by the tragedy – none more so than Val, who had persuaded Sam that this was an ideal opportunity for them.

In the end he had not needed much convincing, as the child's great-grandfather, Charlie Pearson, was a valued employee at Walker's mill, having worked in the packing department ever since he was a lad. Charlie was now retired, and he and his wife, Alice, had been delighted at the turn of events. They were still in touch with their great-grandchild as Sam and Val took the little boy to see them regularly. This compensated, to a great degree, for the loss of their beloved granddaughter, and her parents, who had emigrated to Canada some years previously.

And then, in the autumn of 1959, when Russell was one year old, Val had discovered that she was pregnant again. She had believed that she would never be able to carry a child to full term, but this time she had done so. Their baby daughter, Lucy Elizabeth, had been born on the first day of June, 1960, a most welcome addition to the family.

The child's christening, a private baptism service at the local church, had taken place the previous Sunday. Beatrice had been shocked at the behaviour of Russell during the service, and afterwards at the little party held at the home of Sam and Val.

'Our little Rosemary behaved beautifully,' said Beatrice. 'I was so proud of her.' Rosemary was the daughter – the only child, so far – of Jonathan and his wife, Thelma.

'She is four years old,' said Joshua, 'and she's learnt that there are times when you have to be quiet. It's done her a world of good going to that playgroup. You can't compare her with a two-year-old. They're into everything then. Our Jonathan and Samuel were a handful at that age, if I remember rightly.'

'Then I don't think you remember rightly at all,' retorted his wife. 'They were very well-behaved little boys. I could take them anywhere; people used to say how good they were and what a credit to us.'

'Aye, maybe so. I'll grant that they behaved themselves pretty well when we took them places but they could be little tearaways at home, both of 'em. And Jonathan used to egg Samuel on. I remember then pulling up the flowers in the garden, saying they were helping Albert with the weeding. And you must recall the time they got into your make-up drawer. What a mess!'

'Mischievous, that's all,' countered Beatrice. 'They grew out of it.'

'And so will Russell. He'll settle down and get used to baby Lucy being around. He had their undivided attention until the new baby arrived and they probably made even more of him because he was adopted, to make sure he knew that he was loved and wanted.'

'And what will happen when he finds out he's not their child? Not their birth child, I mean. Isn't that what they call it? I know they refer to birth mothers nowadays. And there's a school of thought that believes you should tell the child the truth; tell him that he was a special baby because he was chosen by them. How would he react to that?'

Joshua sighed. 'Goodness me, Beatrice! I don't know. It's up to them, isn't it, what they decide to tell him? Let's cross that bridge when we come to it. They will have to sort something out because Charlie Pearson and his wife are taking an interest in the little lad. Only natural they should.'

'Maybe so, but it's a complication we could do without, if you ask me.'

Joshua longed to tell her that nobody was asking her but he held his tongue. 'I admit he's a lively lad,' he said, 'but I dare say that other little lad that was there – Walter's kiddie, Paul – was a handful when he was that age. I remember Walter saying so, but he's four now and he behaved very well at the christening. And so did the other children.'

'Yes, I forget who they all are,' said Beatrice. 'So many children, all over the place.'

'You know very well who they are,' said Joshua. 'Walter and Cissie have two children: Paul, and Holly – Holly is nearly three. A bonny little lass, the image of her mother. Cissie used to work at our place, you know.'

'Yes, I've heard you say she worked in the burling and mending room,' said Beatrice dismissively. 'Rather a . . . common sort of girl, I thought. I'm surprised that she and Valerie are such good friends. Chalk and cheese, aren't they?'

'Maybe so; I know Cissie isn't as ladylike as her friend but she's a grand lass and her heart's in the right place. The two girls have been friendly since they started school together when they were four years old. It's a long time. That's why Val asked her to be godmother to Russell, and to Lucy as well. And Walter is godfather to Russell; you remember that?'

'Yes, Walter Clarkson. He's one of your protégées, isn't he?'

'He's a good worker; been with us since he left school, apart from his National Service, of course. He's in charge of the weaving sheds now – a very responsible young man. And the other little girl belongs to Janice and Phil, the couple from Harrogate; Sarah, they call her. Val says she's just one year old. Nice little lass; Val and Cissie are her godmothers.'

'Janice; she's the girl from Blackpool, isn't she?'

'Yes, she's from Blackpool but she and Phil have a restaurant in Harrogate now – Grundy's, they call it; that's their surname and it's nice and easy to remember. I believe they're doing very well. Perhaps we could go over and have a meal there sometime?'

'Maybe we could.' But Beatrice did not sound too enthusiastic. 'I must admit that Janice seems a very pleasant girl – friendly, in a quiet sort of way. Not as loud and raucous as that other one, that Cissie!'

'Well, it takes all sorts,' replied Joshua, 'and the three lasses are good friends, despite their different backgrounds or whatever. They've got more friendly since Janice moved to Yorkshire, of course. That's a holiday friendship that has lasted.'

'And it's not the only one either,' said Beatrice feelingly. 'I must admit, though, Joshua, that it's turned out all right with our Samuel and Valerie – much better than I expected. It's a good thing it was Valerie he fell for and not the other one, Cissie!'

Joshua laughed. 'You're right there. I don't know how I'd fancy Cissie as a daughter-in-law!' Secretly, though, he liked Cissie. She reminded him of Marilyn Monroe, with her mass of blonde hair, big blue eyes and frivolity. He agreed, though, that his son had made the right choice with Valerie. 'Samuel's got good taste,' he added. 'And it'll work out all right with little Russell an' all. Sam and Val are good parents.'

He remembered only too well what Beatrice was referring to. It had been in the August of 1955, when Walker's mill closed for a week's annual holiday, that the two girls, Val and Cissie, had gone to Blackpool, staying at the boarding house – more of a private hotel by that time – run by Janice's mother. Sam had also gone to Blackpool with two friends for a golfing holiday, although they had sampled the attractions that the resort had to offer as well.

Sam and Val had met at the Winter Gardens ballroom when he had asked her for a dance. He had not recognized her as an office girl from Walker's mill but she had known him at once. She had told him that she was one of their employees but it had made no difference. The two young people were immediately attracted to one another and Sam had known that this was the girl he wanted to marry. There had been opposition, as he had expected, from his mother and his brother, but he had stood firm and they had married in the spring of 1957. And Valerie Horrocks, after a frosty reception from some members, had been accepted wholeheartedly into the Walker family.

In their semi-detached home, a half-mile or so from his parents' home, Sam and Val were also talking about Russell's behaviour. Not only at the christening, but the way he was behaving most of the time, especially since the arrival of baby Lucy three months ago.

Both children were in bed now, at seven o'clock. Fortunately Russell usually settled down to sleep when he had had his drink of milk and a biscuit and a bedtime story. By that time, of course, Lucy had been bathed and settled in her cot and he had his parents' undivided attention, which was what he wanted and expected at other times as well.

It was the Wednesday evening following the christening, and he had been particularly troublesome that day when Val had taken the two of them to the local shops.

'He hates having his reins on,' said Val, 'and I don't like it much either. He pulls like mad and I feel as though I'm taking a puppy for a walk. But he won't hang on to the handle of the pram. He just goes tearing off ahead and I can't let him do that, especially near the main road. And he's a nuisance in the shops. I feel embarrassed when I have to keep telling him not to touch the fruit or the sweets, and not to race around. I can see people looking at him and thinking, *What a badly behaved child!* I have to let go of his reins in the shop, and no way could I leave him with the pram while I go inside. I hardly ever take my eyes off the pram, of course. I see ladies peering in and smiling at Lucy. You never know, do you? You hear of babies being kidnapped but there's nothing else I can do while she's so small.'

'You worry too much, darling,' said Sam. 'Drink your sherry and try to relax.'

The two of them were enjoying a few moments' peace and quiet before they started their evening meal. It was a hectic time between five thirty and seven: Russell's tea time, then Lucy's feed and bath, then bedtime for the two of them. Sam shared the chores with his wife, knowing that she was not finding it easy with the two small children.

'I know you take very good care of Lucy,' he went on to say, 'but I think you're getting far too worked up about Russell. He's only just two. Haven't you heard parents talk about the "terrible twos"? I remember you told me that Cissie's little boy went through that stage, didn't he?'

'For a time, maybe, but he never seemed jealous of little Holly. You should see Russell's face when ladies look in the pram and say what a lovely baby Lucy is. He scowls and jumps up and down and starts jiggling the pram.'

'But it's rather foolish of people to admire the baby and ignore the little boy, isn't it? They should have more sense.'

'I don't suppose it occurs to them . . . I don't know, Sam.' Val shook her head in bewilderment. 'Cissie seems to be making a much better job of motherhood than I am. And to think what she was like before! A real flibbertigibbet – that's what my mother used to say. But look how she's settled down to it.'

'Nonsense! You're doing splendidly,' said Sam. 'You must try not to get so upset.'

Val sighed. 'I suppose so. Anyway, let's have our tea, shall we?'

She still called the evening meal 'tea', as they had done at her home, even though it was always a cooked meal of some sort. Sam took sandwiches to work for his midday snack, while Val made do with a sandwich or a quick toastie.

That evening it was a chicken casserole with mashed potato and carrots, the sort of meal that could be left in the oven to cook slowly once it was prepared. Apple tart was to follow with fresh cream. Val admitted that the tart had been bought from a local bakery.

'I wouldn't expect anything else,' Sam told her. 'Goodness me! I don't expect you to bake as well as looking after these two. They're a full-time job.' He tried to assure her again how well she was coping while they enjoyed the meal.

'He was dreadful in church, though,' she said, harking back to the christening again. 'Shouting and running up and down the aisle, then I think the penny dropped, somehow. You managed to restrain him and he seemed to realize that he had to be quiet. It might have been the way your mother glared at him! I could see she was horrified. "And our little Rosemary was so good," she said afterwards. I suppose we'll never hear the last of it. And Paul seemed to know how to behave as well.'

'They're two years older; it makes a lot of difference. They both go to Sunday school, don't they? And to a playgroup. They'll be starting school soon. Children seem to start long before they're five.'

'Goodness! How time flies. It doesn't seem long since Paul and Rosemary were born. Heaven help the teachers when Russell starts school if he doesn't calm down!'

'Don't be silly, love. It's ages off yet. But maybe . . . do you think he could go to a playgroup soon? Perhaps early next year? They take them at about two-and-a-half, don't they?'

'They like them to be toilet trained,' said Val. 'And thank goodness he's doing very well in that respect. He seems to know what's expected of him. That's one blessing, I suppose. Lucy gets through a mountain of nappies. I must say that Bendix washer is a godsend.'

'And you're happier now she's having a bottle, aren't you?' said Sam.

'Yes, I have to confess I am. I know some women love breastfeeding – Cissie did – but I found it rather messy; I never felt clean. Anyway, I had no choice when my milk dried up.'

'And now I can help with feeding times,' said Sam with a chuckle.

'I'm very pleased that you're willing to do that. I really mean it, Sam. A lot of men think it's nothing to do with them, that it's the woman's job. But times seem to be changing, gradually.'

'Yes, I don't think my father helped very much with us,' said Sam.

'No, nor did mine,' agreed Val, 'and my mum went out to work – only part-time, mind – when we were all at school. She never expected my dad to do anything in the house.'

Both Val's parents had been employed at Walker's mill. Bert still worked there in the packing department, although Sally Horrocks had finished long ago. Beatrice Walker, of course, had never gone out to work since she married the boss, and she had a woman to help with the running of the house as well.

'Anyway, it's my job to wash up now,' said Val, starting to

clear the table. 'You go and read the paper and I'll soon get rid of this lot.'

Val was thoughtful as she squeezed the washing-up liquid into the bowl and started to tackle the plates.

What a typically married couple we've become, she thought. Their recent conversation had been all about the children – mainly Russell's bad behaviour – nappies and washing machines, playgroups and children starting school . . . What a difference a couple of years had made.

They had been married for three years now – almost three and a half, to be exact. The first year had been a carefree and blissful time as they'd learnt more about each other. A time for entertaining friends and family members in their new home, making improvements to the house and garden, enjoying holidays together and, especially for Val, her first trip abroad, to Paris.

It was during their second year of marriage that Val – more particularly so than Sam – had started to feel that it would be lovely to have a child to make their married happiness complete. For a while, it had seemed that this was not to be. Disappointments month after month, and then a miscarriage at six months had made her feel depressed and inadequate. Returning to her job in the mill office, however, had done her a world of good. She had been feeling quite contented with her lot and resigned to letting things take their natural course.

And then everything had changed dramatically. It had seemed so right, an answer to their hopes and prayers, to adopt the baby who had been so tragically orphaned. And now, a little more than a year later, they had not one but two children. A boy and a girl, which many couples would regard as the ideal family.

But it had all happened so quickly that sometimes Val could hardly believe what had taken place. It had all started off so well with Russell. She had felt so proud pushing the pram around the neighborhood – an elegant Silver Cross pram, a gift from Sam's parents – and stopping to chat to passers-by who admired the bonny baby boy, seven months old at the time of his adoption. He had settled down so well with the two of them and he had already had a routine of feeding and sleeping.

Val had missed the early months, of course – a time when the child is so dependent on his mother for everything and when mother and baby form a bond, although it was said that this did not always happen. Val did feel, though, that she had formed a kinship with little Russell. His eyes would light up with recognition when he saw her, and it was the same with Sam as well. He smiled and gurgled, cut his baby teeth with the minimum of trouble and caused them very few sleepless nights.

Then there was the shock, albeit a pleasant one, of finding she was pregnant again. She had been worried at first that she might lose the baby, but all had gone well, despite her having to cope with an active little boy who was starting to walk at just over a year, and to talk as well, or at least attempt to do so.

He could certainly make himself understood now. One of the first words he had learnt to say was 'no!', but she gathered from talking to other mothers that this was not unusual. There came a time when a child changed from being dependent and obedient to wilful and difficult, realizing that he – or she – was a person in his or her own right, with ideas of his or her own which did not always agree with those of Mummy and Daddy.

Then baby Lucy had arrived, three months before Russell's second birthday. Val had been forewarned about the possible resentment and jealousy of an older child, and she had done her best to make sure that Russell was given as much love and attention as the new arrival. Unavoidably, though, much of her time was spent caring for the baby: breastfeeding at first, comforting her when she cried and making sure that she was always warm, dry and comfortable.

Val had formed a bond with the baby girl at once. It had seemed like a miracle that she and Sam had produced their own child. She was an adorable little girl with dark hair – quite a lot of it – like her mother's, and even at a few weeks' old she had a definite resemblance to both of them.

It was inevitable that Val's family members said, 'She is just like you, Val', whereas Sam's family, especially his mother, proclaimed that she was 'a real Walker'.

Val loved her more than she had imagined she could love

anyone; a different sort of love, though, from the love she felt for her husband or her parents. She loved Russell, too, of course she did. She wondered now, though, if those first few months made a vital difference. Was it possible to love an adopted child as much as a child who was one's own flesh and blood? It was a question she asked only of herself and not without a feeling of guilt. Until the arrival of Lucy, she would have said that she loved Russell just as much as she would her own child. But, now, she was not sure . . .

She became exasperated and worried when he defied her, quite blatantly sometimes, with a calculating look on his little face, as if daring her to chastise him. She felt at times that she almost disliked him, as well as feeling that she had no idea how to cope with him. She would never smack him; she knew that was not the answer, but cross words or even kind words seemed to make no difference.

She remembered how Sam's mother had objected to the adoption, pointing out that the child's background was far from desirable. The father had been estranged from his own parents and had married the mother only a few months before the child was born. A wild, irresponsible young fellow, according to some who knew him, although the child did seem to have been well-cared-for during his first few months of life.

Val and Sam had argued that that this would make no difference, that their nurture of the child would counteract that of nature and any undesirable traits that he might inherit. But Val, to her consternation, was now wondering if there might be some truth in what Beatrice had said. Was Russell already showing signs of the wildness and wilfulness that had been evident in his natural father? Or was he just a mischievous, determined little two-year-old like many his age?

Val sighed as she dried the pots and put them away. Time would tell, and in the meantime she must do her utmost to love and care for him as much as she cared for Lucy.

TWO

In the living room above the cafe premises, Phil and Janice Grundy were talking about the christening of Lucy Elizabeth Walker which they had attended the previous day. It had come as a pleasant surprise when Val and Sam had asked them both to be godparents to their baby girl.

Val and her friend, Cissie, had been godmothers to Janice and Phil's little girl, Sarah Lilian, so it had not been too much of a surprise for Janice to be asked, but it was nice that Phil, also, had been invited to be her godfather.

'I was quite taken aback to be asked, but delighted, of course,' he remarked. 'It's great how our friendship with Val and Sam has continued. It was certainly an eventful meeting, that night in the Winter Gardens . . .'

It was in the August of 1955 when they had all met in the ballroom of the Winter Gardens in Blackpool. Val and Cissie had been staying at the Florabunda Hotel at the northern end of the town, and they had invited Janice, who, as the landlady's daughter was helping out as a waitress, to go dancing with them. Val and Sam had become acquainted for the first time that night, although she had known him already as the boss's son. Phil and Janice, also, had met when he'd asked her to dance with him.

Phil had been in the RAF at the time, nearing the end of his National Service, stationed at Weeton Camp, a few miles from Blackpool. If not exactly love at first sight, there had been an immediate attraction between the two of them. Their friendship had developed gradually into the certainty that they wanted to be together for always, and they had married in the spring of 1958.

'And now here we are,' Phil went on, 'old married couples with families. Cissie and Walter as well; we mustn't forget them. Just imagine that! Who'd have thought it?'

Cissie, to her annoyance, had not met 'anyone special' that

evening and had returned home to Halifax to marry her boyfriend, Walter Clarkson, with whom she had been having an on-off friendship for a few years.

'Val has certainly got her hands full with those two,' said Janice. 'The last time we saw little Russell he seemed to be quite well behaved. I do hope he'll settle down again. She looked so embarrassed when he wouldn't keep quiet, then Sam managed to restrain him by holding him firmly; he was wriggling like an eel, though. And the other children were so good; Cissie and Walter's two, and Rosemary and our little Sarah.'

'Don't speak too soon!' said Phil with a chuckle. 'You never know what's ahead. A few months makes a big difference, and the last time we saw Russell it was before the baby was born. A touch of jealousy, I suppose, especially as there's less than two years between them.'

'Yes, Val had given up hope of them having their own child. They hadn't been married all that long but she'd been disappointed so many times. It happened so soon, though, just as they were getting used to having Russell . . . I certainly wouldn't want another baby, not just yet.'

'Message received and understood,' said Phil with a grin. 'You're doing really well, though, love; looking after Sarah and running the cafe as well.'

'Not without help. Marjorie's a real treasure; I couldn't manage without her, and we've been very lucky with the waitresses. And Toby's an excellent chef, isn't he?'

Phil agreed that they had been very fortunate with their staff. They had all worked together as a team and Grundy's had become a popular venue for local people and visitors to the town of Harrogate since the opening two years previously.

When they had met in the summer of 1955, Janice and Phil had discovered that they had similar backgrounds and this, as much as anything, had helped to cement their growing friendship.

Janice had been working as a waitress in the hotel run by her mother, Lilian Butler, marking time until starting her university course in September. Phil, about to complete his National Service, was to return to Ilkley to help his father run the Coach and Horses, a country pub and restaurant, once a coaching inn. His two years in the RAF had interrupted his training as a chef, learnt partly from his father and partly from night-school classes.

They had planned to meet again when Janice started her university course in Leeds, not far from Ilkley. Fate had stepped in, however, and their plans had changed. In early September, Lilian had been taken ill suddenly with a brain tumour. Janice had decided not to go away to college but to stay and run the hotel, to the best of her ability, with the help of the assistants who had worked with Lilian.

Phil, on hearing of their predicament, had come, with the total agreement of his father, to help at the Florabunda Hotel until the holiday season finished in October, when the illuminations came to an end.

Lilian had never fully recovered from her operation and died early the following year. Phil had still been helping there but he'd had his own work with his father to return to, and Janice had known that she could not run the hotel on her own. It had been quite a wrench for the Butler family when they'd sold the hotel and moved to a bungalow near to Stanley Park on the outskirts of town.

Janice had known by this time that her future lay in the catering business. She'd given up all thoughts of university and enrolled for a year's course at a catering college in Blackpool, after which she'd worked for a while at a seafront hotel.

Her friendship with Phil had blossomed into love and they were married in 1958. Phil had had a stroke of good fortune. He had long wanted a place of his own, not wishing to work with his father for evermore. Then his elderly aunt, his mother's much older sister, died and made him almost her sole beneficiary. Not a vast fortune but enough to buy a place that he and Janice could run together.

They had looked for premises close to Ilkley, although Phil had not wanted to set up in opposition to his father. Then, searching a little further afield, they had found just the place they wanted in Harrogate. A shop, with vacant possession, at the end of a terrace, it had once been a bakery. It was a half-mile or so from the town, facing the vast expanse of grassland known as the Stray.

It had needed a lot of renovating but they had opened eventually in the summer of 1958. They had decided on the name Grundy's, their own surname – short and easy to remember. It was a cafe, or tearoom, rather than a restaurant. They served morning coffee – or tea – light lunches and afternoon teas. After a while they started to open in the evenings for private pre-booked parties: family celebrations or small gatherings of friends.

The downstairs dining room, which could seat up to eighteen – although this was rather a tight squeeze – overlooked the peaceful scene of the Stray. The upstairs family accommodation was adequate for the time being: a large living room, kitchen, bathroom and two bedrooms. Sarah, at the moment, was sleeping on a cot in their bedroom but they knew that arrangement could not carry on indefinitely. She would need her own room before long and a bed instead of a cot.

The spare bedroom was used for visitors, not that there were many who stayed overnight. The exception was Ian, Janice's younger brother, who came to stay with them during his school holidays. Not just as a guest, however. He helped in the cafe, mainly as a waiter, but also worked in the kitchen doing odd jobs: washing up, preparing vegetables and being generally useful. Over the last year, during his visits at Christmas and the Easter holidays, he had shown more interest in the cooking and preparation of food. So much so that he had decided, as his sister had done, that his future lay in the catering business.

He had spent one year in sixth form at the grammar school in Blackpool, then, instead of going into the upper sixth, he had enrolled at the catering college in Blackpool where Janice had done most of her training.

'Do you think Ian will come and work here, as usual, during the holidays?' Phil asked now.

'Possibly,' replied Janice, 'but you never know what possibilities might arise in Blackpool. There are so many hotels looking for staff and he'll meet all sorts of different people. Who knows what opportunities might come his way.'

'I was rather surprised he decided to stay in Blackpool to do his training,' said Phil. 'I would have thought, under the circumstances, he might have preferred to go away to a residential college.'

'You heard what he said, though. Dad persuaded him it would be more sensible to stay at home; cheaper for one thing, and the Blackpool college has a good reputation.'

'Even so, it might have done him good to get right away,' said Phil.

Ian was Janice's only brother, six years younger than herself. He had been twelve years old when his mother died and it had come as a dreadful shock to him, as it had to Janice and her father, Alec. Ian, though, had kept his feelings to himself, not speaking much about his sadness. He'd still felt secure in his home background and the love of his father and sister. Although there was quite an age difference, the two of them had been close, more so than many siblings.

Ian had been upset when Janice and Phil got engaged, even though he liked Phil and regarded him very much as an elder brother. He had reacted quite badly when he realized they would be living in Yorkshire after their marriage. He had seemed to imagine they would stay in Blackpool and the status quo would remain unchanged.

The final blow for Ian had been when, two years after his mother's death, his father had remarried.

'He's in a much better frame of mind, though, now,' Janice went on. 'I noticed a great change in him this summer.'

Ian had spent the summer break working with them at Grundy's before starting his college course.

Janice was aware of how much he had matured. Just turned seventeen, he was a good-looking lad, dark-haired like his father but much taller and slimmer, with grey eyes that were more often thoughtful than shining with humour. Janice and Phil had told him how pleased they were that he had finally decided on his future career.

'I thought at one time you'd fancied being a car mechanic,' Phil had reminded him just before he started his course.

'Just a passing phase, that time I stayed with Uncle Len,' Ian had responded. 'I enjoyed tinkering about with cars but Len owns his own garage and it would be ages before I could do that. I got really interested in your business while I was

working here, and then I thought, yes! That's what I'd like
to do; train to be a proper chef, like you are, Phil. But I suppose
it's also something I've inherited from my mum and my
grandma before her.'

'You never had anything to do with the hotel, though,' Janice
had said, 'or boarding house, as it used to be called.'

'No, but I was too young, wasn't I?'

'I dare say Mum would have wanted you to go to university
like she wanted me to do, to have all the chances she and Dad
never had – that's what she used to say. It was always her idea
rather than mine that I should go, but it wasn't to be . . .'

'Dad never had much to do with the hotel, either, did he?'
Ian had said.

'Not with the running of it, no, but he was always there to
lend a hand when she needed him. He used to carry the luggage
upstairs and do any odd jobs that arose. And he had his own
job of work to go to each day; he still does, of course.'

Alec Butler worked as a maintenance engineer for an electrical
company. He had originally lived in Burnley, where he worked
in the cotton mill. But after meeting and falling in love with
Lilian at her mother's boarding house, he had given up his job
– and chance of promotion – to come and live in Blackpool.
That had been back in the early thirties, and there had been no
question of Lilian moving to Burnley. She could not be spared
from the boarding house where she worked for her mother, with
hardly more than pocket money for pay.

Florence Cartwright, always known as Florrie, had been a
hard taskmaster, like many of her ilk. Widowed during the Great
War, she had moved to Blackpool from Wigan with her two
children and had become a seaside landlady, largely self-taught
with only skills in cooking and baking that she'd learnt from
her own mother.

And so it had been with her daughter, Lilian. She had left
school at fourteen and started work in the North Shore boarding
house, no matter what other ideas she might have had regarding
her own choice of work. What Florrie Cartwright said went
without question.

Lilian had worked uncomplainingly, though, before and after
her wedding, and had carried on with the business after her

mother's death. She had insisted, however, that it should then
be known as a private hotel rather than a boarding house. And
she had given it a name, Florabunda, partly in memory of her
mother and partly because she loved Florabunda roses; something which Florrie would have called ostentatious and having
ideas above one's station!

'You'll be more highly trained than any of us once you've
finished your training,' Phil had told Ian, who was starting on
a two-year course. Janice had done only one year. 'Times have
changed tremendously. In your grandma's day the folk who
ran hotels – well, boarding houses – were self-taught; skills
were handed down, mother to daughter, through the generations. It was mainly the women, of course, who were in charge
of such places.'

'Yes, I remember Grandma Florrie,' Janice had said. 'You
won't remember much about her, Ian. She never had a proper
cookery lesson in her life and she handed on what she knew
to our mother. Mum did go to some night-school classes as
well, though, to learn about what she called more fancy dishes.
In Grandma's day it was just plain, wholesome food: Lancashire
hotpot, Shepherd's pie, sausage and mash, fish and chips . . .
but the same visitors used to come back year after year.
Florrie Cartwright had a good reputation and so did Mum when
she took over.

'Mum changed things quite a lot, though. For one thing, she
changed the tariff to bed, breakfast and evening meal instead
of providing three meals a day, like they did in Grandma's day.
It must have been jolly hard work: cooked breakfast, midday
dinner and what they called "high tea". Anyway, when it changed
it gave the workers some free time in the middle of the day,
and it gave the visitors the whole day as well so they could go
further afield if they wanted to, although hardly any of them
came in their own cars.'

'And there would be a change in the menu, too,' Phil had
added. 'I don't suppose your grandma had ever heard of "starters",
Janice!'

'Good gracious, no! She would have thought that was a very
odd idea. No, it was just dinner and pudding – usually rice, or
fruit tart with custard, or steamed puddings. I don't suppose

anyone bothered about their waistlines! Of course, people did a lot more walking then. Mum tried to get away from the stodgy sort of puddings – she did more trifles or ice cream, or meringue dishes. And gateaux, but she used to buy them ready-made. That was what I specialized in at college: cake and pastry-making. I wanted to become more professional.'

'And so you did,' Phil had told her. 'Your fancy cakes and pastries are really out of this world. There are hardly ever any left at the end of the day.'

'And I've even managed to perfect my choux pastry, with Marjorie's help. The eclairs and choux buns are very popular. I think we're a good team, Phil, with you concentrating on the main savoury dishes – not forgetting Toby and Marjorie, of course.'

'And we mustn't forget Ian, either,' Phil had said, grinning at his young brother-in-law. 'You've worked really hard for us and I like to think we've taught you something as well. But you're going to learn more about the catering business from the real experts . . . You're still quite happy about staying in Blackpool, are you?'

'Yes, I'm OK about it now. It makes sense to live at home rather than in digs. And I'm learning to live with the situation; with Dad and Norma, I mean.' He'd given a rueful grin. 'I never really disliked Norma, you know. Actually, she's jolly nice. But it was such a shock when Dad said they were getting married. I didn't think he would ever want anybody else after Mum. And she's so different from Mum, not just in looks but in . . . everything.'

They had known what Ian meant; they'd had this sort of conversation before.

A few months after Lilian's death, one of Alec's workmates had invited him to go along to a social club he attended. It was not the sort of thing Alec had done before. He had enjoyed an occasional pint at the local pub, and he and Lilian had gone out to a cinema or maybe to a church social evening when she was not too busy with the hotel. It had seemed that Alec and Lilian were all in all to one another; certainly Ian had thought so.

Alec found that he enjoyed the club and the camaraderie of

the men – mostly men although some of the wives went along as well. He played darts and became a member of the team, and played bowls during the summer season.

Norma served at the bar and joined in the other activities as well. Alec had been attracted to the dark-haired, vivacious widow, although he was wary at first. But her overtures to him were only friendly, to make him feel welcome there; she was that sort of person.

Their growing friendship had developed into something more and they had married barely two years after his wife's death, which seemed a very short time to Ian. She had sold her own home and come to live at the bungalow. Norma worked in the dress department at a store in Blackpool and was always well-groomed and fashionably dressed. A most attractive lady all round, and she had done her best to be friendly and understanding towards Ian, who was in his early teens.

Although he was never openly rude or antagonistic towards her, she knew of his resentment. Then, one Christmas, he had fled from his home and gone to stay with Janice and Phil. They had tried to make him realize that life would be much easier if he learnt to adjust to what had happened. And now, a couple of years later, things were much better.

'Yes, we've always found Norma very pleasant,' Janice had said in answer to his remark. 'She was great when we opened up here, helping me to choose the crockery and furnishings. And she makes Dad happy again. We mustn't resent him finding a new lease of life, Ian. He's only in his early fifties and Norma's about the same age.'

'No, like I said, I'm OK now,' Ian had reassured her. 'I expect I'll be out a lot more when I start the course. Actually, I'm really looking forward to it, now that I've made up my mind.'

'And Sophie will be looking forward to her college course as well,' Janice had said. 'We'll miss her here, unless she comes to work for us during the college breaks, although she might have a lot of studying to do.'

'Yes . . .' Ian had looked woebegone for a moment. 'We've said we'll write to one another and meet up when we can, but who knows?' He'd shrugged and given a sad smile.

'Cheer up,' Phil had told him. 'You're only very young, both of you, but if it's right it will work out for you, like it did for Janice and me.'

'We're only friends,' Ian had said. 'Well . . . a little bit more than that but nothing serious, if you know what I mean. But I like her a lot.'

Sophie Miller was Ian's first girlfriend. She lived not far from Grundy's and had worked as a waitress, along with some other friends, during the school holidays. That was how she and Ian had met. Sophie was eighteen, a year older than Ian, and would very soon be starting a teacher training course at a college in Leeds, living there in a hall of residence.

'What will be, will be,' Phil had told Ian. 'Just try to look forward, not back, and make the most of whatever comes along. I'm sure you'll go far, Ian; you've got what it takes.'

Ian had returned to Blackpool soon after to prepare for his new venture.

And now, a couple of weeks later, Janice and Phil were wondering how he was going on, both he and Sophie at her college in Leeds.

'It will do Ian good to meet a whole lot of different people.' said Phil. 'He met Sophie when he was feeling all lost and sorry for himself. She was good for him but, as I told him, what will be, will be . . .'

THREE

As Christmas approached Grundy's began to get very busy, particularly in the evenings. When they had first opened they had concentrated on the daytime trade: morning coffee, light lunches and afternoon teas. That had been plenty to cope with when they were finding their feet and waiting to see if their new venture would prove popular.

Quite soon Grundy's had become well known in the area, and it was then that Phil decided they would open in the evenings, but only in a small way, for private parties that must be pre-booked. The customers were given a choice of menus from which to choose in advance and the system had worked very well. They were particularly busy on Saturday evenings and often opened two or three other evenings each week. They always closed on Sunday for the whole day. Sunday was still, by and large, regarded as a day of rest, whether one chose to think of it as the Sabbath Day or just a time for relaxation.

By the end of October they were almost fully booked for evenings in the month of December. They always closed down entirely over the Christmas period, finishing at teatime on Christmas Eve and reopening on 28 December. They had always wanted this time of year to themselves to see their families and, particularly now, to spend time with their little daughter, Sarah.

'If these bookings continue we shall need larger premises,' Phil remarked to Janice at the beginning of November as he pencilled in yet another date. He was laughing as he said it but she could tell that an idea was taking shape in his mind.

'Do you mean it?' she asked. 'Really?'

'Well, it's a thought,' he replied. 'We always knew the cafe area was small and it does OK for the daytime trade – for people popping in for a quick snack or a chat over a cup of tea or coffee. But the evenings are proving more popular than I dared to hope. And we can't accept bookings for more than sixteen, or eighteen at a pinch. They need space to move around.'

'But we don't have the space, do we? There's the kitchen at the back, and the storeroom, so we can't extend any more there. And upstairs it's our own private place.'

'Yes, I know, but we've said that we really need another bedroom. Sarah ought to have her own room soon, and that means we won't have a spare room for when Ian comes to stay, or anyone else for that matter. I was wondering . . . if we could find a house nearby . . .?' He stopped, looking at Janice quizzically.

'Go on,' she said, smiling at him encouragingly but with a touch of amusement. 'I'm trying to keep up with you. You and your big ideas!'

'Well, we could turn the upstairs into a restaurant, just for the evening functions. And this is a good residential area; I'm sure we could find a house nearby – it would have to be quite near – and use these premises just as our workplace.'

'Phew! You're certainly ambitious. But there's a lot to consider. Can we afford it? I know we're doing quite well but we mustn't bite off more than we can chew. And think of all the work involved. A lot of structural work, and wouldn't we need another kitchen upstairs?'

'Possibly. I haven't really thought about the details. Perhaps it's just a pipe dream. Let's wait till after Christmas and see what the bookings are like in the New Year.'

'Yes, we've quite enough to think about at the moment . . .'

Janice felt somewhat bewildered. She hadn't realized that Phil had such grandiose schemes. She was quite contented with the way things were, especially as Sarah, at fifteen months, was starting to walk and needed watching most of the time.

She was a good child, though, and Janice was able to fit her work around mealtimes and rest times. She made sure she had time to devote to Sarah each day – to take her for a little walk, to supervise her meals now she was eating more than baby food, and to make bathtime and bedtime a happy time for both of them.

'Yes, we'll think more about it in the New Year,' she said to Phil, not wanting to dismiss his idea entirely. 'We have this Christmas to consider first. Christmas Day is on a Sunday, which is our day off anyway.'

'And people might have Tuesday off work as well as Monday,' added Phil, 'in lieu of Boxing Day. So we should certainly do the same. Close at teatime on Saturday – Christmas Eve – and open again on the following Thursday. That will give us a few days to ourselves.'

'I'm pleased that Ian is coming to help us again,' said Janice. 'I thought he might have been offered work at one of the Blackpool hotels. A lot of them do a special four-day Christmas break. But he decided he wanted to come here as usual.'

'And we'll be glad of his help too,' agreed Phil. 'We're fully booked every evening the week before Christmas. We'll certainly be ready for a few days' break after that.'

'I don't suppose we are the only attraction,' said Janice. 'No doubt he'll be meeting up with Sophie again, although he hasn't actually said so.'

'And she hasn't said that she wants to help out here, either. It might be expecting too much of her after her first term at college. She'll probably be ready for a rest. We could take on a couple of students, though, like we've done before; those sixth formers from the girls' school are keen to earn some pocket money. Or do you think we can manage without them?'

'You never know from day to day with the morning and afternoon trade. Sometimes it's crowded and other times we only get a few. A lot depends on the weather. It's a fair distance to walk from town if it's raining. Some women like to pop in for tea or coffee when they've done their shopping – those that live locally. Some ladies make it a special meeting place. Groups of them come in the same day each week; older ladies, though, the ones who have no children to look after.'

'Or no work to go to,' added Phil. 'I know there are quite a lot of ladies of leisure in Harrogate who don't need to work.'

'And we don't get any riff-raff, either,' remarked Janice. 'Oh, dear! That sounds terribly snobbish, doesn't it? But you know what I mean, don't you? It's a very genteel sort of place, where people come to retire. I'm so glad we managed to find it. A real stroke of good fortune, wasn't it?'

'Good fortune followed by hard work,' added Phil. 'Don't let's forget that we've made it a success, the two of us and our excellent staff. Anyway, let's think about Christmas. What are we going to do? Same as usual? We usually go to see my parents on Boxing Day. OK with you?'

'Of course,' agreed Janice. 'We're always made so welcome and they'll be looking forward to seeing Sarah again. It's amazing the difference only a few weeks makes when they're at the baby stage. I'm not too sure about going to Blackpool, though. It's a long way to travel for a day, although I suppose we could stay overnight? But Ian will be with us and he'd have to go back with us, probably sooner than he intended. And there wouldn't be room for us all in their little bungalow. Isn't life complicated?'

'Only if we make it so,' replied Phil, always ready to come up with a solution to a problem. 'We must see your dad and Norma, and they'll be anxious to see Sarah again. Supposing they were to come here instead of us going there? No, I know we haven't much room either, but they could have our bedroom. We could make do on the couch for one night . . .'

'No, I've a better idea,' said Janice. 'They must have the spare room. Ian won't mind camping out in the living room; we've got a comfy couch. That is if they want to come . . . Did you mean the day after Boxing Day?'

'Yes, of course. I didn't mean Christmas Day. We like that day to ourselves. I know it will mean extra work when they come but don't worry about that. I shall see to the cooking and Ian will be here to help me. Then you can have some time with your dad and Norma. What do you think?'

'Yes, it's a good idea. Depending on what they say, of course. They might have other plans. They've a lot of friends, people from the club, and there's Norma's sister . . .'

'Well, we'll ask them and see how they feel about it.'

Alec and Norma were delighted when Janice invited them to go to Harrogate on the Tuesday after Christmas and to stay overnight. She had phoned one evening in mid-November when they were on their own, Ian having gone out to meet some friends, as he quite often did since he had started at the college.

'How very kind of them,' said Norma, 'especially as they'll be so busy over the Christmas period. I think Janice has really accepted me, hasn't she? I know it must have been hard for her, losing her mum and then embarking on a career change.'

'I don't think there was ever much opposition from Janice once she'd got used to the idea. She's a sensible girl, and she had Phil with her, of course. Their friendship was starting to develop so she had other things to think about. I'm glad they decided to make a go of it. We liked Phil straight away, Lilian and me, when she brought him home. I know Lilian would be pleased to see them happily married and doing so well.'

'And there's been a change in Ian, hasn't there, since he started at the college?' said Norma. 'He seems much more relaxed and at ease with himself now.'

'Yes, I'm relieved he's settled down and decided what he wants to do. I was quite surprised, though, when he decided to go into the catering business. But I know he's always admired Phil; he looked on him as an elder brother, although he had it in his mind that they would stay in Blackpool and run a guest house here after they were married.'

'Yes, poor lad! He lost his mum and then he found out his sister would be leaving. I'm not surprised he resented me at first.'

'Yes . . . I'm sorry. He could be damned awkward and moody. And I must admit I wasn't quite sure how to handle it. You were so patient, love, and understanding, when I'm sure you must have felt like throttling him!'

Norma laughed. 'Well, we're OK now, Ian and me. He'll be over there in Harrogate, helping them out, won't he, when we go? He'll probably think he's got away from us for a while until we turn up again, like a bad penny!'

'He won't bother. Like you said, he's much more relaxed about everything now. And don't forget, he'll be seeing his girlfriend, Sophie, while he's there. He doesn't say very much about her – can't expect him to – but we've seen letters with a Leeds postmark, haven't we? I'm sure he'll be looking forward to seeing her again.'

'They're only young, though, Alec. And Sophie's a year older than Ian, isn't she? She's at a coed college, I believe; there are young men there as well as girls. She'll no doubt meet lots of different people. It's too much to expect that she won't meet someone else, and Ian too, of course. He goes out a lot more than he used to. Where is he tonight?'

'I don't know,' replied Alec, 'and I didn't ask. We can't treat him like a child any more. He's never all that late coming in and he never has too much to drink.'

'He shouldn't be in pubs at all, should he?' said Norma. 'He's only seventeen.'

'Yes, I know, but he looks older and I'm sure bar staff turn a blind eye unless there's any trouble. I know I have to let go of the reins and trust him, and I'm sure he won't let us down.'

FOUR

C issie Clarkson pulled her chair closer to the fire and took a long drag at her cigarette. With a cup of tea on a stool at her side, she was relaxing after taking Paul to his infant school, just five minutes' walk away.

The house felt quiet without him, although Holly was still at home, now playing quietly on the hearth rug with her dolls and teddy bear. She had always been a quieter, much more gentle child than Paul, although the two of them had got along well together, probably because they were quite close in age. Paul was now four-and-a-half and had started school three months ago. Holly would be three on Christmas Day, now only a couple of weeks away. She missed her brother and didn't understand why she couldn't go to school with him.

'Mummy . . . when can I go to school, like Paul?' was her constant cry.

And Cissie tried to placate her, saying, 'Soon, love; perhaps after Christmas, when you're three. It won't be long.'

She hadn't told her, though, that it would not be the school that Paul attended. There was a playgroup not very far from the school and Cissie had made enquiries there. Yes, they would be willing to take Holly; in fact, they took children as young as two-and-a-half, provided they were no longer in nappies and were quite happy about being parted from Mummy. Cissie's neighbour, Megan, who lived a few doors away, took her little girl, Kelly, there each day, so Cissie felt sure that Holly would settle in spite of being separated from her brother.

'And then what will I do with so much free time on my hands?' Cissie asked herself. Not all that much time, really, because the playgroup was only in the morning, although the children could stay for lunch, if the parents wished, at a nominal charge.

Paul stayed for school dinners, as did most of the children. He went off each Monday morning with his five shillings of dinner money – two half-crown pieces – in an envelope tucked away safely in his pocket. He enthused about the dinners: meat and potato pie, big fat sausages, spaghetti in tomato sauce and sometimes even fish and chips. And the yummy puddings: jam roly-poly, spotted dick, jelly and custard . . . He even liked the rice pudding, which some children hated, served with a dollop of red jam that they stirred to make the rice turn pink. Paul seemed to like them all. He had never been a picky eater but Cissie wondered if her culinary efforts did not match up to the dinners served at school. Fortunately they were cooked on the premises in the school's own kitchen, not delivered in tins as was the case at many of the schools.

Cissie had settled down well to her duties as a housewife and mother, to the surprise of many of her friends, who remembered her as a carefree, sometimes irresponsible girl. She had, in fact, surprised herself. Paul had been born only six months after their marriage. Cissie, at first, had regretted what had happened and resented her loss of freedom. Her bitterness, however, had been short-lived, and when Holly was born eighteen months later her new-found joy in her marriage was complete.

There had been one or two upsets and misunderstandings but they were on an even keel again now and looking forward to Christmas.

Paul was in a constant state of excitement about all that was happening at school. Next week would be a very busy time, with the school concert and then a party for all the children, when they expected a special visitor with a sack of presents.

Cissie had received an invitation to the concert but she was sorry that Walter, like most of the fathers, would be unable to attend as it was in the afternoon. She had provided Paul with a striped tea towel, as requested, for his part in the performance.

'It's to wear round my head, Mummy, 'cause I'm one of the people who live in Bethlehem – that's where baby Jesus was born – an' I can wear my dressing gown.'

He'd explained that he didn't have anything to say. The important parts like Mary and Joseph, the shepherds and the kings were for the older children, but she understood that every child took part, if only in a small way. And they all sang the carols. Every night they were entertained with Paul's rendition of 'Away in a Manger' and 'We Will Rock You', with Holly joining in as well.

'And we're making all sorts of surprises to bring home, Mummy, but it's a secret.'

He had asked for the inside of a toilet roll and an empty washing-up liquid – or similar – bottle, so she was looking forward to seeing the masterpieces that were being created.

'I can't wait for this one to start school!' her friend, Val, had said with feeling when she had seen her the previous week. 'Well, not school; playgroup, perhaps, if they'll take him. They might teach him to behave himself. I'm blessed if I can!'

Cissie had taken Holly on a bus up to Queensbury to visit her friend. Val had found it difficult to get to Cissie's home with six-month-old Lucy in the pram and Russell to cope with as well.

Cissie felt concerned to see her friend so harassed but Russell really was a little demon. She could not recall that Paul had ever been so bad, although he had had his moments. They had not been in the house very long before Russell had snatched Holly's doll and thrown it across the room, making the little girl cry. No harm had been done as the doll had landed on the carpet with its china face intact.

Val had chastised Russell, shaking him a little and telling him he was a very naughty boy.

'Now say you're sorry to Holly.'

'Sorry . . .' he'd said, looking sheepish for a moment, then he'd snuggled up to Val, wanting attention. She'd ruffled his reddish golden hair and given him a quick hug.

Holly had stopped crying when she saw her precious Belinda was not hurt, and the two children were persuaded to 'play nicely now', with building bricks and toy cars while their mothers had a cup of tea.

'He'll settle down, you'll see,' Cissie had tried to convince her friend, although, secretly, she thought the child was getting out of control. Val was such a sensible person; one she had thought could cope with almost anything.

Russell was a bonny little boy but, understandably, he did not resemble either of his adoptive parents. Val was dark-haired and so was baby Lucy, and Sam's mid-brown hair had no trace of auburn. It seemed as though Russell would be red-haired with, possibly, a temperament to match. Only time would tell.

'I certainly hope he'll settle down soon,' Val had said in answer to her friend's remark. 'I keep thinking about what Sam's mother said; that he might inherit bad traits from his real parents; his father, she meant, of course. She was very much opposed to us adopting Russell. Sam's dad tries to show no difference in his attitude to the two of them, but I'm afraid that Beatrice makes it quite obvious that Lucy is the favourite. She makes such a fuss of her and Russell can't help but notice it.'

'She should have more sense, silly old cow!' Cissie had said in her usual forthright way. 'So . . . are you looking forward to Christmas?'

'I suppose so . . .' Val had answered doubtfully. Then, 'Yes, of course I am,' she'd amended. 'It's more fun when you have children, although Russell is rather young to understand fully about Father Christmas and Lucy is still a baby.'

'Father Christmas will be visiting both of them, though, won't he?'

'Oh, yes, we took Russell to Bradford to see him. He was rather overawed for once but he managed to say that he wanted a car and a fire engine. We told him Father Christmas would come if he was a good boy and he was very good for that day. We'd left Lucy with my mum so he had our undivided atten-tion. He's having a pedal car for Christmas,' she'd whispered, although the children hadn't seemed to be listening to the conversation. 'That was Sam's idea; he had one when he was a little boy and he loved it. What about you? What is he bringing to your house?'

'Paul wants a tricycle, and Holly . . .' The little girl had looked up at hearing her name. 'Holly, tell Auntie Val what you want Father Christmas to bring,' Cissie had said.

'A doll's pram,' Holly had replied, 'and a baby doll with lots of nice clothes. And Paul wants a tricycle.'

'Well, we'll have to wait and see, won't we?' Cissie had said. 'It's her birthday, of course, on Christmas Day,' she'd added quietly, 'so we'll have to make sure she doesn't miss out. It makes it an expensive time but it isn't her fault, is it, that she was born at Christmas? Now, am I going to have a look at my goddaughter before we go?'

Lucy had been upstairs having her afternoon nap. 'Of course,' Val had said. 'It's time she was awake. I'll go and get her.'

She'd returned with the wide-awake baby, who'd had no objection to being nursed and fussed by her Auntie Cissie.

'Isn't she lovely, Mummy?' Holly had said, gently stroking the baby's cheek. And Lucy had smiled at her, her little face lighting up as though she knew her.

Russell hadn't looked up. Cissie had been aware that he was scowling. He'd started to make loud 'brumm, brumm' noises with his cars, crashing them into the table legs.

Cissie had handed Lucy back to her mother. 'Show me your favourite car, Russell,' she'd said to the little boy. 'I like this one.' She'd picked up a bright red sports car. 'I wish I had a car like this.' But he'd shook his head and scowled again. Val had looked annoyed but knew better than to force him to comply. It would do more harm than good.

'Well, it's time we were going,' Cissie had said cheerfully. 'We mustn't be late meeting Paul from school. Come along now, Holly. Say bye-bye to Auntie Val and Russell . . .' Cissie had bent down to give the little boy a hug but he had not responded.

Val had kissed Holly's cheek then put her arm round her friend. 'See you again soon, Cissie. Love to Paul and Walter . . .'

'Russell's a naughty boy, isn't he, Mummy?' Holly had remarked as they walked to the bus stop. 'I don't think I like him very much. But I like Lucy.'

'Perhaps he was just feeling a bit cross,' Cissie had answered. 'We do sometimes, don't we?' She had thought to herself, though, that Holly's reaction was no doubt the same as that of many other people. Poor Val! Cissie hoped that her friend had not made a dreadful mistake.

Cissie, in common with many other mothers who were watching, brushed away a tear as the children performed the age old nativity play. Holly, sitting next to her, was enthralled by it all. The angelic-looking Mary, gazing tenderly at the doll in her arms, and Joseph standing proudly by her side; the shepherds with tea towel headdresses slightly awry; and the kings, resplendent in gold cardboard crowns and robes created from mothers' old evening gowns. Paul, as he had said, was 'just a person from Bethlehem', but he sang lustily and was clearly enjoying it all.

There was a fun part to the concert as well as the story of baby Jesus. Children dressed as Christmas crackers, fairies and teddy bears, and rousing choruses of 'Santa Claus is Coming to Town' and 'Rudolph the Red-nosed Reindeer'.

The party also was a great success, according to Paul – a yummy tea of potted meat sandwiches, jelly and ice cream and sticky buns. And Father Christmas was there with presents for all the children. A Ladybird book for each of them; Paul's, to his delight, was about various models of cars and vans. He confided, however, that he didn't think it was the real Father Christmas.

'We saw a man who looked just like him talking to Mrs Jones afterwards,' he said. 'He'd taken off his red coat but his face was all fat and jolly.'

'You're probably right,' agreed Cissie. 'He has a lot of helpers because he can't be in so many places at once, can he?'

'No, I s'pose not, said Paul thoughtfully.

She wondered how long it would be before the penny dropped entirely. Not for a few years, she hoped. It was good to keep the magic as long as possible.

On the last day of term, he brought home the surprises they had made, including a card with a rather lop-sided snowman with a printed greeting inside. *To Mummy and Daddy. Happy Christmas, Love from Paul.* It had been copied from the blackboard as the children were still in the very early stages of reading and writing, but his printing was clear and not too wobbly. A calendar depicted a bowl of flowers made from gummed paper shapes. The toilet roll middle had been used to make a cracker containing dolly mixtures and the washing-up liquid bottle was transformed into a table decoration: Father Christmas with a red crepe paper coat, a hat and a cotton wool beard.

'It's to put on the table on Christmas Day when we have our dinner,' Paul announced proudly. And Cissie agreed that it would look lovely and add just the right finishing touch.

FIVE

Ian was enjoying his catering course now he had become accustomed to the newness and the challenge of it all. It was vastly different from being at school; they were treated as adults rather than adolescents. Many of them, of course, were older, having decided on a career change, and others were similar in age to himself, in their late teenage years. There were girls – or women – as well as men, about fifty-fifty in proportion. This, also, was a change for Ian. He had attended an all-boys' grammar school and had never had a great deal of contact with girls, apart from at the youth club once a week.

He did not find it easy to make new friends. At school he had had his own set of mates, like-minded boys Gary, Steve and Mike. They had played football together and watched their favourite team, Blackpool, play most weekends. They were all chess addicts, meeting at each other's houses for games between the four of them. The other three had stayed on in the upper-sixth form while Ian had branched out in another direction. He still saw them occasionally, although they had found another fourth member to play chess with them. Ian missed them but knew that he must settle down and concentrate on his new course of studies.

He was looking forward to spending Christmas in Harrogate once again with his sister and brother-in-law. At first, he had regarded his visits there as an escape from the situation at home with his father's new wife, Norma, and the changes that their marriage had brought about. Also, he had missed his sister, Janice. Although they were six years apart in age, they had been good friends, and he had liked Phil as well. He had watched him at work in the kitchen and had admired his skill and dedication to his career, so much so that Ian had decided this was what he wanted to do. So now, in mid-December, he was ready to show his sister – and brother-in-law – how he had progressed in his studies. And, of course, he would see Sophie again.

She was his first girlfriend. He had been surprised and flattered when she had agreed to go out with him; she was a year older than Ian and was already in the sixth form at her grammar school. When they became friendlier, however, he realized that she, also, was not very experienced with regard to the opposite sex. They were still just good friends, happy to enjoy kisses and loving embraces but nothing more than that. Ian knew, though, that Sophie was at a coed college and he wondered if she might meet someone else there who was more mature and worldly-wise than he was.

Ian's course was comprehensive, covering all aspects of catering. Hotel management, bookkeeping, the full range of cookery – baking, pastry-making, meat and fish dishes, preparation of vegetables, desserts and puddings, cakes and fancy gateaux, and the planning of menus. There were sixty students in all, divided into groups for the different lessons and lectures.

Ian had not made any particular friends, although he found everyone was pleasant and amiable. Many of the students were not local and were in digs. It was not a residential college so they had to find their own lodgings. This was not difficult as there were many boarding houses willing to take students during term time, and private houses, too, where the owners were glad of the extra income.

Ian knew he was fortunate, in one respect, to be living at home. It was cheaper and no doubt more comfortable than many of the digs, although he did not have the freedom that some of the other students were experiencing, being away from home for the first time. Some, like himself, were local, others from nearby towns in Lancashire, and some from quite a distance away as the college had a very good reputation.

It was during the second week of December that Ian was invited to a get-together that some of the students were planning at one of the seafront hotels.

A group of first-year students were working in pairs at pastry making. Ian was paired with a young man whom he had seen around but they had never worked closely together. He introduced himself to Ian.

'I've noticed you at lectures,' he said, 'but we've never actually met, have we? Not properly. I'm Darren, Darren Parkinson, and you are . . . Ian, I think?'

'Yes, that's right,' he replied. 'Ian Butler. 'Pleased to meet you at last.'

'Yes, same here.' The two young men grinned at each other but did not shake hands as they were all sticky with pastry.

'I think you're a local lad, aren't you?' said Darren. 'I thought someone said you lived in Blackpool.'

'Yes, so I do. I'm a day student. It has its pros and cons. It's cheaper living at home, of course, with my dad and stepmother, and I don't have far to travel each day. I usually cycle here but it's near enough to walk.' The college was less than a mile from his home. 'On the other hand, I sometimes feel that I miss out on the social side with going home each night. I haven't had a chance to get to know anyone really well. Don't get me wrong, I'm not unsociable but I suppose . . . well . . . I'm not really the sort to push myself. I've stayed to one or two things but on the whole I've been concentrating on getting on with the job in hand. What about you, Darren? You're in digs, I suppose? I don't think you're a local lad?'

'No, I'm from Bury.'

'Yes, I guessed you were from somewhere in mid-Lancashire.'

'The accent's a giveaway, isn't it? Not that I want to disguise it. Why should we?'

'No, you're right. There's a Blackpool accent too. Apparently we don't pronounce words like "moon" and "school" correctly. We tend to say "mewn" and "scewl". I don't think we know till it's pointed out to us. My brother-in-law noticed. He's from Yorkshire, and that's another different accent.'

'Yes, we're all different, aren't we?' Darren commented. 'That's what makes life so interesting. Anyway, as I was saying, my home's in Bury so I'm in digs in Hornby Road; it's only a short walk away. I'm the only student there. Mrs Riley – she's the landlady – takes visitors. It's a small boarding house but she likes to take a student or two. She feels she's doing her bit for the local college.'

'But you're the only one there?'

'Yes, at the moment. Actually, it's a double room with two twin beds so there's room for another one. Might you be interested?'

'Me! Oh, no. Like I said, it's cheaper living at home and I

think Dad would take a dim view if I said I wanted to move. Why? Would you like someone to share with you?'

'Possibly, if it was the right person. The grub's good. Cooked breakfast and a very satisfying evening meal, same as the visitors have. Of course, there are none there at the moment. She stayed open till the end of the "lights" as they call it – the end of October. And she'll open for visitors again around Easter time. So at the moment I'm dining with the family: Mr and Mrs Riley and their daughter, Alison. She's seventeen, a year younger than me.'

'Oh, that's nice for you then,' observed Ian.

'Not really.' Darren shrugged. 'Not my type. Anyway . . . you were saying you haven't got around much yet; not had a chance to meet many of the students. Would you like to?'

'Well, yes . . . I suppose I would. I mean . . . yes, that would be great.'

'I guess I'm pretty much the same sort of person as you,' said Darren. 'I keep myself to myself a lot of the time, then realize I must make more effort. I got talking to two lads who lodge near to me and they've invited me along to a "do" they're organizing at a hotel on the prom; the Pier View opposite Central Pier – not a very original name! Do you know it?'

'No, I can't say I've noticed it but there are thousands of hotels, aren't there?'

'So would you like to come along? They said I could bring a friend.'

'Yes, I would like that. Thanks very much.'

'It's Wednesday next week, at eight o'clock. That's just before we break for Christmas. There'll be quite a few private parties going on next week, I suppose, but this one is Guy and Ant's idea. They sing and play the guitar so they'll be entertaining us. There'll be about eighteen or twenty there, they said. A few drinks, of course, and they've arranged for us to have a buffet supper. So you'll come?'

'Yes, I'd love to. But there's one snag . . . I'm only seventeen; not old enough to drink!'

'Who's to know? You look older than that. And don't tell me you've never had a drink?'

'Of course I have.'

'Well, then, what's the problem?'

'There isn't one.' Ian laughed, feeling very pleased and happy. 'Will there be girls there as well? Not just for the lads, is it?'

Darren gave him what seemed to be an odd look. 'Well . . . yes, I should think so. They didn't actually say but I assume there will be. Does it matter?'

'No, I just wanted to know. I shall look forward to it . . .'

They had been working companionably together as they talked, and the apple pie they were preparing was now ready to go into the large oven, together with those of the other students.

'I think that's a jolly good effort of ours,' said Darren, admiring the carefully crimped edging to the pie, the decoration of pastry leaves on the top and the milk and egg glaze which would ensure a golden glossy finish.

'Yes, very well done, you two,' said the woman tutor passing by their table. 'Now, clear away, wash up and leave everything tidy. That's the most important part of food preparation, as you know. It's getting near the lunch break – half an hour or so. Your pie should be ready to take out before you go.'

The students' efforts were made use of in the cafeteria at midday. Ian and Darren were highly satisfied with their creation. It smelled very appetizing too.

'I wish my brother-in-law could see that,' Ian remarked as they made their way to the dining area. 'He'd be quite impressed.'

'The Yorkshireman?' enquired Darren. 'Why? Is he in the catering business?'

'Oh, yes – he and my sister run a cafe in Harrogate. They opened it soon after they got married a couple of years ago. That was really what inspired me. I've been over to help them during the school holidays. Just as a general dogsbody to begin with, although I did quite a lot of waiting on at the tables. And I got really interested in what was going on in the kitchen. So . . . here I am, hoping to be a qualified chef myself one of these days. What about you, Darren? What made you decide to go into catering?'

'Dunno, really. I've always enjoyed my food. My mum's a smashing cook and I used to help her in the kitchen along with my sister – she's two years older – but my mum said that cooking wasn't just for girls. My dad didn't agree. He's a real male chauvinist; he lets Mum wait on him hand and foot but she doesn't seem to mind. He's a mechanic, a foreman at a local garage and he comes home all mucky and oily. He cleans up before he has his meal but that's him finished then for the day. He didn't half go on at me when I told him what I wanted to do for a career! I won't tell you what he said. Well, I expect you can guess! Not a job for a proper man and all that. I reminded him about Graham Kerr – you know, the Galloping Gourmet chef on TV – but he said he'd never heard of him. So, that's my story . . . Now, let's see what they've got to tempt us today.'

Neither of them needed more than a snack as they would be enjoying a good evening meal. They chose the soup of the day, which was tomato, with a crispy roll, followed by a piece of lemon meringue pie.

Ian found it was good to have someone to chat to over the meal. It was strange that their paths had never really crossed until now, although they had known one another by sight in the way that they knew most of the students. Ian was pleased that he had found a mate with whom he was compatible, or so it seemed at first acquaintance.

'See you around then,' said Darren as they went their separate ways after lunch to different lectures. 'If we don't meet again I'll see you on Wednesday night at the Pier View. Around eight o'clock, OK?'

'Yes, thanks again. I'll look forward to it. Just casual dress, I suppose?'

'Yes, come as you are, but without the chef's apron, of course!'

Ian laughed, feeling very light-hearted and as though he really belonged, at last.

Darren grasped his arm in a friendly gesture as they parted. 'See you then. Cheerio for now.'

'Yes, bye for now. I'm glad we've got to know one another,' he added a little self-consciously.

'Me too!' Darren grinned as he walked away.

Alec and Norma were pleased that Ian had been invited to a college gathering. They had been concerned that he had not really become part of the social scene. They knew he missed his mates from school and he had not spoken much about the students he had met.

Alec did not warn him about the dangers of drinking too much. He thought he was a sensible lad who knew his limitations; anyway, he had to find his own way around in the big wide world.

Ian dressed with care on the Wednesday evening. He had a fairly new suede jacket in a light tan colour that he had bought with his earnings from Grundy's. It went well with his black trousers, pale blue shirt and a slim tie in a darker shade of blue.

'Gosh! You look handsome,' Norma remarked when he was ready to leave. 'All the girls will be giving you the eye tonight.'

'Oh, I'm not bothered about that.' He blushed slightly. 'It's just nice to be invited somewhere.'

'Well, have a good time,' said his father. 'We'll probably be in bed when you get back but you've got your key. Now, you must get a taxi back. Here, take this.' He handed him a ten-shilling note.

'Thanks, Dad. I'm walking there, though. It's a nice mild night.'

It was a good mile to the hotel near Central Pier, but Ian walked briskly and arrived just after eight o'clock. He stepped through the swing doors and was greeted by the sound of chattering voices and laughter and the aroma of cigarette smoke and ale. It felt and looked warm and cosy with a rich red carpet, wood-panelled walls and comfortable armchairs and benches upholstered in a red plush fabric. There was a bar at the side with several people waiting to be served. As he stared around wondering where to go, Darren appeared.

'Hi there. I was just coming to meet you.' He took Ian's arm. 'We're through here.'

He led the way to a room at the rear of the building, similarly furnished and with a smaller bar. There appeared to be about ten or twelve there already, both men and girls. Ian recognized several of them. Some looked up and said, 'Hello', while some said, 'Hello, Ian', which made him feel more at home.

Darren led him to a table where two lads were sitting and two girls who might, or might not, have been their girlfriends. Ian wasn't sure but he knew them by sight.

'Nancy, Sally, Bob and Jack . . .' Darren introduced them casually. 'And this is Ian.'

They all greeted him in a friendly way and he sat down on a bench with his back to the wall.

Darren sat down next to him. 'We've decided to have a kitty,' he said. 'We'll all put some money in then there's no arguing about whose round it is. OK with you?'

'Yes, sounds like a good idea,' said Ian. 'What do you suggest?'

'Well, we've each put a pound in. Is that OK?'

'Yes, fine.' Ian took out his wallet and put a pound note on the table with the rest of the money. The groups at the other tables seemed to be doing the same.

'I'll go and get a round in while it's not too busy,' said Darren. 'What'll you have?'

'Oh, a shandy, please,' said Ian, playing it safe.

'OK, what about the rest of you?' The other four gave him their orders and Darren went off to the bar.

Ian watched him standing there looking very confident. Ian would have felt self-conscious ordering drinks. Darren was a good-looking lad, more well-built than Ian, with a pleasant, round face and fair, wavy hair that he did not damp down with brilliantine. Ian had dark brown hair which was perfectly straight.

Darren returned with the drinks and they all raised their glasses and said, 'Cheers!'

By this time several more had arrived and the noise level had risen. Ian tried to do a quick head count. Eighteen, nineteen . . . which was more for less the number Darren had said. He recognized most of them.

There was a small platform at the opposite end from the bar and in a few moments two young men carrying guitars made their way there.

'Guy and Ant,' said Darren. 'Do you know them?'

'I've seen them around . . .'

'They're from Preston; they were at school together there.'

They tuned up their guitars, then one of them stepped forward.

'Hello, folks,' he began. 'We're pleased you've all come, and Ant and I will do our best to entertain you.'

There was a rousing cheer and hearty applause.

'OK, then. We'll start with "Peggy Sue" – that's one of Buddy Holly's – then "Walkin' in the Rain" – the fabulous Johnny Ray's song . . .'

They sounded very professional. Guy sang the melody line and Ant harmonized below; they had pleasant, light tenor voices. The audience listened appreciatively then joined in with the repeats.

They entertained for almost half an hour, progressing to several Elvis numbers then Cliff Richard's 'Livin' Doll'.

'Enjoying yourself?' asked Darren.

'Very much so,' replied Ian. 'Glad you invited me; wouldn't have wanted to miss this.'

'My pleasure,' said Darren. He put an arm round Ian's shoulders for a moment, then, just as quickly, he withdrew it.

The other four, Nancy, Bob, Sally and Jack, appeared to be casual boy and girl friends. Glancing around, Ian noticed other couples, but there were more men there than girls, some of the lads sitting together in a group and others, like himself and Darren, looking as though they might be mates.

There was a pause in the entertainment while they went to the buffet bar and chose what they wanted to eat from the selection on offer: assorted sandwiches, sausage rolls, pork pies, chicken drumsticks, crisps and salad items. They replenished their glasses and sat down to eat while a man who was the resident pianist at the hotel sat down and played popular tunes of the day.

There was a space between the tables making a small dance floor, and some of them, mainly the girls and a few lads, got up and danced, jigging and twisting and shaking to the livelier numbers: 'All Shook Up', 'Jailhouse Rock' and 'Mambo Italiano'.

Ian and Darren sat in a companionable silence. There didn't seem to be any need to talk. Ian was enjoying himself more than he had thought he would, feeling carefree and just a little light-headed after his third shandy. *Watch it*, he said to himself. *Orange juice next time.*

Then the pianist started to play a song by Elvis, 'Let Me be Your Teddy Bear', and most of them sang along. To his surprise and slight shock, Darren put an arm round his shoulders again, singing along with a twinkle in his eye. It passed through Ian's mind that his friend did resemble a teddy bear, with his round face and shock of blonde hair. He grinned at him, feeling a little uncomfortable, then gradually pulled himself away. Probably Darren had had too much drink; he was on Double Diamonds, not shandies.

The evening drew on, Guy and Ant entertained them again, then they introduced a girl, one of the students, who was also a musician. Her name was Stephanie Grey. Guy introduced her, then they accompanied her as she sang several soulful songs that they all knew, but they listened without joining in as she had such a melodic voice. They were all love songs: 'April Love', 'When I Fall in Love', and 'Softly, Softly, Come to Me', which Ruby Murray, with her seductive voice, had made so popular.

'She's good, isn't she?' said Ian. 'I've noticed her at some of the lectures but I'd no idea she had such a lovely voice.'

'Yes, a hidden talent,' replied Darren, 'or not hidden in her case. She's willing to share it with others. It's surprising what might be lurking beneath the surface in all of us. Who knows what talents we may possess?'

Darren had lowered his voice. It was soft and persuasive and Ian was starting to feel uncomfortable. He glanced around. Nancy and Bob, Sally and Jack had eyes for only each other, and at the other tables everyone was listening intently to Stephanie, lads with their arms round their girlfriends and some lads, Ian noticed, sitting close together, as were he and Darren. But no one was taking any notice of what was going on at other tables.

He felt even more alarmed when Darren took hold of his hand, gently and unobtrusively beneath the table. It suddenly dawned on him what this was all about.

'Ian . . .' Darren began, '. . . are you sure you won't change your mind about sharing my digs? I'm sure we'd get on well together, you and me.' His blue eyes were looking intently into Ian's grey ones.

Ian pulled his hand away. 'I'm sorry . . . you've made a mistake,' he managed to say, but his words sounded gruff and hesitant. He was unsure how Darren might take his rejection – he might turn nasty – so he half-smiled at him. 'I'm sorry but I'm not . . . you know . . . like that. I hadn't realized . . .'

Fortunately Darren also smiled, rather sheepishly. He shrugged. 'Well, then, I'm sorry, too, for jumping to the wrong conclusion. I thought, when you said you kept yourself to yourself and you hadn't made many friends, you might be looking for someone . . . like me. Sorry, my mistake.'

Ian was nonplussed. It was the first time, to his knowledge at least, that he had met anyone 'like that'. He had heard about them; homosexuals was the correct word, but he had heard them referred to as 'queers' or 'nancy boys'. He did not want to think of Darren like that. He liked him; he had thought he was forming a good male friendship, such as he had had with Steve and Gary and Mike. He felt and must have looked bewildered. Darren touched his hand again but this time in a matey way.

'Not to worry; no harm done, I hope. Let's forget about it.'

But Ian knew he would not be able to forget about it so easily. His eyes had been opened to something he didn't really understand.

'Actually . . . I've got a girlfriend,' he said, talking quickly and, he hoped, confidently to try to cover his embarrassment. 'You know how I said I go to help my sister and brother-in-law in Yorkshire? Well, that's where I met Sophie. She was helping out as a waitress but she's at college now in Leeds, training to be a teacher. So I'll be seeing her again next week.'

'Good for you,' said Darren. 'Like I said, I'm sorry – my mistake. No hard feelings, eh?'

'No, not at all.' Ian was breathing an inward sigh of relief; it might have been awkward. 'I hope . . . I hope you find what you're looking for,' he added a little diffidently.

'I might; one still has to be careful,' said Darren. 'I had a friend back home but we went our separate ways. Such is life! Now, what about one more drink before we get thrown out? Orange juice again?'

'Yes, thanks.' Ian nodded, still feeling dazed and out of his depth.

Darren behaved quite normally when he returned with the

drinks. He, too, had gone on to orange juice. After a final chorus of 'Now is the Hour' they all started to drift away.

'Shall we share a taxi?' said Darren. 'We go the same way and I don't want to walk. It's OK, you'll be quite safe!' he added.

'Fine,' said Ian. 'I'll pay; my dad gave me the money and you get out before me.'

There were a few taxis outside waiting for the late-night trade. They spoke very little during the journey home.

'Cheerio, then,' said Darren as he got out at his digs. 'Have you enjoyed it . . . in spite of everything?'

'Yes, I have, honestly,' said Ian. 'Bye, then – see you tomorrow, no doubt.' There were two days left before the Christmas break.

The bungalow was in darkness as he let himself in. He went straight to bed, his mind buzzing with all the new experiences and revelations. All the same, he had enjoyed it immensely.

SIX

'Now we can start to think about our own Christmas festivities,' said Janice to Phil at four o'clock on the Saturday, which was Christmas Eve.

There had been a steady number of customers, mainly at lunchtime with last-minute Christmas shoppers, but fewer in the afternoon. The cafe looked bright and full of Christmas cheer. A small tree with glistening baubles stood in the window, tasteful arrangements of holly and ivy, trimmed with red and green ribbons, graced each table and the walls were adorned with clusters of tiny silver stars. A large red poinsettia on the cash desk added the finishing touch.

Only Janice and Phil, Ian and Sophie remained at the end of the afternoon. Toby, the assistant chef, had gone home after lunch, as had the other waitress. Sophie Miller, Ian's friend, had been only too pleased to help out again to earn a little towards her college expenses.

They tidied up the tables for the last time for a few days – they would open again on Thursday – and stacked the pots in the dishwasher.

'Will you stay and have a cup of tea with us, Sophie?' asked Janice. 'I think we deserve one, don't you?'

'No, thanks all the same,' Sophie replied. 'I've quite a lot to do at home. All my presents to wrap, for one thing. I'm very much behind with all that. And I promised I'd help Mum with a few jobs ready for tomorrow . . . I'll see you tonight, though, Ian, like we arranged. We're going to the Christmas Eve Service. Did Ian tell you?'

'Yes, he did,' said Janice, 'and we're coming along too. I said to Phil that it would be a nice thing to do, so I asked the lady next door if she would babysit. I'm afraid we don't go to church as often as we should. I know we're closed on Sundays but we tend to regard it as a day of rest for us. And there's

Sarah, of course.' She smiled, rather apologetically. 'But it's all too easy to make excuses for not going, isn't it?'

'Yes, I suppose so,' said Sophie. 'Mum and Graham said they'd go along as well tonight. Mum said, like you did, that it's a good thing to do . . . So I'll see you later, Ian. I'll meet you outside the church at about eleven o'clock. OK?'

'Yes, see you then,' Ian said as Sophie put on her coat and made for the door. 'No, wait a minute – I'll walk home with you.'

'Don't be silly,' she retorted. 'I'm a big girl, aren't I? I'm not going to get lost.' She blew him a kiss and went out into the darkness of the early twilight.

Ian went upstairs to the comfortable living room. There was a coal fire blazing in the hearth. The place was centrally heated but they preferred the cosiness of a fire in winter. A large tree stood in the window and Phil had switched the lights on, only partially drawing the curtains so that it shone out into the darkness like many other trees in the neighbourhood.

A pile of presents lay beneath it, the majority of them for little Sarah Lilian, now aged fifteen months. She was too young to know about Father Christmas but Janice insisted that she should have a stocking to open in her cot. Even though she didn't understand the significance, Janice did, and she would have just as much pleasure from it as her daughter.

Ian had been there since Tuesday. He had spent the weekend in Blackpool, not wanting to be seen to dash away too quickly, taken a train to Harrogate on Tuesday morning and met Phil at the station as usual.

'We'll be glad of your help,' Phil had told him. 'We're particularly busy in the evenings with Christmas meals, so perhaps you could give us a hand at the tables then? Not every evening, though,' he'd added with a smile. 'You'll be pleased to know that Sophie is working with us again, and I know you'll want to spend some time with her.'

Ian had been pleased to hear that and he'd hoped that Sophie, likewise, would want to spend some time with him. She had called at Grundy's to offer her services, and Janice and Phil had been pleased to employ her again.

She'd been busy waitressing when Ian arrived but popped up to see him later in the family living room. He'd felt a little shy at seeing her again after so long; it had been about three months. He didn't kiss her as he was embarrassed with his sister being there, but they arranged that they would meet later that evening.

'Unless you want me as a waiter tonight?' he'd asked Phil.

'No, you can start tomorrow,' Phil had said, 'and we'll see how it goes.'

Ian had walked round to Sophie's home, a few minutes' walk away, at half past seven that Tuesday evening. She'd invited him in to say hello to her mother and stepfather, Graham. He had met them occasionally and found them very friendly and welcoming.

When he had first met Sophie they had found that they had this in common. Ian's father had remarried and so had Sophie's mother – and her father as well – but in her case it had been because of divorce. Her father had met a younger woman and they now had a little girl. Sophie said that she got on well with Graham now but she had resented him at first – or had pretended to do so – just as Ian had done with Norma. But all was well again with the two families.

The shyness they had felt at meeting again soon disappeared. Ian had kissed her gently as they walked along a secluded pathway on the Stray. They had decided to walk into Harrogate, find a snack bar that was still open and have a good chat. Ian felt a warm glow of fondness and friendship rather than desire as he looked at her. She was a very pretty girl with dark hair that curled gently beneath her green woollen hat. She'd worn her green and white striped college scarf and he had said how dashing it looked.

'So you're enjoying college life?' he'd asked.

'Yes, very much so. What about you? How's the catering course going?'

'Great; I'm really getting into it. I think I'm becoming quite proficient; well, I hope I am.'

'Good. Will you be helping Phil in the kitchen?'

'I might, if he'll let me. I can make a decent apple pie. And we've made Christmas puddings; I gave mine to Norma. But I expect Phil and Janice made theirs ages ago.'

There was a jolly, seasonal feeling to the town. Coloured lights shone from the trees along the Stray; a large Christmas tree stood in the main square and shop windows were still ablaze with lights, displaying toys, stylish clothes and a myriad of tempting ideas for gifts.

They'd found a snack bar on the main street that was still open, sat at a corner table at the back and ordered strawberry milkshakes and slices of chocolate log with cream that looked delicious.

'Now, tell me about college,' Ian had said. 'Have you learnt how to teach a class of children?'

She'd laughed. 'Well, I'll get there eventually, I suppose. We've had our first teaching practice, being left in charge of a class, but only for part of the time; for PE and story time and just a few lessons. The rest of the time we spent observing the teachers. The kids were nice and friendly, five- and six-year-olds and not too difficult to handle. It was a poor area, though, and an old-fashioned Victorian building; quite an eye-opener really. But I got good reports from my tutors and the class teacher, so I'm quite pleased with myself.'

'And what about the . . . er . . . social side of the college? I suppose there are all sorts of things to do?'

'Yes, whatever takes your fancy. There's a film society – they show really ancient films! And there's country dancing, amateur dramatics and a choir, if you can sing. Actually, I've joined that because I enjoyed singing at school. And there are dances on a Saturday night at some of the halls of residence; they take it in turns.'

'And . . . do you go to them?'

'Yes, why not?' She'd answered him a trifle pertly. 'But I haven't met "anybody", if that's what you want to know,' she'd added with a wry grin. 'We did say, didn't we, Ian, that we didn't want to get serious, that we'd just see how things go?'

'Of course we did.' He realized he must be careful what he said or he might lose her altogether. 'I just wondered, that's all. You might as well enjoy whatever's going on while you're there.'

'There are more girls than men,' she'd said. 'Five women's halls and three for the men. And, on the whole, the men are about two years older than us because they've done their

National Service. There are not enough to go round! Only joking,' she'd added.

'Yes, National Service,' Ian had said. 'That's something I've just escaped. It's coming to an end in December, isn't it?'

'Yes, so it is. Would you have liked to have gone?'

'Not sure. It would certainly have been an experience. Phil was in the RAF, you know, stationed near Blackpool. That's when he met Janice. So it turned out well for him. Some of the lads at our college have been excused because they're already in the middle of their training.'

'So what about the social life at your place?' Sophie had asked. 'Do you take part in it?'

'I miss out on a lot of it because I'm living at home. Some of the others have made more friends because they meet together in the evenings. Actually, I did go to a party at one of the hotels on the prom last week. A lad I met invited me. There were a couple of the lads playing guitars and singing and one of the girl students sang; she was really good. And there was lots to drink and eat, of course.'

'So you enjoyed it?'

'Yes, I did, in spite of everything!'

'What do you mean?'

'Well, I had a strange experience . . .' He'd gone on to tell her, in hushed tones, about Darren and how he had made tentative suggestions towards him. 'Honestly, I was scared stiff at first! I was worried he might turn nasty when I spurned his advances but he was OK about it. I've seen him since then and he's not said anything else, thank goodness!'

Sophie had laughed. 'And you had no idea he was that way inclined?'

'No, why should I? It's something I've not really thought about very much. Don't know much about it, to be honest. There was a lad at school who seemed rather . . . odd, and we were suspicious about one of the masters. But . . . it's a punishable offence, isn't it?'

'Supposed to be, but I rather think a blind eye is turned a lot of the time, if the couples are discreet about it. They're starting to call them "gay" now, rather than "queer". It sounds better somehow, doesn't it?'

'I suppose so.' Ian still felt confused about it all. 'I thought that gay meant bright and cheerful?'

'Well, now it stands for "good as you" as well as its proper meaning, and it's not just men, you know, who can be that way inclined.'

'You mean . . . women as well?'

'Well, yes; apparently there are girls or women who some-times fancy one another. There were two mistresses at our school who were always together. One taught PE and the other taught French; as different as chalk and cheese, but they were very close friends.'

Ian had looked bewildered. 'I can't imagine it.'

'No, neither can I,' Sophie had agreed. 'But I'm not really bothered. Live and let live is what I say. There might come a time in the future when no one is bothered about it. Apparently it's never been a punishable offence for women because Queen Victoria refused to believe that women would behave like that, so they never passed an Act of Parliament about it.'

'How do you know all this?' Ian had asked.

'Oh, it's surprising what girls talk about when they get together! Anyway, let's change the subject. What are your plans for Christmas?'

'It'll be a quiet Christmas Day so that Janice and Phil can relax after all the extra work. And it'll be fun with little Sarah; not that she understands all about it but I'm sure she'll be excited. I'm her godfather, you know, so I take a great interest in her. Then I expect we'll go to Ilkley on Boxing Day to visit Phil's parents. Then on the Tuesday my dad and Norma are coming and staying overnight. It'll be the first time they've done that. So it'll be like Christmas Day all over again, I suppose. But we'll be able to spend some time together, you and me, won't we?'

'Yes, sure. But I'll be catching up with some of the girls from school. My friend, Sharon, is at a training college in Manchester, and Dawn has started her nursing training at the hospital here. Anyway, you're waiting on for some of the evenings, aren't you?'

'Just Wednesday and Friday, Phil suggested, so maybe we could go somewhere on the Thursday night? But I'll see you during the day, of course.'

'Yes, that sounds OK. Come on, let's go. We've been here ages and they'll want to close. We don't want to get thrown out!'

They'd walked home hand in hand, happy to be together but not saying very much; they had already done a great deal of talking. Ian was reflecting on what a friendly and uncomplicated girl Sophie was. Not sophisticated as some girls were – or pretended to be – but already she seemed more knowledgeable about the ways of the world than he was.

He'd walked all the way home with her and they'd exchanged a couple of loving kisses at her gate.

'Thanks for a lovely evening,' she'd said. 'See you tomorrow.'

'Yes, see you, it's been great.'

He'd had a spring in his step as he walked back. Life was good and full of promise, and he was growing more mature and sure of himself with each passing day.

They had met during the daytime, going about their duties, then went out again on the Thursday evening. There was a rerun of the film *Calamity Jane* showing at one of the smaller cinemas and, as Sophie was a fan of Doris Day, Ian had agreed readily to the idea. He'd enjoyed it, too, and they'd spent another happy evening together.

Their next outing was rather different; the carol service at the local church, which was not far from either of their homes. And tonight they were with their respective families.

Phil and Janice's neighbour, who owned the florist's shop next door, had willingly agreed to babysit. She didn't go out much in the evenings but this was very near and she was fond of all three of them.

Janice and Phil, Sophie's mum, Jean, and Graham said hello to one another when they met outside the church. Janice and Phil had attended it only very rarely since Sarah's christening but they were made to feel very welcome by many of the parishioners who knew them.

The six of them sat in a pew about halfway down. There was a good number of people there already and more arriving every minute as the organist played a selection of Christmas music from 'The Messiah' and some of the less familiar Christmas carols.

There was a warm and friendly atmosphere. The church dated

from the Victorian era, with high-backed oak pews and flat cushions and kneelers of cherry red. Sprigs of holly and small
Christmas roses decorated the windowsills and a display of richly
hued chrysanthemums of gold, russet and orange graced the altar.

They knew it would be a short service, starting at eleven
fifteen and ending at midnight. There was a hush in the congregation as the organist played the introduction to 'Once in Royal
David's City'. They all stood as the choir walked round the
church and the sweet and clear voice of a young boy chorister
sang the first verse, then the choir joined in and, lastly, the
whole congregation.

It was a simple service with Bible readings telling of the
birth of Jesus, the visits of the shepherds and the wise men,
and familiar carols which everyone sang wholeheartedly. There
was an anthem from the choir, 'Sing Lullaby', and a seasonal
sermon – not too long – from the vicar, speaking of love and
friendship made more meaningful with faith in Jesus. Then, at
twelve o'clock the church bells rang out, proclaiming the start
of Christmas Day.

There was a good deal of hand shaking and hugging and
kissing from the folk who knew one another, and several people
came to greet others who were not such regular attenders. There
was no doubt that they were welcome there, along with hopes
that they might come again on less auspicious occasions.

Ian and Sophie's families stood outside the church, the two
youngsters looking unsurely at one another.

'You're very welcome to come home with us for a glass of
sherry,' said Sophie's mother to them all, seconded heartily by
Graham.

Janice and Phil said thanks all the same, but they must go
and relieve their babysitter; another time, maybe.

'But you'll stay for a while, Ian?' said Janice. 'I know you
would like to.'

He nodded thankfully. 'But I won't stay long.'

'Well, you've got your key but we'll probably still be up
when you come back.'

The four adults exchanged handshakes and kisses and Christmas greetings, then Ian, a little shyly, followed Sophie into the
house.

'I wanted to give you this,' he said, taking a small gift-wrapped parcel from his pocket. 'Don't open it till tomorrow. Oh . . . it's tomorrow now, isn't it? Christmas Day, I mean.'

'But I'll save it,' said Sophie, putting her arms round him and giving him a quick kiss – her mother and Graham were in the kitchen, 'and open it with the others. Thanks ever so much.'

There was a pile of presents under the tree, as there was at Janice and Phil's. 'And this is yours,' she said, handing him a parcel tied with gold ribbon. 'And this is for little Sarah.' That one felt soft and cuddly.

'Thanks for mine, and I know Sarah will love it, whatever it is.'

Ian was almost bursting with happiness as he walked home. The four of them had drunk a glass of sweet sherry, then he and Sophie had exchanged a few fond kisses on the doorstep as they said goodbye. He was on top of his own little world.

SEVEN

'Well, I hope Russell will behave himself today,' said Val to Sam as they were preparing to leave for Christmas dinner at his parents' home.

'There's no reason why he shouldn't,' said Sam. 'He's been as good as gold so far today.'

'And is it any wonder with all those presents? I know he's been good but how long will it last, especially with your mother's eagle eye on him? He's aware of it, you know.'

'Aren't we all?' said Sam. 'But she'll be in a good mood today with it being Christmas – at least, I hope so. My father knows how to get round her with expensive perfume and jewellery and all that. I don't think he should pander to her so much but I suppose it's anything for a quiet life!'

'Well, I'll be glad when we're back home again,' said Val. 'I can never relax completely when I'm there. It's OK, don't worry,' she went on, aware of his concerned look. 'I shall do my best to enjoy it. It'll be a jolly good meal and your dad's always the life and soul of the party. And Thelma will be there, thank goodness.'

Her sister-in-law, Thelma, married to Sam's brother, Jonathan, had been a great help to Val when she had first met Sam's family, assuring her that Beatrice Walker's bark was worse than her bite and that one had to humour her, to a certain extent. Thelma and Val had become very good friends and Val was always glad of her bolstering presence on these family occasions.

Christmas dinner at the Walkers' was quite an ordeal for Val, especially since they had had their family. She had insisted, though, and Sam had agreed, that her own parents must not be overlooked on these festive occasions. And so, each year since they were married in 1957, they had spent Christmas Day, or at least part of it, with the Walkers and Boxing Day with her family, the Horrockses, or vice versa.

And this year it was the Walkers turn for the important day. Tomorrow, at her old family home, it would be much more relaxed and enjoyable.

'You look very nice,' said Sam as Val turned round from the dressing table after putting the finishing touches to her appearance – combing her dark hair and coaxing it into a curl, applying a touch of bright red lipstick and green eye-shadow to her brown eyes. 'Beautiful, in fact.' He grabbed hold of her and gave her a quick kiss. 'You look stunning in your new dress. Worth every penny!'

The cherry red dress, made from a soft woollen fabric in the new length, just above the knee, complemented Val's dark colouring. It was a present from Sam from Schofield's store in Leeds. And today he had given her a surprise present: a silver and garnet necklace which fitted perfectly with the V-shaped neckline of her dress.

'You don't look so bad yourself,' she replied, returning his kiss. She had bought him a Jaeger jumper of moss green cashmere as a surprise, and fortunately he was delighted with it. He was wearing it today as it would be quite an informal occasion.

'Come on, now; no time to be canoodling,' said Val. 'Lucy's all ready, aren't you, darling? Nice and dry and clean and tidy, just the way Grandma likes her!' She picked up seven-month-old Lucy, who had been sitting contentedly on their bed, propped up against a pillow.

'What a pretty little girl!' said Sam. 'Do you know, she looks more like you every day.' The child was dark-haired like her mother, with the same warm brown eyes. 'Come on, then, my two lovely ladies. Let's go and find Russell.'

Russell had been playing happily by himself with his new Dinky cars. He had a playpen, which Val did not like overmuch as she thought it seemed as though they were treating the children like zoo animals, but it was sometimes necessary to separate the two of them. Russell was such a little terror, into everything.

'Come on, young feller,' said Sam, lifting him high in the air. 'Time to go and see your gran and granddad.'

Russell wriggled, shouting, 'No! Want car, big car.' He had

seemed quite contented but, on seeing his parents, decided he would exert his authority again; it sometimes worked with Mummy, but Daddy was there as well.

'No!' said Sam. 'We're going out now. You can have a ride later.'

'No! Want a ride now!'

Russell's main present had been a pedal car, bright red, with shining mudguards, a horn and headlights, looking very much like his daddy's Ford Consul. He had 'driven' up and down the front path with Sam assisting him as he could not quite manage the pedals as yet.

'Now, be a good boy, please, Russell,' said Val. 'See, you can take your police car. And what about a few Smarties? Not too many, though; they'll spoil your dinner.'

She knew it was bribery but she didn't want a scene before they'd even set off. Russell nodded and seemed quite happy to conform, for the moment. They gathered together the small mountain of belongings they needed to take with them: bottles and baby food for Lucy; nappies and baby wipes and cream for Lucy, as Russell, to Val's relief, had dispensed with nappies at an early age; Lucy's carry cot and blanket and gifts for all the family.

Finally they were ready and the drove away to the home of Joshua and Beatrice Walker. It was only a mile or so distant, but too far to walk with all the paraphernalia. Sam parked the car in the spacious driveway, noting that his brother, Jonathan's Ford Zephyr was already there. Sam carried Lucy in her carry-cot and Russell held Val's hand as she rang the bell at the imposing oak door. The sound of the chimes echoed through the house, and in a moment the door was opened by Mrs Porter, dressed as usual in black.

'Hello there, Valerie,' she greeted her cheerily, 'and little Russell too, though he's not so little now, are you, young man?' The child looked quizzically at her. 'And here's Mr Samuel and Lucy . . . A happy Christmas to you all.'

Val had told Mrs Porter soon after their first meeting that she must call her Val, or Valerie, which was what the lady seemed to prefer. She knew she could never get used to being called Mrs Sam, or Miss Horrocks, as she was at that time. Mrs Porter seemed to understand, although she kept strictly to protocol with the rest of the family.

Mrs Porter was a sort of housekeeper and cook to the Walker family – the only servant they had apart from a cleaning woman and a part-time gardener – but she did not live at the house. She was a widow, now in her late sixties, and lived not far away with her brother, who was also widowed. She had worked for the Walker family for many years, her hours flexible to suit the requirements of Mrs Walker.

The days were long gone when mill owners such as Joshua would employ a host of servants: a live-in housekeeper, maybe a butler for the more affluent families, a cook and scullery maid, and at least one upstairs maid.

Beatrice, in fact, was quite capable of running a household on her own. She had been the eldest of several children in an ordinary working-class family and had done her share of housework, cooking and looking after her younger siblings. But she had a position in society now as a mill owner's wife, and a housekeeper was necessary to maintain the image she had of herself.

Mrs Porter usually came in the afternoon to prepare and cook the evening meal for Beatrice and Joshua; they dined early, around six o'clock, when he returned from the mill. Occasionally, if they were entertaining guests, she would stay later, free to go when she had stacked the dishwasher, to be emptied the next day.

Most afternoons, Beatrice was occupied with what she thought of as her good works. She was chairman of the local Townswomen's Guild, an influential member of the church council and served on the committees of several charitable organizations. Before she departed in a chauffeur-driven taxi from a local firm – Beatrice had never learnt to drive – she would discuss with Mrs Porter such matters as menus for the week and the orders to be given to the various tradesmen who called: the butcher, fishmonger, baker and greengrocer. There was also a weekly order for household commodities from the local Co-op.

The exception to the rule was Sunday when Mrs Porter came in the morning to prepare and cook the midday meal. Always a roast – pork, lamb or Joshua's favourite, roast beef with Yorkshire pudding – ready for when the Walkers returned from the morning service at church. They never missed this weekly ritual. Beatrice regarded it not just as a social but a Christian duty, and as an example to set to others.

Today was not only Sunday but Christmas Day, and Mrs Porter had been there for several hours in charge of the huge turkey – although Joshua had put it in the oven at a very early hour – the roast potatoes, the vegetables and stuffing and the Christmas pudding which she had made a few weeks ago. One of several, in fact, because Beatrice liked to donate a large one for the church lunch, given for the needy of the parish, and one for Mrs Porter to take home to be enjoyed by herself and her brother.

Joshua and Beatrice were very generous employers. Mrs Porter was well paid for her services and Beatrice had learnt not to act the grand lady or patronize the woman, who was well aware of Beatrice's humble beginnings. Alice Porter was very satisfied with the status quo. Her wages paid for little extras for herself and her brother, Cyril, and she and Beatrice got along quite well together, so long as Alice, with her tongue in her cheek, remembered her place.

She ushered Sam and his family into the comfortable lounge where Beatrice was sitting, in pride of place, in the largest armchair near the fireplace. A coal fire blazed in the hearth, adding to the warmth and cheerfulness of the scene. Val, despite her misgivings, felt that it was a very pleasant and welcoming scene.

Beatrice, as always, reminded her of the queen mother, sitting there regally, dressed in her favourite shade of lilac – an exquisite two-piece suit of the finest wool – with a necklace of amethysts around her plumpish neck. Val made a guess that this was a Christmas present from Joshua.

She smiled graciously as Val bent to kiss her cheek. 'How lovely to see you, Valerie, dear, and . . . little Russell.' She patted the little boy's ginger hair and pecked at his cheek. 'Hello, Russell,' she said without a great deal of enthusiasm. 'Has Father Christmas been to your house?'

He nodded unsurely, seeming tongue-tied. Val did not

pressure him to 'give Grandma a kiss' or to answer her question, not sure what was going through his little mind. She wanted it to be a happy and peaceful day.

And, by and large, it turned out to be so. They all greeted one another warmly, petty grievances and disagreements set aside on this day of goodwill to all mankind. There were nine of them altogether, although only eight sat down to dine around the Edwardian table in the dining room as baby Lucy had already been fed and laid in her carrycot near to Val. Russell sat in a high chair, one that had been used years ago by Jonathan and Samuel. Rosemary, the four-year-old daughter of Jonathan and Thelma, was able to sit at the table with a couple of cushions on the chair.

The table was a picture of elegance, such as one might see in the pages of *Ideal Home*. The cutlery was heavy silver, a long-ago wedding present for Joshua and Beatrice; the cloth a heavy cream linen with a crocheted border – a family heirloom – with napkins to match in silver napkin rings. There were wine glasses of lead crystal but the tablemats added a more homely Dickensian touch with scenes of coaches and horses, coaching inns, red-coated horsemen and jolly Pickwickian characters. Beatrice had created the centrepiece – a silver bowl containing a red poinsettia surrounded by holly and ivy, and small chrysanthemums of yellow and white. This unfortunately had to be moved when Mrs Porter brought in the vegetables in their Rockingham china dishes.

The meal was the traditional Christmas fare: slices of white meat from the plump breast of the turkey and a little of the brown meat from the huge legs of the bird. There was sage and onion stuffing; Beatrice had suggested chestnut stuffing as this was thought to be the correct accompaniment to turkey, but she'd been overruled by Joshua, who preferred to stick to what he knew and liked. Crisp roast potatoes, a selection of vegetables including the traditional sprouts – not loved by all but a 'must' at Christmas – followed by the Christmas pudding with brandy sauce. A mellow white wine was served with the meal, with orange juice for the children.

Val tried to enjoy the delicious food as much as she could, with an eye all the time on Russell. His meal was in his own plastic bowl so Beatrice's precious china was in no danger. She hoped he would not perform any of his naughty tricks such as turning the bowl upside down when he thought he had eaten enough or banging the spoon so that the gravy flew in all directions. He had been scolded time and again but these were things he did when he wanted attention, especially if Val was occupied with Lucy.

Fortunately he behaved impeccably. Val could see Beatrice watching him from the other end of the table but he seemed unaware of anything but the tasty meal he was clearly enjoying. He managed very well with his spoon and pusher, preferring to do it by himself rather than being helped. He was an independent child for much of the time, until he decided that he wanted to be noticed. He created a laugh all round when he finished his dinner, giving a contented little sigh and shouting, 'All gone!' as he sometimes did at home. Val, at that moment, felt a surge of love for him.

They pulled crackers and wore the paper hats – all except Beatrice, who did not want to spoil her hairdo – read out the silly jokes, then sat back full of bonhomie after a very satisfying meal.

Thelma spoke to Mrs Porter as she cleared away the dishes. 'That was a wonderful meal, Mrs Porter; thank you very much.' She glanced across at Beatrice, lest she should be thought to be speaking out of turn. 'Val and I will sort out the kitchen and make the tea and coffee, won't we, Val? Then perhaps Mrs Porter could go home?'

Val voiced her agreement as Thelma looked across at her mother-in-law. 'Is that all right with you . . . Mother?' she asked.

Val knew that Thelma, like herself, had difficulty in calling Beatrice 'Mother' or 'Mum'. Val avoided the issue by not using any name at all except 'Grandma', which was acceptable now they had the children.

'Yes . . . thank you, Thelma and Valerie,' said Beatrice, looking a little put out that she had not been the first one to say thank you to the woman who had done all the work, but she did so now.

'Thank you very much, Mrs Porter. That was an excellent meal. You go off home now and enjoy the rest of the day with your brother.'

The lady was pleased to be dismissed and thanked the two

young women for offering to step in and attend to the rest of the chores.

Thelma laughed. 'It's nice to escape for a little while, isn't it, Val?'

'Yes, it sure is! A bit of peace and quiet.'

'Well, I'm really grateful,' said Mrs Porter. 'Just stack the pots in the dishwasher; they won't be used again for a while. But be careful with milady's best china! Sorry, I'm forgetting my place, aren't I?'

They all laughed. Thelma and Val had come to regard Alice Porter as almost one of the family. Nothing was ever said but the two of them knew that the woman was well aware of their mother-in-law's pretensions, just as they were.

When she had first met Thelma, Val had imagined that she might be aloof and self-restrained. She had reminded Val of a snow princess in a fairy tale: she was tall and slender with finely drawn features and pale blonde hair in an immaculate pageboy style. But as she became more acquainted with her, she realized that her looks belied her personality. Thelma was warm and friendly with a sense of humour, which Val guessed was necessary with her rather straight-laced husband. Thelma had taken Val under her wing, knowing that she had a family background that Beatrice considered far inferior to that of the Walkers; moreover, she was one of their employees. Thelma, on the other hand, had met with full approval because her father was a solicitor. But Val had proved herself to be worthy of a place in the Walker family. Even Jonathan now recognized that she was an admirable wife for his brother.

The girls busied themselves in the kitchen when Mrs Porter had gone, carefully stacking the dishwasher with the precious china then making pots of both tea and coffee to end the meal, a northern custom that Joshua insisted upon. They poured out and handed round the beverages, then it was time for the ritual of giving out the Christmas presents.

They were in a huge pile beneath the Christmas tree, large ones and small ones all wrapped in gaily patterned paper and ribbon and gift tags.

Lucy, after a short nap, was sitting on Val's knee looking bright and alert as though she knew what was going on. Russell, quiet for once, was leaning against his daddy's knees. Val was pleased he was behaving so well and hoped against hope that this would continue. She was more relaxed now and the tension she always felt on meeting Beatrice had receded.

'Rosemary, dear, would you like to hand out all these nice Christmas presents?' Beatrice said now to the little girl whom Val guessed was her favourite grandchild.

She was an angelic-looking child with pale blonde hair and delicate features like her mother. She was dressed in a dark-red velvet frock with ribbons in her hair. She smiled and nodded, looking delighted at the idea. Both she and Russell had been eyeing the presents with interest.

'I'll read the names on the labels and then you can take them round,' said Thelma. 'Now, let's see . . . This one says, "To Russell, with love from Grandma and Grandpa".'

Russell actually remembered to say thank you and started to tear off the paper at once.

'I think we'd better wait till Rosemary has given them all out,' said Val. 'Then we can all open them together. OK, Russell?'

He started to scowl, then thought better of it as he watched what was happening. Presents for everybody, and there might be some more for him! 'OK,' he said.

The children had received their main family presents in the morning – the ones that Father Christmas had brought – although they had been told that Mummy and Daddy had had a part in it as well, lest they should grow up believing that the magic man in red would bring everything they wished for without question.

These gifts were from family members to one another: to Jon and Thelma from Sam and Val, and vice versa; to Mum and Dad from Sam and Val . . . and so on. There were presents from great-grandparents and aunts and uncles who were not there but who liked to remember the children at Christmas, and when Rosemary had finished her task the unwrapping began.

Soon the carpet was littered with the discarded paper, ribbons, tinsel and gift cards. The gifts had been so carefully wrapped and were now torn apart by the children's eager little hands. The adults, though, were slightly more patient and thanked one another delightedly for the cashmere jumpers and pullovers, leather gloves, boxes of exclusive chocolates that one only bought at Christmastime, perfume and boxes containing special beauty products.

The children received sensible presents of jumpers, dresses and woolly hats, but there were more interesting things as well: jigsaw puzzles, games, building bricks, colouring books and crayons. Russell and Rosemary were wildly excited and Lucy stared at it all in wonder. When Russell started a game of screwing up the paper and throwing it around, encouraging Rosemary to do the same, Val and Thelma decided it was time to put an end to the merriment. They gathered up all the debris and took it away.

The two children were persuaded to 'play nicely and quietly' with a jigsaw puzzle while the adults enjoyed a glass of sherry and listened to the queen's speech. Fortunately, peace reigned while Her Majesty was speaking but came to an end when Russell started to snatch at the pieces and shove them in the wrong places, much to Rosemary's annoyance.

'He's spoiling it!' she shouted. 'He can't do it; he's too little!'

'Can! Can do!' he retorted, and Val intervened just as he was about to punch his cousin.

'Don't be cross with him, Rosemary,' said Thelma. 'He's only two and you're four-and-a-half, aren't you? Put the jigsaw away now and you can do it another time.'

Russell was red in the face and scowling. Val knew that he was also quite tired as he had been up since the crack of dawn. She looked appealingly at Sam and he read her thoughts.

'Well, folks,' said Sam. 'Sorry to break up the party but I think it's time we were heading back home.'

'Oh, surely not so soon,' said Beatrice. 'You haven't been here all that long.'

But Sam knew from the glances she kept levelling at Russell that she would not really be sorry to see them depart.

'Long enough, Mother,' he said, then realized that his remark was rather tactless. 'I mean . . . I did say that we wouldn't stay for tea. Lucy will be very tired by then, and this little man . . .' he patted Russell's head, '. . . is getting tired as well, and that's when he starts to get . . . a little bit difficult.'

Beatrice nodded. 'Just as you say, dear. But it's been lovely to see you all.'

There was a good deal of commotion then as coats were put on, all the presents gathered up and put in a big carrier bag, and there were hugs and kisses and promises to 'see you soon'.

'Give Gran a kiss,' said Val to Russell.

He looked a little unsure but dutifully pecked at her cheek. Beatrice put an arm round him, just for a moment. 'You've been a good boy, for most of the time,' she said.

Joshua picked him up and lifted him high in the air. 'He's a grand little fellow, aren't you, Russell? You've got a lovely little family there,' he said as he put the child down and kissed Val's cheek. 'Well done, Valerie, my dear.'

Eventually all the goodbyes had been said and they were in the car and ready for off.

Val let out a deep sigh. 'Thank goodness that's over!'

'Why? It wasn't too bad,' said Sam. 'No temper tantrums and no fisticuffs. I thought he did rather well. He's getting better, I'm sure he is.'

'He's scared stiff of your mother, and who can blame him?' said Val.

Sam thought it best not to answer.

Lucy was ready for a sleep when they arrived home but Russell had recovered from his tiredness. He raced around, waving his arms and whooping loudly. Val knew he was glad to be home in an environment where he could be himself; he had exercised restraint for long enough. She managed to quieten him with a jigsaw puzzle that was easier than the one he had attempted with Rosemary. It featured his favourite things: cars and buses and a big red fire engine.

'I'll ring Janice now,' she said as peace was temporarily restored. 'I'll thank her for the children's presents, wish them a happy Christmas and see how my little goddaughter's getting on. Keep an eye on Russell, won't you, Sam?'

Sam, ensconced in an easy chair and almost asleep, opened one eye and nodded.

EIGHT

'That was Val on the phone,' said Janice, late on the afternoon of Christmas Day, 'thanking us for the children's presents, so I thanked her for Sarah's, of course. They've been to Sam's parents for dinner; quite an ordeal, I should imagine. I'm glad I haven't got a mother-in-law like Beatrice! I really look forward to seeing your parents, Phil. They've always been so easy to get along with, and they make Ian welcome as well.'

'Yes, they're a pretty easy-going couple,' agreed Phil. 'Make the most of your relaxing day tomorrow, love. Mum and Dad will insist on doing everything themselves. You'll be busy with your dad and Norma the following day but I'll do most of the cooking, like I promised, and Ian will want to show off his new skills.'

'I've told him to invite Sophie for tea on Tuesday, when Dad and Norma are here. They haven't met her yet. Not that there's anything serious between Ian and Sophie but they seem to get along well together. They won't have seen one another for two whole days, and it seems ages when you're young, doesn't it?'

'Oh, I don't know so much,' said Phil. 'They're coping with their separation pretty well. Ian's enjoying his course and there seems to be a lot going on at Sophie's college. It remains to be seen if their friendship will stand the test of time. These teenage romances don't always survive.'

'Ours did,' said Janice, 'or perhaps I should say that mine did. You were my first real boyfriend, although I don't know what you'd been up to before we met.'

'Not a great deal,' said Phil with a laugh. 'And I've certainly no cause to complain now.' He gave her a quick hug and a kiss. 'What are we having for tea?'

'Tea!' Janice stared at him. 'Do you really think we need any tea after that enormous meal?'

'Well, a late tea, or perhaps an early supper. Ian will no doubt be hungry again when he gets back.'

Ian, after dutifully listening to the queen's speech, had gone out for a long walk to get some fresh air and burn off the excess pounds gained with eating two helpings of Christmas pudding.

'OK, we'll get Sarah bathed and into bed first, and then . . . turkey sandwiches, I suppose, and I'll cut the Christmas cake. Then it'll be telly, won't it? The usual variety show. Who's on this year?'

The scene was similar to thousands of others throughout the country. Some family gatherings would be considerably larger, sometimes leading to frayed tempers and squabbles as the host and hostess tried, often unsuccessfully, to please everybody.

Cissie's and Walter's families, the Fosters and the Clarksons, had been friends for a considerable time and they always spent Christmas Day together, one year at the Fosters' home and the following year at the Clarksons'. This year it was the turn of the Clarksons.

The men, Joseph Foster and Archie Clarkson, had worked together at a woollen mill for many years – not Walker's mill but another one at the other side of the town. Their wives had worked for a while as weavers but were now glad to stay at home and be housewives. The men, also, were sidesmen and keen workers at their local church. Their wives, Hannah and Millie had, therefore, struck up a friendship; a somewhat cautious one, however, for Hannah Foster could not entirely conceal her envy of Millie. Both sets of parents, though, had always hoped for a marriage between Cissie and Walter, their only children, and this had taken place five years ago in 1955.

Now there were two grandchildren and it was a source of quiet amusement to Cissie and Walter as they watched their parents, especially the mothers – and more especially Hannah Foster – competing with one another over the gifts they bought for their grandchildren, Paul and Holly.

'Come along now, you two,' said Cissie when it was nearing twelve o'clock on Christmas Day. 'It's time we were getting ready to go and see Grandma and Granddad.'

'Which ones?' asked Holly, stopping for a moment as she wheeled her new doll's pram up and down the hallway.

'Grandma Millie,' answered Cissie, and she was not really surprised to hear Holly exclaim, 'Goody!' She suppressed a smile; it did not worry her that Walter's mother was the favourite granny. She knew that her own mother loved both children very much, but Millie was far more easy-going and relaxed in her relationship with the children, something they must have noticed, albeit unconsciously. Cissie and her mother had never got along together all that well, although there had been an improvement in their relationship since the arrival of the children.

Paul had just come in from the garden where he had been riding his new tricycle up and down the path. 'Daddy's getting the car out,' he said, 'and he's putting my bike away in a special place in the garage.'

'Can I take my pram to Gran's?' asked Holly.

'No, there won't be room in the car,' said Cissie, 'but you can take your new dolly. Put her nice new coat on, then she'll be warm.'

It was Holly's third birthday as well as being Christmas Day, so she had received either two gifts or one more special one from relations and friends. She didn't seem to mind; she had been told that she was special because she shared her birthday with baby Jesus. She had heard a lot about him recently as she'd learnt the words and sang along with Paul as he practised 'Away in a Manger' and 'Little Jesus Sweetly Sleep' for his nativity play.

'Can I take my table decoration to Gran's?' asked Paul. 'We're not having our dinner here, are we?'

'Oh, yes, she'll love that,' said Cissie, 'but we must remember to bring it back, then we can put it on our own table tomorrow. Now, let's find the presents we're taking for Grandma and Granddad, and Nana and Grandpa as well.'

Officially, Hannah was Nana and Millie was Grandma, but the names often got confused and shortened to Gran.

They packed all their belongings in the boot of the car, then Walter drove the short distance – a mile or so – to his parents' home. It was a semi-detached house, quite a modest one with small gardens to the front and rear. This was a bone of contention, however, to Hannah Foster, as their home was a terraced house in a row of others just like it, opening straight on to the street. Both families, though, did own their own properties.

The Clarksons also owned a car, whereas the Fosters did not. Joseph had not learnt to drive and had never been interested in doing so as he lived close to his place of work. It peeved Hannah that they had to accept lifts from their friends, although they never refused to do so, and they usually spent the annual summer holiday together using the Clarksons' car.

Cissie's parents had already arrived and Hannah was seated in the best armchair by the fire. The two men were chatting amiably and Millie was busy in the kitchen. She appeared when she heard their voices, wiping her hands on the large white apron she was wearing to cover her best frock.

She bent down to hug and kiss Holly first of all. 'Happy birthday, Holly, and happy Christmas as well. Isn't it exciting?'

She also embraced Paul. 'Happy Christmas, love. My goodness! Aren't you growing? You'll be as tall as your daddy before long.'

'Grandma, I've brought something special,' he said. 'It's a table decoration. We made them at school and it's to stand in the middle of the table when we have our dinner. Would you like it?' He carefully removed it from its bag and handed it to his gran.

'Well, isn't that lovely!' she exclaimed, taking hold of the Father Christmas, a washing-up liquid bottle wearing a red crepe paper coat and hat, with eyes nose and mouth drawn on a cardboard face, rosy red cheeks and a cotton wool beard.

'Have you made it all by yourself?'

'Well, most of it. The teacher helped a bit. We all made one.'

'Look, Nana.' Millie held up the figure to show to Hannah. 'Isn't he lovely? He'll match my red tablecloth.'

'Very nice,' said Hannah briefly. 'Aren't you going to come and give Nana a kiss, Paul?'

He dutifully did so, and so did Holly. As if he was aware of a slight tension in the air, Paul said, 'We only made one, Nana, and Grandma can't keep it. She can use it today, then we're taking it home to put on our own table tomorrow, aren't we, Mummy?'

'Yes, that's right, love,' said Cissie. 'Hello, Mam, Happy Christmas.'

There were greetings all round, then coats were removed and room was made in the small lounge for the newcomers.

There were two downstairs rooms and a small kitchen. The front room – the lounge, or sitting room – was kept for best and only used on special occasions. The larger back room was the dining and living room, which was used most of the time. Today a coal fire burned in the cream-and-green-tiled fireplace in the lounge, a few paper streamers showed that it was Christmas, and the small artificial tree that Walter remembered from his boyhood stood in the window with the same fairy on the top.

'Do you need any help, Millie?' asked Cissie. Her mother-in-law had said she should call her Millie and Cissie had got used to doing so. Hannah had felt obliged to ask Walter to use her Christian name, something that would have been considered outrageous a generation ago.

'No, thank you, dear,' said Millie in answer to the question. 'I'm managing all right but it's nice of you to ask. Perhaps you could help to set the table in a little while, you and Hannah?'

Hannah sniffed. She was supposed to be a guest today. She gave a faint smile. 'Yes, I don't mind helping if you're busy.'

Paul pulled at his mum's arm. 'What about the presents, Mummy? Shall I hand them out now?'

'Perhaps we should wait till we've had our dinner, Paul,' said Millie. 'I'm rather busy at the moment. I'm just going to see how the turkey's cooking and then I've to see to the potatoes and vegetables. So shall we wait till later? We've got some nice presents for you as well.'

'That's a good idea. It'll be something else to look forward to,' said Cissie, 'after we've enjoyed Grandma's nice dinner. You can play with your Lego now, and Holly's brought her new dolly.'

The two men were still chatting and Walter went to join them on the settee. They started to talk 'shop' about the conditions in their respective mills.

'Come on, Mam,' said Cissie after a little while. 'Let's help Millie with the table.'

The folding table was extended to its full size to seat eight of them, and Cissie fetched extra chairs from upstairs to make the full number.

'The tablecloth and cutlery are in the sideboard drawer,' said Mille, coming in from the kitchen looking hot and flustered. 'You know where they are, don't you, Cissie? And the wine glasses are in the little cupboard at the top. They might need a wash; we haven't used them for ages. And you can use two bigger glasses for the children's orange juice. The tablemats are in the bottom drawer and here's the special serviettes I've bought. I'll leave you to see to it, then. I've just the gravy to make and I'll get Archie to carve the turkey.'

'I'll go and tell him,' said Cissie, making for the lounge. She returned with her father-in-law and Paul, proudly holding his table decoration.

'Just wait a bit, love, while we set the table,' said Cissie, 'then you can put it in the middle.'

Hannah gave her usual sniff and slight shrug, as if to infer that it was all rather disorganized.

Cissie ignored her as she opened the drawers to get the cloth, tablemats and cutlery. The tablecloth – used only at Christmastime – had a gay design of holly and red poinsettias. The knives, forks and spoons were in daily use, and Cissie chose the ones that looked the most presentable. The tablemats featured brightly-coloured flowers – a different design for each mat. Cissie placed a paper serviette at the side of each fork. These had been bought with the children in mind, with pictures of Santas and snowmen on them. Nothing matched but it all looked very bright and cheerful.

'Now, Paul, let's have your Father Christmas,' said Cissie. 'Put him there, right in the middle. Look, Nana – doesn't that look smashing?'

Hannah agreed readily, for once, that it was 'Just the job!' She really did think the world of her grandson.

'All shipshape here now, Mam,' said Cissie. 'You go back to the lounge and I'll see if Millie wants any more help.'

There was, in fact, scarcely room for them all in the small kitchen. Archie was carving the huge turkey and Millie was making a final check on the potatoes and vegetables.

'I'm going to put it all straight on to the plates,' she said. 'I know it's more correct, like, to put the veg in dishes to help yourself, but I always think it goes cold. They can come back for more. Put the stuffing and the apple sauce on the table, though, Cissie; not everybody likes them. Then you can put out the dinner for the little 'uns. You know how much they can eat!'

When all the meals had been dished out on to the plates, Millie took off her apron and wiped her hot face. 'Would you go and tell them it's ready, Cissie, love?' she said.

They all came into the dining room. Cissie put two cushions on Holly's chair so that she could reach the table. Paul was able to manage with one cushion and they were both reasonably competent with a knife and fork, Paul having learnt the skill at school dinners. Holly tried determinedly to copy him, as she did with most things, not wanting to be left behind, but Cissie sat next to her to help when she struggled a little.

Millie was wearing a woollen dress in a delicate shade of lavender which toned well with the purplish rinse she had on her greying hair. She was a plumpish woman but well-corseted. She always tried, with success, to make the most of her appearance.

'New dress, Millie?' asked Cissie. 'It suits you; that colour's just right for you.'

'Thank you, dear,' said Millie, looking pleased. 'Yes, it's a Christmas present from Archie. I chose it myself, of course, but he chose this brooch. That was a lovely surprise.' The floral brooch with shiny mauve stones and seed pearls glittered on the lapel.

Cissie noticed her own mother looking a little put out at the compliment to Millie. She could not pay a similar compliment to Hannah as she was wearing the paisley patterned dress that she had worn last Christmas. The two women were not at all alike in looks. Hannah was thin but large-boned, with angular features, and did not bother to 'tart up' – as she called it – her iron-grey hair with a coloured rinse. She had a perm about three times a year, and it was obvious from the tight curls that she had recently visited the hairdresser.

Cissie searched around in her mind for something to say to

her mother. 'What has Dad bought for you, Mam?' she asked after a moment's hesitation. She knew that her father was always generous with his birthday and Christmas gifts; he did not dare to be otherwise.

'Oh, I've got a new coat,' said Hannah, preening herself a little. 'We got it from C and A but it's from their more exclusive range. It's a heather mixture tweed with a fur collar.'

'And very nice it is, too,' said Millie. 'It suits you, Hannah.'

Hannah gave a satisfied nod, seemingly mollified now.

The two older men, and Walter, were tucking into their meal, enjoying the food and taking little heed of the conversation between the women. Archie Clarkson and Joe Foster were not dissimilar in looks, both with grey hair, now receding, and a bald patch on top. Both were of a hefty build, though not over-weight, and both of them wore spectacles. They were similarly dressed, too, in V-necked pullovers that had been Christmas presents from their wives.

'Smashing meal, Millie,' observed Joe. 'These roast potatoes are just the way I like 'em, all crisp and brown and soft inside . . . Mind you, Hannah can do a nice roast potato an' all, can't you, love?' he added, looking anxiously at his wife.

Hannah nodded briefly. 'This sage and onion stuffing is delicious, Millie,' she said. 'Have you made it yourself?' she asked, knowing very well that Millie had done no such thing.

'Good gracious, no! Of course not,' replied Millie. 'It's good old Paxo. You can't beat it, even though it's out of a packet. But I must admit it's tasty.' She looked across the table at her grandchildren. 'They seem to be enjoying their dinner, bless 'em, and aren't they managing well on their own?'

'Holly needs a bit of help,' said Cissie, cutting the child's turkey into small pieces. 'Paul learnt to use a knife and fork at school dinners and Holly's doing her best, aren't you, love?'

The little girl nodded. 'And I'm going to school soon, like Paul. Not the same school, though; the one where my friend Kelly goes.'

Millie looked surprised. 'Well, now, fancy that!'

'First I've heard of it,' muttered Hannah. 'She's only three, our Cissie. They don't start school till they're four, and that's too soon in my opinion.'

Cissie held back a sharp retort and took a deep breath. 'It's not really school . . . but Holly likes to think it is,' she added quietly. 'It's a playgroup for younger children. They take them at two-and-a-half if they're ready, so Holly's quite old enough. Like she said, her friend Kelly goes. Her mother, Megan, is a friend of mine so we'll be able to go together. It's on the way to Paul's school so it's very handy.'

'Oh, that's nice,' said Millie. 'You'll feel lost with both of 'em gone, though, won't you?'

'Yes, I know. The house felt really strange when Paul first went to school and I know I shall miss Holly an' all, though the playgroup's only in the mornings.' She decided to take the bull by the horns and be damned to the reaction. 'I'm thinking I might get a part-time job while they're both out in the mornings. Like I said, the house'll feel empty and it'll be summat for me to do.'

'What?' exclaimed Hannah. 'Haven't you got enough to do, looking after yer home?' She nodded knowingly. 'Aye, I thought you'd get fed up with housework sooner or later, but it's what we have to do when we get wed.'

Cissie was surprised when Walter made a comment. He was looking at her, and she was pleased to see his almost imperceptible wink and half-smile. 'Cissie's a jolly good mother and wife, Hannah,' he said. 'None better, and I'm not going to complain so long as she's there to see to the kiddies, and I know she will be. Anyway, it could only be for a few hours a day.'

Hannah gave her usual sniff but made no comment.

'Well, it that's what you want to do, dear, then I don't see why not,' said Millie, a little cagily. 'It would give you a bit of pocket money for yourself. I know money doesn't go far when you've got two children. They grow out of everything so fast, don't they?'

'Walter's got a good job, though, hasn't he?' said Hannah. 'He's been promoted.'

'Nothing's sure these days, Hannah,' said Walter. 'Dad and me and Joe were just talking about the mills.'

'You wouldn't want to go back to the mill, dear, would you?' asked Millie. 'I know you were very clever with all that mending you did but I'm sure it must have got a bit monotonous and very hard work, too.'

'No, I wouldn't, Millie, but I couldn't anyway. Walter says they're not taking any new staff on just now and they're not replacing folk when they leave, are they, Walter?'

'That's true, and it's the same where Dad and Joe work.'

'Aye, it's all this new-fangled stuff from America; that's where it's come from,' said Joe. 'Nylon and terylene and crimplene and all that sort of stuff. Synthetic fibres, they call them. There's not as much call for wool now and the orders aren't coming in as they used to. It's the same at Walker's, isn't it, Walter?'

'Yes, I'm afraid it is. The bosses have been talking about where they can make cuts.'

'But your job's safe, isn't it, Walter?' asked his mother.

'I hope so,' he replied with a wry grin. 'Anyway, let's change the subject. What about your Christmas pud now, Mum? I think we've all finished.'

The three women cleared away the plates, Hannah a little condescendingly but aware that it might look bad if she didn't help.

'Thank you, Hannah,' said Millie. 'A little help is worth a lot of pity, as my mother used to say, God bless her. Cissie'll help me to dish out the puds, won't you, love? A smaller portion for Holly but I expect Paul can manage as much as us, can't he?'

'You bet he can! He loves his puddings. Rum sauce an' all. It smells real good, Millie.'

'And they're actually homemade, the pudding and the sauce,' said Mille with a sly grin.

'Not like the stuffing, eh?' Hannah was now safely back in the lounge.

'Take no notice of her,' said Cissie. 'She always has to stick her oar in. She's enjoying it, though, I know she is. She cleaned her plate, didn't she?'

'Oh, I know your mother only too well,' said Millie. 'We're the best of friends, you know. I suppose we all have our funny little ways. Now, let's take these puddings in.'

The puddings, well laced with rum and the rum sauce to add more flavour, were well received by everyone.

'Delicious, Millie!' said Hannah, and there was no doubt that she meant it. The rum and the small amount of wine she had had with the meal had put her in a more mellow frame of mind. Cissie exchanged a knowing glance with Millie as she answered, 'I'm so pleased you enjoyed it, Hannah.' She couldn't resist adding, 'It's homemade.'

'The only problem now is the washing up,' said Archie. 'We'll have to get one of them dishwashers, Millie.'

'Nonsense!' exclaimed his wife. 'I've never been worried about a few pots. Let's stack 'em up and forget 'em for now. They'll keep till later. Come on, let's get on with the exciting part, shall we? The presents! Are you ready, Paul and Holly?'

The children, with Cissie helping, handed round the gifts. It was always difficult to buy for the men but Archie and Joe seemed well pleased with the lambswool scarves, the always useful socks, and large boxes of their favourite sweets, liquorice allsorts. Hannah and Millie enthused over the gift boxes of toiletries: soaps, talc and bath oil, perfumed with gardenia fragrance for Millie and lavender for Hannah – luxuries they would not buy for themselves. Both mothers were treated exactly the same.

Cissie was not surprised to receive useful presents from her mother, who never ceased to remind her that she was a house-wife: a cookery book, and apron and oven gloves – although they did have a pretty design of butterflies. And, more acceptable, a large box of Milk Tray chocolates.

Millie had chosen a very attractive manicure set, with hand cream and a set of small bottles of nail varnish. Cissie thanked them both profusely, not giving the slightest hint as to which present was the more popular.

The two grandmothers had conferred together about what to buy for the children. And, of course, it was Holly's birthday, so she had to have extra presents. They had gone on a shopping expedition together, ending up at their favourite store, Marks and Spencer. They had each chosen a pretty dress for Holly with matching cardigans, then Millie had chosen fancy socks and underwear, and Hannah a bright woollen hat and gloves, making sure that she spent just as much as her friend.

Millie bought a duffle coat for Paul, a bright blue one to

wear when he was not in school uniform, and Hannah bought him checked trousers and a blue jumper.

There were 'fun' presents as well: colouring books and crayons, a book with clothes to cut out and fit on a cardboard doll, games of Snap and Happy Families, Ladybird books and boxes of Jelly Babies and Smarties.

Paul and Holly were delighted with their gifts but were ready to go home. They had kept quiet long enough while the grown-ups listened to the queen and then had a cup of tea and a slice of Christmas cake.

'Thank goodness that's over for another year,' said Cissie when they had arrived home and settled down. 'No . . . I suppose I don't really mean that, do I? Your mam makes us so welcome and it's nice for us all to get together . . . I suppose.'

'And next year it will be your mother's turn,' Walter reminded her.

'Perish the thought! Let's enjoy the rest of the day, shall we? Your mam's given me some turkey to make sandwiches and there's Holly's birthday cake, complete with three candles.'

Walter gave her a hug and kiss. 'Thanks, Cissie, love,' he said.

'Why? What for?' she asked.

'Well . . . for everything. I sometimes forget to say it like I should. Happy Christmas, love.'

NINE

During the second week in the New Year, Janice and Phil had an unexpected visit from their next-door neighbour. Isobel Tarrant owned the florist's shop adjoining their property, aptly named Bella's Blossoms; the lady was usually known as Bella to her friends.

Janice answered the knock at the door at just turned seven o'clock, pleasantly surprised to see her.

'I hope I'm not disturbing you,' she said. 'I know you're usually very busy, but I have some news to share with you.'

'No, we're not busy at the moment,' said Janice. 'Sarah's bathed and in bed and Phil has no party in tonight. The evening bookings have dropped off a bit since the New Year so it's nice to have some time to ourselves. Come on up, Bella . . .'

Janice took their visitor into the living room where Phil was reading the evening paper. He, too, was pleased to see Bella. She was a good neighbour, busy during the day but willing to babysit on the odd occasions when they went out. Janice brought flowers from her shop to add a touch of colour and brightness to the cafe.

'A glass of sherry, Bella?' asked Phil, always an agreeable host.

'Yes, that would be lovely,' she replied. 'Thank you.' She looked a little anxious as she sat down in an armchair.

'Not bad news, I hope?' said Janice when they were all seated.

Bella took a little sip of her sherry. 'This is delicious. I don't often indulge myself with treats like this . . . No, not bad news,' she went on. 'I suppose it's good news, in a way, but I must admit that it took me a long time to make up my mind.'

They both looked at her enquiringly.

'I'm moving,' she said. 'I've decided to sell the shop and go and live with my sister. She's been urging me to do it for quite a while but I was very undecided.'

'Oh . . . I'm sorry to hear that,' said Janice. 'We'll both be sorry, won't we, Phil?' Bella had become a friend as well as a neighbour.

'We certainly will,' said Phil, 'but you have to do what is right for you. And . . . you've really made up your mind, have you?'

'Well . . . yes. I shall be sixty-five my next birthday; retiring age, although I know I could stay on longer if I wished. I really enjoy working in the shop. It's been a real godsend to me since my husband died; that's eight years ago now. We were married quite late on in life, you know. I'd turned forty and James was rather older. We never had any children but we were so happy together. It helped me to come to terms with losing him, to a certain extent, with having the shop to run. But it's getting harder, especially on these winter mornings.'

'Where does your sister live?' asked Janice. 'Will you be moving far away?'

'No, not all that far. Dorothy lives in Thirsk; well, on the outskirts of the town. It's a lovely market town and she's in a very nice part of the countryside. She's a widow, too; has been for about five years. They were married a long time, her and Bill. They had two children, and she's got grandchildren, of course, but they don't live anywhere nearby. She keeps busy with her WI meetings and her church, and she's got friends, but she says it's not the same as family. We've always got on well together, Dorothy and me; she's two years younger and there were only the two of us.' Bella stopped speaking, looking pensive and a little unsure.

'It's a big step to take, giving up your home and your liveli-hood,' said Phil, 'but I'm sure you've considered all that, haven't you?'

'And you feel you would be happy living with your sister?' asked Janice.

'Yes,' replied Bella. 'I've thought about all the pros and cons. I know I'll be giving up my home but Dorothy's house is far too big for her now. She's never wanted to move, though, since Bill died; I suppose all the memories are there . . . I'm sure I'll be happy there. She says I can have my own rooms: bedroom, of course, and a living room to myself for when I want to be on my own. But I expect we'll have our meals together and sit together in the evenings. We'll have to see how it works out, won't we?'

'And what about your premises?' asked Phil. 'Do you intend to sell it as a going concern, for someone to take over the florist's shop and the goodwill? You've built up a good business there, haven't you?'

'Yes, I suppose I have. But how many people would want to buy a florist's shop? It might sell straight away; on the other hand, I could be waiting for ages. It might be best to sell it as a shop with living accommodation, like yours was when you bought it. Vacant possession as well, because I shall move in with Dorothy as soon as I put it up for sale. I wanted you to know before the notice goes in the window.'

'Have you got an estate agent?' asked Phil.

'Yes, he'll be coming round and taking photos and setting the wheels in motion. I shall be sorry to leave in a way. I've made friends round here, and I shall miss you, of course. But we'll keep in touch, won't we?'

'Of course we will,' said Janice, 'and we wish you all the best, don't we, Phil?'

'We certainly do . . . Another glass of sherry, Bella?'

'Oh, no, thank you, dear. One is quite enough for me. I won't stay much longer. I know your time together is precious; you both work so hard.'

She left after they had chatted about this and that: Sarah's progress and how the cafe was faring after the Christmas and New Year period.

'Well, that's a surprise, isn't it?' said Janice. 'I shall miss Bella but I'm sure she's doing the right thing. It must be a cold sort of job in the winter; there's not much heat in the shop because of the flowers.'

'Yes . . .' said Phil thoughtfully. 'It's a good shop, though – nice and roomy.' He looked enquiringly at Janice. 'Are you thinking what I'm thinking?' he asked with a half-smile.

'I haven't thought much at all yet, except about Bella leaving. But I can guess the way your mind is working!'

'Do you think we could?' Phil's eyes were shining with

enthusiasm. 'It's an ideal opportunity, the shop next door becoming vacant. We were talking about extending, weren't we?'

'Only tentatively,' said Janice. 'You were doing most of the talking and I was listening! But I really thought it was more of a pipe dream. I know you mentioned that we might look for a house nearby so that we could turn the upstairs into a restaurant.'

'But this would make more sense, wouldn't it? If we were to combine our place and Bella's shop it would give us a much larger dining area. And we'd have lots more space to play with upstairs – two extra bedrooms, maybe. You know that Sarah really needs a room of her own.'

'It would mean a lot of structural work, though; knocking down walls and goodness knows what else.'

'It could be done. Lots of people buy the premises next door when they want to expand. It's too good a chance to miss, Janice.'

'Oh, stop, Phil! You're making me dizzy! Do you really think it's possible?'

'I don't see why not. We're doing well . . .'

'There's been a lull since Christmas . . .'

'But it's picking up again. I've quite a few evening bookings, and in February we could do Valentine evenings.'

'We'd have to close down, though, while the work was going on.'

'Not necessarily . . . Well, maybe for a week or two. But it would be worth it in the long run.'

'Let's sleep on it, Phil,' said Janice. 'I'm overwhelmed at the moment. We'd need to talk nicely to our bank manager and find a firm of builders who are reliable. There are so many cowboys on that sort of job.'

'Very true, but the firm we had before were OK, weren't they?'

'This is a much bigger job, making two premises into one. It's certainly ambitious, Phil.'

'Yes, I know, but what is it they say? You have to speculate in order to accumulate.'

'That's all very well, but I don't want us to get into deep water and find we've taken on too much.'

'Don't worry, we won't. I'm a good swimmer! But, as you say, we'll sleep on it. Let's have a cup of tea and forget about it for now. Then we'll see what tomorrow brings.'

But Phil knew that he would feel exactly the same the following day.

In January, a new term started in colleges and schools all over the country.

Ian and Sophie said goodbye as they finished their holiday jobs at Grundy's, promising to write and to meet . . . who could say when? The next long holiday would be at Easter. Ian didn't know if Phil would need any assistance at that time of year. Besides, the holiday season would be starting in Blackpool and the students were often engaged temporarily by the seaside hotels.

It was with mixed feelings that Ian retuned home. He had enjoyed Christmas with Janice and Phil, and when his dad and Norma had visited they had all got along well together. Sophie, who was by no means a shy girl, had made a good impression on them. Ian had benefited from her friendship. She had brought him out of the protective shell he had formed around himself and helped him to come to terms with his feelings about his father and Norma.

He was sad to part from Sophie; on the other hand, he was looking forward to getting back to college and the course that he was enjoying so much. He had mixed feelings, too, about seeing Darren again. Would there be any constraint or embarrassment between them? he wondered. He had found the incident unnerving, and it had worried him, probably more than it might have worried other lads who were more worldly-wise than he was.

However, when he found himself in the same group as Darren, the young man behaved as though nothing untoward had happened. Like Ian, he was ready to apply himself to the next part of the course. It promised to be an interesting term.

Every so often the students put on a three-course meal, sometimes at lunchtime, sometimes in the evening, to which people from outside the college were invited. A reasonable charge was made for the meal and it was a chance for the students to show off their skills, not only in the cooking and presentation of it but in the serving and waiting at the tables. The next such occasion was to be towards the end of March, and Ian decided, as it was an evening meal, that he would invite his dad and Norma to come along.

'It's not free, though,' he told them. 'And you need tickets because the numbers are limited.'

'We'd love to come, wouldn't we, Alec?' said Norma. 'And I'm sure it'll be worth every penny.'

They had received a letter from Janice and Phil at the beginning of February with some very interesting and surprising news. They were buying the florist's shop next door and were extending their business.

'It's all in the early stages yet,' Janice had written. 'We managed to get a bank loan, but don't worry, we're not overreaching ourselves. The cafe and the evening bookings are doing well and we're sure we're making a good move. We need more living space anyway, with Sarah growing up. At the moment we are in consultation with the builders to sort out the best way to tackle this project, so they should start work quite soon . . .'

'By heck! That's an ambitious move,' said Alec. 'But I always thought Phil was a go-ahead sort of lad. Well, jolly good luck to them! I hope they're not biting off more than they can chew.'

'Phil knows what he's doing,' said Ian. 'He said he wanted to build up the evening trade and make Grundy's a name that everyone knows about. I hope it goes well for them.'

Ian had other things on his mind, though. Sophie had not been writing as regularly, though he knew she was busy with her college work and he was not the world's best letter writer. It wasn't really possible to contact her by phone, which would have been simpler. Then, in mid-February – just before St Valentine's Day – she wrote to say that she felt it was only fair to tell him that she was seeing someone else, a fellow student she had met at one of the weekly dances. *I hope we can still be friends*, she wrote, *but we'd decided, hadn't we, that we didn't want to get serious?*

Ian found himself confiding in Norma, rather than his father, when she commented that he looked a bit down in the dumps.

'Yes, I am,' he replied with a wry grin. 'Very aptly put, actually. Sophie has dumped me.'

'Oh, I'm sorry to hear that,' said Norma. 'Sophie's a lovely girl – we like her very much. But you're only . . .'

'Yes, I know,' Ian interrupted her. 'I'm only young and she was my first girlfriend . . . but I really liked her. I suppose I knew this might happen, though, with her being at a college with so many men around.'

'Yes, that's true. But there are girls at your college, aren't there?'

'Yes, of course, about as many girls as men. Some are older; they've done other jobs before but some are around my age. I've not been interested, though.'

'Well, sometimes someone comes along when you least expect it. You never know what's round the next corner. You make sure you enjoy your leisure time as well as your work. We know you're working very hard but make some time to have fun, eh?'

Ian smiled at her. 'Yes . . . thanks, Norma. I'll try.'

There were times when he found that he liked her very much.

At the other side of the Pennines, Holly Clarkson was enjoying her first term at Sunnybank playgroup. She referred to it as school, not to be outshone by her elder brother. Every day she came home singing a new song or reciting a little jingle they had learnt.

'I'm a little teapot, short and stout; here's my handle, here's my spout . . .' she chorused, complete with actions.

They were provided with milk and biscuits at a mid-morning break and the session ended at half past twelve when the mothers – or sometimes grandmothers – came to collect them.

Cissie was pleased at the way Holly had settled into the playgroup, but she had never really doubted that she would. She had been a very easy child so far, usually obedient and with a very loving nature. Seeing her friend, Val, struggling at times with Russell, Cissie realized how fortunate she had been with her own children.

The house felt strangely empty, though, with the two of them out every morning. It had been quiet when Paul started school but now it was even more so. Cissie had more time to do her household tasks and more time for herself. It was blissful, at times, to sit down for half an hour to read a magazine and enjoy a cup of coffee and a cigarette. But Cissie was really an energetic person and she soon realized that this would not do. She had thought about getting a part-time job, as she had mentioned to her family at Christmas, but she had not really considered how this would work in practice. Holly was away for only three-and-a-half hours, nine till twelve thirty. There was little time for her to do a job and be back in time to meet Holly.

She had toyed with the idea of asking Walter's mother to meet her, if and when she got a job, but that did not seem fair; her mother-in-law was a busy person and she had her own daily routine. There was her friend, Megan, though . . . It had occurred to her, fleetingly, that she might be able to help, then Cissie had put the idea to one side. It would be too much to ask of her friend.

Megan lived a few doors away from the Clarksons. She had a daughter, Kelly, who was a little older than Holly, and a much younger boy.

'You're quite keen on getting a job, aren't you?' she said one day towards the end of February, when they were walking home after leaving the children.

'Well, it was just an idea,' said Cissie, trying to sound nonchalant. 'It's been so bloomin' cold though just lately that I've been glad to get home to the fire. But spring's on its way so I might see what I can do. It's not so easy, though, with . . .'

'With the children, I know,' said Megan. 'But stop worrying about Holly. I'll meet her from playgroup, then she can have a bit of lunch with me and Kelly. I suppose you're thinking of just a morning job, not all day?'

'Good heavens, no! I say, that's real good of you, Megan. I'm not desperate to get a job but it would help with extras and I might have a bit of money to spare for myself. Walter doesn't say much but I know things are not too good at the mill. You never know who'll be next for the chop.'

'Not Walter, surely?'

'Probably not, but you never know. Thanks, Megan; I'm really pleased about that.'

'I sometimes think I'd like a job myself – get out of the house for a bit – but Ryan's only just turned one so it'll be a long while before I can do it. Harry earns good money, though; not the poshest of jobs but he doesn't complain. And it's surprising what they pick up on their travels. Some folk have more money than sense!'

Harry Price was a refuse collector – or dustbin man – who often came home with spoils of the job: almost new household goods that people had thrown out. Megan had recently acquired a radio and a food mixer.

'So what do you fancy doing then?' she asked. 'What sort of job? You wouldn't want to go back to the mill, would you?'

'I can't, even if I wanted to; there's no jobs going there. I'd like a change. Not a cleaning job! I don't really like cleaning our own house but I do it 'cause I want it to look nice. Perhaps a shop job; I've never done that sort of work but I could learn. I'm not stupid. I'll have a look around when I'm in town and see if there's any adverts in the paper.'

'Good luck hunting then,' said Megan. 'I'll be ready to help as soon as you need me.'

Cissie's favourite place in Halifax was the old Victorian market hall. It was a colourful and interesting place, always busy what-ever the time of day. The aroma from the various stalls filled your nostrils as soon as you entered. Pleasant smells, though, from the cheese and fish stalls, and the scent of flowers, fresh fruit and vegetables.

It was one of Holly's favourite places, too. There was a tempting sweet stall and Cissie, who had never been the sort of mother to worry too much about her children eating sweets, always treated her to some of her favourites – Jelly Babies, midget gems or chocolate drops – making sure they took some home for Paul as well.

Cissie, too, was unable to resist the homemade fudge and treacle toffee, and some of Walter's favourite peanut brittle.

She found it a real treat now, however, to be able to browse around the stalls on her own without Holly tugging at her, wanting to look at the toy stall or the bakery where Cissie would let her choose a cake for her tea. Holly was a well-behaved child, though, not the sort that you often saw in town yelling their heads off and being pushed and pulled around by harassed mothers.

Cissie was enjoying her freedom but she was still looking out for a job. One morning in mid-March she was paying her weekly visit to the market. She had bought some fat pork sausages for tea and a piece of brisket beef for the weekend from one of the many butchers' stalls, along with potatoes, carrots and sprouts, apples and bananas, fresh crusty bread and a selection of cakes, a chunk of Wensleydale cheese and their weekly treats from the sweet stall.

Her bags were heavy; too heavy for her to walk home – she would have to get the bus. But before that she would have a sit down and a cup of coffee at the little cafe in the centre of the market. It was always busy with shoppers and workers from round about who popped in for a quick snack. There were various toasted items, currant teacakes, sandwiches, soup, cakes and pastries on offer, but Cissie only wanted a cup of coffee – and a cigarette – to help her to relax before going home then collecting Holly from the playgroup. As usual, she had spent longer than she should have mooching around, so she had little enough time to spare.

The waitresses were friendly and cheerful and the service was brisk. She was revived by the strong, sweet coffee and a few drags of her cigarette, then she was ready for off again. She paid the bill and picked up her heavy bags. It was only as she was going out that she saw the notice on the wall near the entrance: *Staff required. Apply within.* And to think she had almost missed it.

She retraced her steps and spoke to the woman on the cash desk. She knew that this was Mrs Laycock, the owner, who did her share at anything that needed doing: helping in the small kitchen area, serving at the tables and dealing with the money. She knew Cissie quite well by sight because of her frequent visits there.

Cissie pointed across to the notice. 'I've only just seen that and I'm looking for a job; only part-time, though. Is it for a waitress?'

'I've only put it up this morning,' said Mrs Laycock, 'and

you're the first to enquire. Yes, we need a couple of waitresses. Moira's leaving us – she's having a baby – and we'll need another one 'cause we're always busier in the spring and summer. Part-time, you said, love?'

'Yes, only mornings, while my little girl's at playgroup. I'd have to collect her at about . . . two o'clock, I suppose. My friend said she'd look after her if I got a job.'

'Well, it looks as if you've got one, love, if you'd like it. We'll give you a try, anyway, but I'm sure you'll be fine. I've seen the way you look after your little girl. Never any trouble, was she?'

'No, she's a good little lass.' Cissie was feeling quite over-whelmed. 'Gosh! Can't believe this. You're really saying I can have the job?'

'Well, let's say a week's trial, to be fair to all of us.' Mrs Laycock smiled at her. 'Can you start Monday, nine o'clock? Oh . . . and can you manage Saturdays?'

Cissie hesitated before saying, 'I'm sure I'll be able to sort it out. Thanks ever so much. I'll see you Monday, then.'

'Wait a minute . . .' Mrs Laycock laughed. 'I don't even know your name, do I?'

'I'm Cissie – Cissie Clarkson, and I live on Jubilee Road.'

'Oh, yes, I know it. Not too far away. And I'm Ada; we don't stand on ceremony here, so long as we all pull our weight. I'll look forward to working with you, Cissie.'

TEN

Easter that year was at the beginning of April. By that time Cissie was working happily at her new job. She had not really thought, when taking the job, about Saturday mornings or the school holidays. The playgroup stayed open but Paul would need someone to look after him.

Walter had agreed to take care of both children on Saturday mornings. He did not work on that day and did not mind as long as he could attend the football match on Saturday afternoon.

Walter's mother, and Cissie's mother – rather less willingly – agreed to have Paul during the school holidays. It was only for the mornings and he was a well-behaved child, most of the time. Hannah Foster actually enjoyed the mornings when he was in her care, but she never stopped reminding Cissie that she was doing her a tremendous favour.

'Cissie says that Holly has settled down very well at her playgroup,' Val remarked to Sam soon after Easter. 'She's been there since January and she loves it. I wonder if I should try Russell at the playgroup near to us? He's such an active child and it's hard to keep him occupied all the time. I know he gets frustrated. Maybe it would be good for him to have children of his own age to play with. Do you think so, Sam?'

Sam raised his eyebrows. 'Maybe, maybe not. You can try it if you like. I know you've got your hands full with both him and Lucy. But Holly's such an easy little girl, isn't she? Not much trouble. That always amazes me when I think about Cissie! I dare say Holly would make friends with anyone. Russell's quite a different kettle of fish!'

'Oh, Cissie's OK,' said Val. 'She's much more stable since she married Walter and had the children. I think he's been good for her, although I had my doubts at first. And she really loves her job at the market . . . Anyway, it was Russell we were talking about. I'll give him a try at the playgroup. They take them at two-and-a-half and he'll be three in September.'

The playgroup was not the one that Holly attended, and Val was relieved about that. For some reason, Russell liked to taunt Holly, and she was such a sweet-natured little girl. Val didn't want any trouble with her best friend.

The playgroup was called Happy Days and was only a few minutes' walk from their home. It was in a much more pleasant setting than Sunnylands, which was in a Methodist church hall with only a concrete area to play in outside. The helpers had to watch the toddlers continually for fear of grazed knees or worse, so they spent most of the time indoors.

Happy Days was in a large detached house with an attractive rear garden, equipped with a slide, swings and a sandpit. The owner of the house, Kate Whittaker, had two children under school age, a four-year-old girl and a boy roughly the same age as Russell. She had done the necessary training in childminding, and Val felt that not only would Russell be in safe hands, but that, hopefully, his behaviour would improve. Although she felt guilty for even thinking it – and she wouldn't dream of saying it to Cissie – the Happy Days playgroup was much more upmarket than Sunnylands with, presumably, children who were biddable and easy to control. Russell might well learn by example.

He seemed to understand when she and Sam told him he was going to a lovely place where he could play with a lot of other boys and girls.

'There's a slide and swings and lots of toys,' Val told him. 'Some nice ladies to look after you, and I expect they'll have milk and biscuits like they do at Holly's playgroup.'

'Like orange juice best,' he replied.

'Well, I expect they'll have orange juice as well . . .'

'Is Holly there?' He grinned at his mum.

'No, Holly goes to a different place.'

'Are you coming, Mummy?' He was looking a little puzzled.

'I shall take you and leave you there for the morning,' she told him. 'You know, like you go to stay with Grandma some-times. And then I'll come and meet you and we'll go home for lunch. OK, Russell?'

'OK.' He nodded. 'Is Lucy coming?'

'Oh, no; Lucy's only a baby, isn't she? And you're a big boy.'

He nodded again. 'Bigger than Lucy.'

He seemed quite contented about it all as he walked at the side of Val, who was pushing the pram. It was the Monday following Easter week. He had been pretty good just lately. There had been Easter eggs from various members of the family and he had enjoyed the treasure hunt that Sam had arranged in their garden, searching for miniature eggs.

He seemed overwhelmed when Val introduced him to Kate.

'Hello, Russell,' she said. 'We're glad you've come to join us. And what a lovely red jumper! Did Mummy make it?'

He shook his head. 'No . . . Grandma.'

'Oh, I see.' Kate looked a little anxiously at his unsmiling face but realized it was all very new to him. 'Well, say bye-bye to Mummy and we'll go and meet some of the other boys and girls . . . He'll be OK,' she added quietly to Val. 'It's a bit strange at first. What we do is give them a week to settle down, then we'll know whether it's a good idea . . . or not. As I said, Mrs Walker, he is rather young. My little boy, Gareth, is the same age, so maybe they'll get on together. Don't worry; we'll take good care of him.'

Val kissed Russell's cheek. 'Bye-bye, love. Mummy will see you soon.'

He didn't answer, but she was used to his silences when he was not very sure about something. Kate seemed like a very capable person, used to dealing with all sorts of children.

Val spent an anxious morning wondering how he was going on and whether it had been a good idea. When she went to meet him at half past twelve he was ready and waiting with his coat on, along with several other children.

'Mummy!' he shouted when he saw her, which gave her a stab of joy and love for him. He could be lovable at times, which helped to convince her that they had done the right thing in adopting him. At other times she was still full of doubts, but she told herself he was sure to improve.

'Has he been a good boy?' Val asked Kate, making sure that Russell could hear.

'Well . . . it's early days, Mrs Walker,' she replied. 'As I said, it takes a while to settle down and get used to the other children. But I'm sure he will. Bye-bye, Russell. See you tomorrow.'

'Bye,' he muttered, holding Val's hand tightly.

She decided not to remonstrate with him, although she guessed that things had not gone too well.

'Did you like it?' she asked when they had walked a fair distance from the house.

'Yes,' he answered briefly.

'So . . . what did you do? Did you play with the other boys and girls?'

'Yes. Played in the sand, and the slide, and we had milk and biccies. No orange juice . . .'

'Oh, well, never mind. Did you drink your milk?'

He nodded. 'Don't like Gareth.'

'Oh dear! Why don't you like him?'

'Don't know, just don't!'

She decided not to question him any more. He was ready for the fish fingers and mashed potato she prepared when they arrived home. He got down from the table and went over to Lucy as she sat in her high chair.

'Now leave her alone,' said Val. 'She's enjoying her rusk.'

But to her amazement he stood on his tiptoes and took hold of Lucy's hand. 'Like Lucy,' he said.

'Well . . . that's nice!' said Val, utterly flabbergasted. 'You're a good boy, Russell.'

He was surprisingly good for the rest of the day, but not very willing to tell his daddy much about the playgroup.

'I think there's something that Kate's not telling me,' Val said. 'I do hope he wasn't a nuisance. Anyway, we'll see.'

The next day, Tuesday, seemed to go all right. Russell went along willingly in the morning, and when Val met him at lunchtime Kate said that he had been much better. 'I must admit he was a little difficult yesterday,' she said, 'but I think we're winning. We usually do. See you tomorrow, Russell.'

On Wednesday, however, when Val arrived to collect Russell, he was ready and waiting with his coat on, looking far from happy.

'Hello, Mummy,' he said in a tiny voice, then he hung his head.

Mrs Whittaker stood at his side, looking solemn. 'Could I have a word with you, Mrs Walker?' she said. 'Let's go in here.'

'Just a minute,' said Val. 'I'd better get Lucy.' She went

outside to lift the little girl from her pram, then followed Kate into the room that she used as an office.

'Now, Russell,' said Kate, 'you sit quietly and look at this book about the three bears while I have a talk to Mummy. Sit down, Mrs Walker. This won't take very long.' She looked at Val understandingly, with a faint smile.

'Oh dear!' said Val, guessing at what she was about to hear. 'Has he been a nuisance? I'm so sorry. What has he done?'

Kate gave a little laugh, although it was clear she was not really amused. 'What hasn't he done! I'm sorry, Mrs Walker, but it seems as though Russell is not ready for playgroup, not at the moment. We knew he was rather young, didn't we? He won't be three until September, and I'm afraid he'll have to wait a while before we try him again.'

'But . . . it's only been three days,' said Val. 'You said he could have a week's trial.'

'We can tell already that it's not going to work, not at the moment. He's disruptive and some of the children are getting upset.'

To her own embarrassment, Val burst into tears. She shook her head. 'I'm so sorry. I really thought this would be good for him, mixing with other children. He's not been an easy child. He was adopted – you probably know the circumstances. We thought we were doing the right thing, my husband and I, although some people did try to warn us.'

Kate leaned forward and took her hand. 'Try not to get upset . . . Valerie, isn't it?'

'Yes, Val . . . I'm usually called Val.'

'I remember you adopting Russell,' said Kate. 'His parents were killed in a car crash, weren't they?' She was speaking quietly and Russell seemed oblivious to their conversation. Val had never known him to be so subdued.

'You're doing a great job, Val,' Kate went on. 'Russell is already toilet trained, and that's a great achievement. It's one of our stipulations, you know. And he's not a messy eater, like so many of them . . . except that he refuses to drink his milk.'

'What did he do?'

'Well, he spilt it on purpose, I'm sorry to say.'

Val sighed. 'And what else?'

'He prefers to throw the sand around rather than making pies! It didn't go in anyone's eyes, but you can see that it could be rather dangerous. And he doesn't like sharing the toys. He listens to stories, though; he seems to enjoy that. But, as I said, Val, it's too soon. Let's wait until he's three. I'm sure there'll be a big improvement by then.'

'I wish I could feel so sure.' Val stroked Lucy's dark hair as she sat on her lap. 'I suppose there's been a bit of jealousy since Lucy arrived. She was quite a surprise to us. We'd given up hope of having any children of our own – at least, I had – and then I found out I was expecting Lucy.'

'And now you've got a lovely little family,' said Kate. 'Russell's not the only troublesome child in the world, you know. You've heard people talk about the "terrible twos", haven't you? When they find out that they can say "no!" instead of doing as they're told. But I'm sorry I have to say no to Russell at this moment. You do understand, don't you?'

'Only too well,' replied Val, feeling a little more composed by now but still very ashamed of Russell's behaviour. 'Thank you for trying, anyway . . . Come along, Russell. We're going home now, and you won't be coming here again for a while.'

'Goodbye, Russell,' said Kate. 'We'll perhaps see you again when you're three.'

'Bye,' muttered Russell. 'Come on, Mummy. Want to go home.'

Russell was quiet as they walked home, and Val, deep in thought, did not feel like talking to him. She decided there would be no point in telling him he was a naughty boy or asking him what he had done to make the ladies cross and upset the children. He seemed to have got the message and was suitably abashed, but she doubted this would last very long. Perhaps, as Kate said, he was rather too young and the discipline they had to maintain seemed strange to him. All the same, it was clear that he needed to learn how to get along with children of his own age.

He ate his lunch of sausage and mash, then played quietly with his cars before watching a children's TV programme, snuggling close to Val on the settee.

She met Sam in the hall as he came in from work, before he

had time to speak to Russell. 'Don't ask him what he did at playgroup. I'm afraid he's been sacked!'

Sam laughed. 'Well, that didn't last long, did it? Too much for them to handle, was he?'

'It's not funny, Sam,' said Val, although she could not help smiling a little. 'I was really upset when Kate told me; quite ashamed of him. I don't want people thinking we can't control him.'

'What did he do?'

'Oh, create mayhem! Throwing sand around, spilling his milk, not sharing the toys . . .'

'Well, he's never really had to share, has he? He usually plays on his own; Lucy's too small to play with him yet.'

'And she's such a good little girl, isn't she? I hope he doesn't make her naughty when she gets older.'

'Now, don't start anticipating trouble. We've just given him a try there. I suppose he can go again later?'

'Yes, when he's three.'

'Well, that's not very long; only five months or so.'

'It would be nice to go shopping in peace. He's quite a handful in the shops, you know.'

Sam gave her a hug. 'Well, I think you're doing splendidly. What's for tea? I'm starving!'

'Lamb casserole; it's cooking slowly in the oven. I'll get the two of them to bed, then we'll have a nice, peaceful evening. It's been quite a day.'

'I'll see to Russell,' said Sam, 'while you bath Lucy. I'll read him a story, and not a word, eh, about his transgressions?'

'No, he's been pretty good since we got home. Let's hope he's learnt a lesson.'

Val went shopping quite near to their home most mornings of the week. They had a weekly order delivered from the local Co-op but there were not many mornings when she did not need to shop for fresh bread or meat or vegetables. It was a breath of fresh air for her and the children, and she felt that the walk was good for her.

She could only go to the town of Halifax, down in the valley, when Sam was available to take them in the car. Val was able to drive but it was not possible for her to see to the children and concentrate on her driving at the same time.

They set off for the local shops on the Friday morning of the week when Russell had started – and left – the playgroup. She had her shopping list so she would not forget anything, as she was likely to do with Russell demanding her attention. She carried a large shopping bag which would fit on to the handle of the pram, and there was room at the end of the pram for some things below Lucy's feet.

There was a tempting display of fruit and vegetables outside the greengrocer's shop for customers to help themselves.

'Oranges, Mummy,' said Russell, grabbing hold of a large Jaffa.

'Put that down, love,' she said. 'You're not supposed to touch unless you're buying it.'

'I like oranges . . .'

'I know you do. We'll get some of those small ones that are easy to peel, then you won't get in a mess.'

She put six tangerines in a bag, then chose some apples and bananas.

'What's these, Mummy?' Russell scooped up a handful of garden peas.

'They're peas. Put them down! I've told you not to touch.'

'I like peas . . .'

'Yes, I know, but we have frozen peas. These need shelling and it takes too much time. We'll get a cauliflower and some carrots.'

'Don't like carrots.'

'Well, they're good for you. My mummy used to tell me that they helped you to see in the dark. Look . . . you can put some in this bag . . . That's a good boy; that's enough.' He behaved better when he was occupied and thought he was helping.

'Come on, now; we'll go in the shop and pay for these things.'

Lucy was sleeping peacefully, as she did when lulled by the movement of the pram. Val left the pram where she could see it from inside the shop. If she left Russell there he was likely to shake the pram until Lucy woke up. The shopping bag was heavy when she had paid for the fruit and vegetables and she balanced it on the pram handle as they went on to the bakery.

There was an appetizing aroma of freshly baked bread coming from the baker's shop. They made most of their own produce, and there was, as usual, a queue of women waiting to be served. She took the shopping bag inside with her, fearing that it might prove too much of a temptation if left on the pram; not everyone in the world was honest.

There were tempting cakes displayed in the window and on the counter behind the glass partition: almond tarts, jam and lemon tarts and Yorkshire curd tart – Sam's favorite. Cream cakes, too, iced fondant cakes, Swiss rolls and fruit cakes full of sultanas and cherries.

Val enjoyed baking her own cakes and had become quite proficient in the years since her marriage. But it was nice, occasionally, to have a special treat made by professionals, such as Mr and Mrs Gregson who owned the bakery.

Val's thoughts turned then to Janice and Phil and their plans for their cafe in Harrogate. Janice had rung in great excitement, saying that they had acquired the florist's shop next door and were extending their business. Janice made superb cakes, such as the ones on sale here. The last Val had heard was that they were planning to start their new venture at the end of May.

She pulled herself back from her wandering thoughts and glanced out of the window. Lucy, who had been fast asleep, seemed to be stirring. The blanket was moving a little as she kicked her legs. Val hoped she would not wake up fully until she had finished her shopping here.

Russell was pulling at her sleeve. 'Look, choccies, Mummy,' he said, pointing to the rear of the shop. They sold homemade chocolates as well as cakes – delicious fudges, marzipans, creams and pralines, caramels and nougats, all covered in plain, milk and white chocolate, to be chosen individually and packed in special white and gold cartons.

'Yes, I know, Russell,' said Val, 'but they're not for children. They're for grown-ups and they're very expensive . . .' Occasionally she had indulged in a few, and sometimes Sam bought them for her.

'See, Russell – you can choose a cake for your tea. What about one of those pink ones with a cherry on top?'

But Russell was not to be dissuaded. He had wandered to

the back of the shop again. She left him there as he couldn't touch the chocolates behind the glass.

At last, it was her turn to be served. She bought a crusty loaf, some currant teacakes, a large curt tart as a treat for Sam, two iced fancies for the children, a cream cake for herself and a large fruit cake. The lady who was serving provided her with a carrier bag and she spent a few moments arranging her purchases.

'Come along, Russell,' she said. 'Time to go.'

But he would not budge. 'Want choccies,' he said.

'No, they're not for you. I'll buy you some sweets when we go to pay the paper bill.'

Bribery, she knew, but one or two women were watching, no doubt thinking, *What a troublesome child!* She took hold of his hand and practically dragged him from the shop. Fortunately he was not crying, as some children might do. He was rarely reduced to tears.

She stepped outside, then stood stock still in shock and amazement. The pram had gone. She stood open-mouthed for a few seconds, then stared around wildly. Had the brake come off? Had it somehow rolled away? But no, it was nowhere in sight.

She dashed back into the shop. 'My baby!' she cried. 'The pram . . . It's gone!'

Russell, at her side, murmured, 'Lucy gone!' but she scarcely heard him.

There was silence in the shop as the few women waiting to be served looked on in horror. Mrs Gregson came out from behind the counter.

'Sit down, dear,' she said, leading her to a chair which was provided for people who were not very good at standing. Val was trembling by this time, then she burst into tears, sobbing uncontrollably.

'My baby, Lucy . . . Oh, what can I do? We must find her.'

'Ring the police. Ring nine-nine-nine,' Mrs Gregson called out. 'Somebody ring, please.'

The other assistant, Molly, was making her way to the phone at the back of the shop.

'No, you carry on serving,' said one of the customers. 'I'll ring.'

'Is there someone we can call, dear?' asked Mrs Gregson. 'Your husband, maybe?'

'Yes . . . yes, Sam,' said Val between her sobs. 'He's at work. Whatever will he say? I shouldn't have left her, but I always do. I never thought . . .'

'Lucy gone . . .' Russell said again, staring around in bewilderment.

'We'll find her, lovey,' said Mrs Gregson. 'The policemen will find her.' She gave him a hug. 'And we'll get your daddy to come and look after Mummy.'

Val haltingly told her the number of the mill office. 'It's Walker's mill,' she said. 'My husband's Sam Walker, the boss's son.' She started crying again. 'Oh, whatever will he say?'

'Now, don't start blaming yourself. Prams are left outside here all the time. And you've been in here lots of times, haven't you, dear? I remember you but I didn't know you were Mrs Walker. Look, try and drink this cup of tea. I think Molly's put some brandy in it.'

'Yes, so I have, and lots of sugar. It's good for shock.'

'Molly, would you ring this number, please?' said Mrs Gregson. 'It's Walker's mill, where this lady's husband works; actually, he's Mr Sam Walker.'

'And I'm Val; everybody calls me Val.'

'And I'm Jean,' said Mrs Gregson. She turned to Molly. 'It might be better if you say that Mrs Walker has been taken ill and could her husband come here as soon as possible. We can explain when he gets here.'

'I'm dreading telling him,' said Val. 'He'll say I've been careless; I've neglected her . . .'

'Indeed you haven't,' said Jean Gregson. 'I'll put a notice on the door to say we're closed for half an hour.' There was a lull at that moment as all the customers had been served. 'It shouldn't be long before the police arrive. It seems a long time when you're waiting but they'll soon be here—' Her words were interrupted by the sound of a police siren. 'Well, now, they're here already.'

A police sergeant and a woman constable came into the shop. Val tried to calm herself as she explained, along with Mrs Gregson, what had happened.

'I kept looking out,' she said, 'like I always do. I could see the blanket moving and I thought she might be waking up. Then

I was busy being served and seeing to my shopping, and when I went out the pram had gone . . .' The words caught in her throat and she gave a sob.

'We'll find her, Mrs Walker,' said the sergeant. 'We'll start a search of the area straight away. I know this is dreadful for you but, believe me, there would be more cause for concern if it was a child of five or six, say, who had been abducted. This is a baby in a pram.'

'More than likely it's a spur of the moment thing,' said the woman constable. 'A woman who has had a miscarriage, maybe, or is unable to have children. It's very unlikely that your little girl will come to any real harm.'

'But you must find her . . .' pleaded Val.

'We'll do all we can, Mrs Walker. I have every confidence that she won't be far away.' The police sergeant, a kindly, middle-aged man, looked sure of himself, and Val began to feel just a little less distraught.

Sam arrived at that moment, knocking at the closed door. Molly went to open it. He dashed across to Val and put his arms round her.

'Oh, Val, darling; thank goodness you're in one piece. I thought you'd be lying unconscious, or worse. But you're upset, aren't you? Whatever's the matter? He looked with concern at the police. 'Whatever is it?'

'Lucy gone . . .' Russell said again.

Val turned on him. 'Stop saying that, Russell! You're driving me mad!'

The policeman explained as succinctly as possible what had happened. 'But we will find your little girl, Mr Walker. We'll start our search right away.'

'And it wasn't Val's fault,' said Mrs Gregson. 'She scarcely took her eyes off the pram. It must have happened in a split second.'

'I'm afraid that's all it needs,' said the policewoman.

Sam held Val close to him. 'I wouldn't dream of blaming Val,' he said. 'She's a wonderful mother.' He looked at Russell, who was unusually quiet and looking contrite. 'She's got her hands full, though.'

'It wasn't Russell's fault,' said Val, knowing it would be all too easy to blame him. She had been distracted by him, pestering about the chocolates, but she had also been a while paying and arranging her shopping, and had taken her eyes off the pram.

'We'll make a start now,' said the sergeant. 'Give us your address and phone number and we'll be in constant touch.'

'And we'd better go home,' said Sam after the police had gone. 'Thank you so much for looking after my wife. We'll let you know as soon as we hear anything.'

'Now, young man,' said Jean Gregson to Russell, 'I saw you looking at the chocolates. All the children do. Very tempting, aren't they? But, like your mummy said, they're not really for children. You can take some home as a special treat, though. Let's choose some, shall we? Not caramels or nougats because they stick to your teeth.'

Russell chose, with Jean's guidance, a strawberry cream, a marzipan, a fudge and a marshmallow.

'Eat them after your tea, only one at a time,' she said.

Russell nodded solemnly. He said, 'Thank you,' without needing to be reminded.

Sam picked up Val's shopping and they went out to the car.

'I hope they find that little lass,' said Jean as they drove away. 'What a nice little family! That lad's a bit of a handful, but . . . oh, dear God, please let them find her!'

ELEVEN

'Oh, how awful!' said Cissie when Walter told her the news about Lucy's disappearance from outside the bakery. 'Poor Val, and Sam, of course, but Val must be going mad with guilt. Well, I know I would be. We've all done it, though; left our prams outside when we've been in a shop.'

The news had filtered around Walker's mill – not to everyone, but Walter, being quite high up in the pecking order, had been told quite quickly.

'I'll ring Val and tell her we're thinking about them,' said Cissie. 'There's nowt we can do, I know, but at least we can tell them how sorry we are. And happen a little prayer might not go amiss.' She cast a glance heavenwards.

Cissie had been brought up to attend Sunday school and church, though sometimes under duress. She rarely went now, but she still believed that 'Him up there' might listen.

They had recently had a phone installed as Walter had had a pay rise, but he was fighting a losing battle trying to stop her from ringing up all and sundry.

'I'm working an' all now,' she reminded him.

Walter had to admit that this was true and it did help a little with the family budget. She was enjoying her job at the market and he had no cause to complain about her neglecting him or the children. She was coping well with her busy life.

'Hello . . .' said Val's anxious voice when Cissie phoned her. 'Oh, it's you, Cissie. Every time the phone rings we think it might be news about Lucy.'

'We're really sorry, Walter and me,' said Cissie, 'but they'll find her, you know. I think our police are great. And how's Russell? I hope he's being a good boy. You've got enough to worry about.'

'Actually, he's being very good. He's very quiet, though, as if he thinks he might have done something wrong. Thanks for ringing, Cissie. I don't feel like talking much, to be honest. We'll let you know when we hear anything.'

'That's OK, I understand. We'll be thinking about you – me and Walter. And I'll say a little prayer tonight.'

Sam had stayed at home for the rest of that day. They had made makeshift meals although neither of them had felt like eating.

Russell was bathed and now in bed. He had shaken his head when Val said he could have one of his chocolates after tea.

'No, don't want it, Mummy.'

He had listened half-heartedly to the story of the gingerbread man that Sam read to him. Val thought she could hear him moving around now. She went upstairs and, to her amazement, he was sitting up on the bed, whimpering.

'Want Lucy . . .' he said.

'I know you do, darling.' Val put her arms round him, feeling a tenderness for him that, to her shame, she did not always feel. 'We'll find her; the policemen will find her.' She tried to sound more positive than she was feeling.

'Where's she gone?'

'We don't know, darling. We think somebody – probably a lady – just decided to take her, maybe because she wanted a baby and she didn't have one of her own.'

'That's naughty . . .'

'Yes, it is; very naughty, like when you want another little boy's car and you run off with it.'

Russell nodded solemnly.

'But this is worse,' Val went on, 'because Lucy's a real live baby, not a toy.'

'But she'll come back . . .?'

'I'm sure she'll be back . . . quite soon. Now you snuggle down and go to sleep.' She kissed his cheek and stroked his hair. 'Night night, Russell.'

'Night, Mummy,' he murmured.

He looked so angelic when he was tucked up in bed, it was hard to believe that this was the same child who could be so obstreperous, causing trouble at the playgroup, demanding attention and determined to have his own way. There had been a change in his behaviour today since Lucy had disappeared. Val regretted that it had taken such a crisis to bring about an improvement. Would it last? But what did that matter, so long as Lucy was returned safely to them.

Both sets of grandparents had been distraught at the news. Joshua Walker had told his wife, half expecting her to make some sort of derogatory comment about Val's carelessness but she did not do so. Beatrice was fond of Val and remarked that she was a very good mother.

'And Lucy's such an adorable child,' she added. 'What a wicked thing to do.'

'Probably some woman who wanted a baby,' said Joshua. 'That's what the police think.'

'That's no excuse. I hope they catch whoever it is and that she gets what she deserves.'

'It's more important to find Lucy, Beatrice. That's all that Val and Sam are concerned about.'

'Yes, I know that . . . and I hope that little lad's behaving himself. Valerie has quite enough to put up with.'

Sam drove round to tell Val's mother what had happened early in the afternoon. She was inconsolable at first, and Sam made a pot of tea and stayed with her for a while, assuring her that the police were on to it right away.

After Bert had arrived home from work and they'd eaten a meal that they didn't really want, they caught a bus up to Queensbury to see Val and Sam.

They arrived just after Val had tried to reassure Russell about his sister. And a few moments later, the policewoman who had been with them in the morning rang the doorbell.

'No news yet,' she said, shaking her head as Sam opened the door, and she saw the momentary light of optimism in his eyes.

'But there's a house-to-house search going on in the area right now,' she told them as they sat drinking yet another cup of tea. 'It's a large area to cover and we have several policemen and women engaged on the search. We're hoping that the pram will be a significant factor. It's a big thing to hide. They are asking if there is anyone new in the area with a baby, or if they've heard sounds of a baby's presence that wasn't there before. I know it's agonizing while you're waiting but we really believe that your little girl will come to no real harm.'

'Has this sort of thing happened before?' asked Sam.

'Not just recently. There was an incident about a year ago. That was a younger baby, snatched out of the pram. The woman had suffered a miscarriage and was suffering from depression. Unfortunately her husband worked away from home and he had just gone back. It was a neighbour who informed us about a baby crying. The child had come to no harm; the woman was well prepared with nappies and baby clothes and feeding bottles, ready for her own baby.'

'And . . . how long was it before the baby was found?' asked Val.

'Oh, less than a week; five or six days, maybe.'

'Six days! That's a very long time.' Val wondered how she could possibly survive six days of waiting.

'Yes, I'm sure it must sound like a long time,' said the policewoman, 'but we will be doing everything in our power to find Lucy, and if you want to contact me then just ring up and ask for me. I'm Hazel, by the way.'

Val nodded. 'Thank you. I know you're doing your best. And we are Val and Sam; it's less formal, isn't it?'

She was starting to regard the attractive young policewoman as a new friend, one who understood the agony they were going through. Val was trying hard to believe that Lucy would be found soon, hopefully safe and well.

'I must leave you now,' said Hazel. 'I know it's no use to tell you not to worry, but try to think positively if you can. It's early days – less than a day yet – and we won't give up till we've found her.'

Val's parents stayed for a little while, although it was difficult to make any conversation that did not relate to the crisis they were going through. Sam offered to run them home and they accepted gratefully.

Sally hugged her daughter. 'Think positively, darling, like that nice police lady said. We'll say a little prayer for you and I'm sure lots of other folk will do the same. Now go to bed early and try to get some sleep. Take a couple of aspirin – they'll help to settle you down.'

Val nodded. 'Thanks, Mum and Dad.'

Bert, with tears moistening his eyes, kissed her cheek. 'Ta-ra, love; we're always here for you, you know.'

Val could not answer for the lump in her throat. She tried to smile at him, then took a deep breath, not wanting to give way to another bout of uncontrollable weeping.

They went to bed when Sam returned and both fell asleep, exhausted by the traumas of the day.

The next day was Saturday, a day when Sam did not go to the mill. They went through the motions, preparing and eating meals, then clearing away, ears constantly alert for a knock at the door or the telephone ringing.

Hazel called to give them an update. A message had gone out on the local radio and there had been a few callers regarding the sound of a baby crying, but they had proved to be false alarms.

Janice called from Harrogate to say how concerned they were about Lucy's disappearance. Cissie had called, full of distress, to tell her the news. Both Cissie and Janice were godmothers to the little girl and Phil was her godfather.

'We're thinking of you all the time,' said Janice. 'It's hard to concentrate on anything else at the moment. I can't imagine how we would feel if it was Sarah.'

'We're trying to think positively,' said Val. 'The police seem very hopeful that she will be found safe and well. What about you? Is everything going according to plan with your extension?'

'Yes, we still hope to be ready by the end of May . . . We'll let you know, and we'll look forward to seeing you – all of you – when we reopen. Thanks for asking, but you've too much on your mind to be thinking about us. I won't keep you any longer, Val; just wanted to tell you how concerned we are . . . Bye, Val . . .'

Val heard the sob in her friend's voice as she rang off.

Sam's parents invited them for Sunday tea and Val knew that it would be churlish to refuse, although her inclination was to stay at home. Beatrice, to give her her due, was full of sympathy and genuinely concerned about Lucy.

'I had a word with our vicar this morning,' she said. 'He told the congregation about Lucy, although a lot of them already knew, and he said a prayer asking God to keep her safe and to be with both of you . . . and Russell, in your time of trouble . . . I must say that Russell is being a good boy,' she added, a note of surprise in her voice.

'Yes, he's missing his sister,' said Val. 'He's been quite upset about it.'

Russell turned to look at his mother for a moment, without speaking, then went back to his game. They had finished their tea and he was playing along quite amicably with Rosemary, helping her, in his own way, to complete a jigsaw puzzle of a farmyard.

Jonathan and Thelma had been invited to the tea party, much to Val's relief. Thelma was a good friend and Val was aware of her quiet sympathy and support. Jonathan was far removed now from the supercilious young man he had been when she had first met Sam. The brothers behaved to one another more as brothers ought to do now, as friends rather than as adversaries.

It was early on Monday afternoon when Val received a phone call from Cissie. Her friend's words fell over one another as she told her some news.

'Val, I've got summat to tell you. You know Megan, my friend, the one that looks after Holly? Well, her husband, Harry, he's a dustbin man, and this morning they found a pram. It was left in a back alley, like, as though it was rubbish to be collected.'

'Where? Where was this?' asked Val.

'In Queensbury. Not the posh end where you live; the other end. Anyroad, Harry went and asked the woman about the pram: was it really rubbish? And she knew nowt about it. It had just been left there. And Harry guessed at once that it must be yours. A Silver Cross, a big cream one . . .'

'Yes, that's right. It must be ours. Oh, Cissie, do you think that Lucy might be there, somewhere near there?'

'Well, the woman knew about Lucy being missing because of the news on the wireless and in the paper, but she'd not seen a baby or heard one crying.'

'So . . . what's happening now?'

'Well, Harry and his mate got in touch with the police and

they'll be following it up right away, so I thought it best to let you know. Sounds hopeful, don't you think?'

'I suppose so,' said Val uncertainly. A pram with no baby in it? But it was hardly likely that Lucy would still be in the pram. She had been missing now for three days.

'It seems as though somebody's dumped the pram because it's too much of a giveaway,' said Val.

A myriad thoughts were racing through her mind. She might be near there or she might be far away. She might be safe and well or she might be . . . She could not bear to let her mind dwell on her worst fear. She tried to speak calmly now.

'Thanks, Cissie. And say thank you to Harry. I don't know him but it's the first real clue we've had.'

'Must go,' said Cissie. 'I've just collected Holly from Megan's. That's when Harry told me about it. I'll get myself some lunch now.'

'How's the job going?'

'Oh, smashing! I'm really enjoying it. Keep yer chin up, Val. There'll be some good news soon – I feel sure of it.'

Val's hands were trembling as she put down the phone. But she picked it up again almost at once to ring Sam at the mill.

'Let's hope it's a breakthrough,' he said quite calmly. Throughout the trauma, Sam had tried to keep his cool. 'Try to keep calm, love. I expect Hazel, or someone, will be calling on you soon to keep you up to date. See you at teatime, darling. I'm sure this is a good sign.'

Val tried to tell herself that Sam was right and that Lucy would soon be found. Russell could not possibly understand all that was going on, but Val was beginning to realize that he was a very astute little boy. She knew he had been listening to her side of the telephone conversations with Cissie and with Sam.

'Lucy coming back?' her asked now.

'We hope so, darling,' Val replied. 'Perhaps . . . quite soon.'

'Want Lucy . . .' he said, as he had repeated so often over the last three days.

Val found it hard to believe that there could be such a change in him. He was subdued and, on the whole, obedient. But the streak of wilfulness was still there beneath the surface. It seemed as though there were times when he wanted to be defiant, then changed his mind. Who could tell what was going through his little mind? Did he, somehow, blame himself for Lucy's disappearance? Or did he think that if he was a good boy then she might come back? Val only knew that she was relieved that she was not putting up with his bouts of bad behaviour at the moment. It was one – very small – blessing in the midst of all their trauma.

As she had expected, it was not long before Hazel called round to tell them the news that Val admitted she had already heard.

'We are concentrating our search in that area,' she said. 'We feel sure that your little girl must be somewhere in the vicinity. It seems as though the woman – or whoever it is – got rid of the pram and is keeping Lucy hidden. If that is the case then she can't hide away for ever.'

Hazel stayed a little while to give moral support to Val. She had been designated as their family liaison officer, and Val certainly felt more hopeful when she was around.

'He's a good little boy, isn't he?' said Hazel as she watched Russell playing with his cars on the floor.

Val could not help but give a wry smile. 'He seems so at the moment,' she replied. 'We're hoping it will last.' Russell was far enough away not to hear the conversation, but Val spoke quietly. 'We've had endless trouble with him, actually. We adopted him when he was seven months old. His parents were killed in a car crash.'

'Oh, yes, I seem to remember the incident,' said Hazel. 'It was very tragic.'

'Yes; we thought we were doing the right thing. I was having difficulty in conceiving. And then, not long after we adopted Russell, I realized I was expecting Lucy.'

'Not unusual,' said Hazel. 'So you had your hands full with two very young children, and Russell . . . He resented his little sister, perhaps?'

'He was a holy terror!' said Val. 'Believe me, there were times when I almost regretted what we had done. But now, we can scarcely believe that he is the same child. He keeps asking about her, about Lucy. Where is she? When is she coming back?'

'Well, let's hope it isn't long before we have some good news. You can be sure that you will be kept up to date about everything. I'll say cheerio for now, Val. Keep your pecker up, as my mother would say!'

Val smiled. 'Yes, and my mother always says that no news is good news. But that's hard to believe when you're waiting, isn't it?'

'Well, perhaps the next news will be good news. Bye for now, Val. Bye-bye, Russell.'

Russell, at the other end of the room, looked up and wiggled his fingers in a wave, as he had done since he was a baby.

'Bye,' he murmured, then returned to his police car.

It was another anxious afternoon for Val, stretching into evening when Sam came home. She was daring, though, to feel a little more optimistic, and Sam agreed with her that the signs were more hopeful. Or was he only saying that to make her feel better?

He went to work on Tuesday morning, leaving Val to face another long day of waiting. She decided to start on a task that would keep her occupied, sorting out her wardrobe and drawers, exchanging her warm winter clothes for her lighter spring and summertime clothing, which had been stored away in a wardrobe and chest of drawers in the spare room. The weather was still chilly at times, though, even though it was April.

It was around ten thirty, when she had been busy at her task for half an hour or so, when the doorbell rang.

'Bell ringing, Mummy,' said Russell.

Val felt her heartbeat quicken, as it always did now at the sound of the doorbell or the telephone.

'Stay there, Russell,' she said. 'I'll go and see who it is.'

She was half expecting that it would he Hazel and, indeed, it was. This time, though, the young policewoman was beaming, her smile seeming to stretch from ear to ear.

'I've come to take you down to the station,' she said. 'We've got your little girl there, waiting for you.'

'Oh . . . thank you so much . . .' Val burst into tears as she flung her arms around Hazel. 'You've found her! She's all right?'

'Yes; a little dazed, of course. She doesn't know what's going on. But she has come to no harm.'

Russell appeared at the top of the stairs, eager to see what was happening.

'Can he come with us?' asked Val.

'Yes, of course he can. And we've phoned your husband. He's meeting you at the station.'

Val dashed up the stairs. 'Come on, Russell. We're going to have a ride in a real police car. You like police cars, don't you? And we're going to bring Lucy home! Isn't that lovely?'

Russell nodded. 'Yes . . . Lucy. I like Lucy.'

Val and Russell arrived at the police station ahead of Sam. Lucy was sitting on the knee of another policewoman, not crying or looking unhappy but seeming a little puzzled. Her brown eyes stared at Val for a moment or two, then she smiled and held up her arms. At ten months' old she was not really talking, just making baby sounds, although Sam had convinced himself that she could say 'Da-da'. Val knew that the 'd' sound was easier for a baby to pronounce than 'm' for Mummy, but she had smiled and said, 'Yes, maybe . . .'

There was no doubt now that Lucy recognized her mother. She gave an excited little chuckle as Val picked her up and hugged her, kissing her downy soft cheek and stroking her dark brown hair. She could not prevent the tears from falling as she sat down with her child on her knee, but everyone understood. How could it be otherwise?

Russell tiptoed up to his mummy and little sister. Very gently, he reached out and touched her little hand. 'Hello, Lucy,' he said, and she closed her fingers around his hand.

'She's pleased to see you,' said Val. 'You're her big brother, aren't you? And you're going to help Daddy and me to take care of her. We mustn't lose her again, must we? What happened?' she asked, turning to the police sergeant who had been in charge of the case.

He was just about to answer when the door opened again and Sam came into the room. Lucy stared at him, just as she had stared at Val for a moment, then she held out her arms.

'Da-da . . .' she said quite distinctly, although whether it was intentional because she recognized her daddy, or just baby talk, no one could be sure.

Sam was delighted, of course, and so was Val as they laughed together, with Russell joining in with the jollity.

'Lucy looks fit and well,' observed Sam. 'She's come to no harm, then?'

'No, no real harm,' replied the police sergeant. 'I was just about to explain everything to your wife as you came in. We discovered her about half a mile from where the pram had been left. It had been abandoned there to put us off the trail, but we felt that it would be only a matter of time before we found your little girl. Hazel was the one who found her.'

He looked at Hazel and she continued with the story. 'Yes, that's right. There was a call from a neighbour to say a baby was crying next door. We'd had a few such calls but this was the one we'd been waiting for. I think the woman knew it was only a matter of time before we caught up with her. She didn't try to deny it. She'd suffered a miscarriage a few weeks ago, the second one she's had in the three years since she married her husband. He's away from home a lot of the time. He's a coach driver for a travel firm, and if it's a long trip to the continent he can be away for two or three weeks at a time. She had been suffering from depression and he took time off work. But she had seemed to be recovering, so he went back to work. He'd been away for just a few days when . . . all this happened. She's told me this herself, quite coherently. As I said, I think she knew she'd be caught.'

'Poor woman, whoever she is,' said Val, remembering how she had felt following her own miscarriage.

'It's a serious offence, though, Mrs Walker,' said the police sergeant. 'We've got her in custody now and she'll be charged with abduction. There may be extenuating circumstances. It's up to the magistrates to decide but we have to do our duty.'

'No, I don't want to press charges,' said Val. 'Do we, Sam?'

'Er . . . I suppose not,' said Sam. 'We've got Lucy back and she's come to no harm. Maybe it was a spur of the moment thing, seeing the pram there.'

'That is what we believe,' said the sergeant, 'but we have to follow the correct procedure. Some people might not be as understanding as you are. If that's what you want, though, we can talk to her, make her understand how serious it is and let her off with a caution.'

Val nodded. 'Yes, I think so. I had a miscarriage, you see,

and one or two other disappointments before that, and I got very depressed for a while. Not that I ever thought of abducting a baby; I was never even tempted. But who can tell what was going through the poor woman's mind?'

'It's true that Lucy was well looked after,' said Hazel. 'She – Claire's her name – had everything prepared ready for her own baby. Nappies and baby clothes, feeding bottles and tins of milk, and a cot with sheets and blankets. It was very sad. She was living in a sort of dream world for a few days.'

'Can I see her?' asked Val. 'Not just now, but . . . sometime?'

'That might not be a good idea, Mrs Walker,' said the sergeant.

'But I do understand,' said Val. 'Sam and I had only been married for a couple of years but I got it into my head that we were never going to have a baby of our own. That's why we adopted Russell. And then, soon after, lo and behold! I was expecting Lucy. So I was wrong, wasn't I? It was only a matter of time. I was impatient. And it might be the same for . . . Claire.'

'It wasn't wrong to adopt Russell, though, was it?' said Sam.

'Good gracious, no!' said Val, horrified at the suggestion. 'He's our son and Lucy's our daughter.'

'And that's enough to be going on with for the moment,' said Sam with a smile. 'Now, it's time we were going back home, isn't it? Time to get this little girl settled in her own home again. We can't thank you enough for all you've done for us; for finding Lucy and taking care of my wife.' He turned to Hazel. 'You just being there for her has made so much differ-ence. I had to carry on working and I was worried about Val being on her own.'

'It has been my pleasure,' said Hazel. 'I could say that it's all in a day's work but it's meant much more than that. And it's been a happy ending. Some of these cases, very sadly, have a tragic outcome. I shall keep in touch with you.'

'And we have your pram here,' said the sergeant. 'We'll make sure it's returned to you, and it's come to no harm either. As Hazel says, we're delighted at the result. Take care now, all of you. Bye-bye, Russell; you look after your little sister.'

Russell nodded seriously. 'Lucy,' he said. 'I like Lucy.'

Val sat on the back seat of the car with Lucy on her knee

and Russell at her side. He held Lucy's hand all the way home, not speaking at all. He broke his silence when Val asked what he would like for dinner.

'I don't think Daddy needs to dash back to work straight away,' she said, 'so you can choose something, seeing as it's a special day.'

'Sausage and mash!' he shouted. 'And ice cream and jelly.'

'I don't know about jelly,' said Val. 'It won't set in time. We can have jelly tomorrow with banana in it. You like that, don't you? But we've got ice cream in the fridge. Pink and white and chocolate. How about that?'

'Yummy!' said Russell, a word he had heard his cousin, Rosemary, and Auntie Cissie's little boy, Paul, exclaim. 'Lucy have some too?'

'Yes, of course,' said Val. 'Perhaps just a little bit, because it might be rather cold for her little tummy.'

Russell leaned across and kissed his little sister's cheek. 'Hello, Lucy,' he said again, looking pleased that she was home. 'I love Lucy, Mummy.'

TWELVE

'Wonderful news!' Janice called to Phil when she put down the phone on that same Tuesday evening. 'That was Val. Lucy has been found, safe and well.'

'Wonderful!' repeated Phil. 'I guessed as much when I heard your side of the conversation. What happened?'

'Oh, she'd been snatched by some woman who'd had a miscarriage and was depressed. Val seemed to be pretty understanding about it all. I don't know that I could have been so forgiving. But Val has been through it herself – the miscarriage, I mean. And apparently Russell is being a very good boy. That's a change, isn't it? I hope it lasts.'

'Yes, he was a little rascal, wasn't he? Anyway, I'm glad it's all ended happily. I can't imagine how we would feel if we lost our Sarah. Well, I don't suppose you can imagine it, can you, unless it happens to you? I don't suppose you told her much about our own plans, did you?'

'No, that can wait. It's too soon to think about sending out invitations, isn't it, because we're not sure ourselves just how long it's going to take.'

The work was progressing well on the conversion of the two properties into one. The builders were now working on the upstairs rooms. It was not too difficult a task for experienced builders to knock down part of the adjoining wall to give access to the rooms next door. When the work was completed there would be four bedrooms, a larger kitchen and bathroom, and a spacious dining-cum-living room.

The downstairs conversion would extend the dining area, making a larger restaurant with a small bar area at one end, a larger kitchen and a cloakroom and washroom facilities for the clients. This would be the last work to be done, and it would involve closing down for a couple of weeks. They were still hoping, however, that the new premises would be ready by the end of May.

It was a big undertaking, certainly a challenge and, maybe, something of a risk, but all had gone well so far. Bella, the owner of the florist's shop, had been delighted when they'd told her what they had in mind, and, because they were friends, she had reduced the price a little, pleased that the premises were to be put to good use.

The bank manager, too, had been obliging, knowing how Grundy's had prospered since the opening two years previously. It was possible that they would need extra staff but, at the moment, they were content with the status quo.

'I wonder if Ian will come and work for us during the summer?' said Phil. 'We could use him if he's available but he might prefer to stay in Blackpool. What do you think?'

'Hard to say,' replied Janice. Her brother had stayed in Blackpool during the Easter break, working at a seafront hotel. 'He has other interests in Blackpool now, hasn't he? I was sorry about him and Sophie, though. They seemed good together.'

'They're only kids,' said Phil, with all the wisdom of his twenty-six years.

'We weren't all that much older,' said Janice. 'I was only eighteen when I met you.'

'Well, we'll see, won't we? I agree that Sophie's a nice lass. I have a feeling that this Alison might be a bit much for Ian.'

'We haven't met her . . .'

'No, but your dad and Norma have. I'm only thinking about what Norma said to you.'

'She said that Alison was rather sophisticated, that's all.'

'And Ian certainly isn't,' said Phil, 'although I don't think he's quite as naive as he used to be. Anyway, time will tell.'

Ian met Alison Riley at the evening meal that the students of the catering college put on for members of the public, mainly those who had been invited along by the students them-selves. The meal took place during the last week of March, just before the college closed down for the Easter break.

'I've invited my landlady and her husband, Mr and Mrs Riley,' Darren told Ian, 'and Alison said she'd like to come as well. I'll introduce you to her, Ian. Who knows? You might fancy each other!'

Ian gave Darren a weak smile. He was still hurting somewhat after the break-up with Sophie, and had told Darren about it. The two of them were quite good mates now, Darren bearing no grudge about the rebuff from Ian. He had still not found anyone to share his digs and was not likely to do so before the arrival of new students in September.

'I'm not really bothered at the moment,' Ian said. 'I've asked my dad and Norma to come and they're looking forward to it. I see that nearly all the tickets have gone. It should be a good "do".'

It certainly promised to be a first-class meal; at least, the ingredients were first rate, but it all depended on the preparation and presentation of the meal by the students, which could make or break it. Members of staff, though, would be on hand to ward off any disasters.

The visitors were asked to choose their menu in advance to make things a little easier for the students and to avoid unnecessary wastage. It was a three-course meal, after which coffee and chocolate mints would be served.

There was a choice of homemade pâté with toast, mushroom soup or melon cocktail for the starter; poached salmon, roast beef or breast of chicken for the main course, all served with seasonal vegetables and the appropriate sauces; and sherry trifle, plum tart with custard, or assorted ice creams for the dessert. All the sauces, of course, were homemade, the only ready-made item being the ice cream.

They were catering for thirty guests and, fortunately, the choices of menu had worked out quite evenly.

The guests started arriving soon after six thirty, as the meal was to be served at seven o'clock. There was a small bar with adequate seating for those who wanted a pre-dinner drink. Others chose to go straight to the dining area, where the tables had been set for two, four or six, to meet with everyone's requirements.

Two students served at the bar, where a limited selection of wines, spirits and ales were on sale. Two more students took orders and served the drinks at the tables.

There were a dozen students responsible for the meal in all: the preparation and cooking, which had begun in the late afternoon, the setting of the tables, the serving and the clearing away. More than a dozen would have meant that they got in one another's way, but all the students would take their turn at one or more of these guest meals during their time at the college.

Ian worked along with Darren, as he often did, making the plum tarts. They both considered themselves to be dab hands now at pastry making. The custard, however, to accompany the tarts proved more difficult. It had to be made with fresh eggs and milk, not ready-made with powder from a tin, or – even more simple – a tin of Ambrosia custard. It was not uncommon for the milk to curdle or the custard to be too thick or too thin.

'I hope to goodness it turns out all right,' Ian said as they prepared the filling of plums. 'Norma always uses Bird's custard powder and I rather think my mum did when we had the boarding house. But Phil always makes the real thing.'

'My mum uses Bird's,' Darren agreed. 'It's just as nice. But we have to show that we can make the real stuff. They call it "English cream" on the continent because it's something they're not used to making. Anyway, let's worry about that when the time comes.' The custard had to be made just before the tarts were ready to be served.

When the first course was ready and the main course was well on its way, half the students took off their cookery aprons to reveal their waiter's uniforms: black trousers and dazzling white shirts with a red bow tie for the men, while the girls wore black skirts and white blouses with a red ribbon at the neck.

The serving of the main course was a tricky business – silver service, which involved the waiter serving each guest individually, over their right shoulder, from a large silver platter. There was a knack to carrying it, and to serving the vegetables and potatoes, trying hard not to drop any on the tablecloth, or, even worse, on the clothes of the customer. The students had practised on each other first before they'd been let loose on the guests. The gravy and the sauces, however, had been placed on the table in dishes for everyone to help themselves.

Ian knew that in many hotels and restaurants, the more common or garden ones, the meal was put straight on to the plate – meat, veg and gravy – in a 'take it or leave it' attitude.

Some others, even quite prestigious hotels, put the vegetables and potatoes in dishes for the clients to take as much or as little as they wished. Far the best way, he thought, and the way his mum had always done it. But the training here could equip them for a position at the Ritz or the Hilton!

On the whole, it was a successful evening with no major disasters. There were certainly no complaints from the customers. The students responsible for the vegetables were aware that the carrots and broccoli might have been a little overcooked, but it was better that way, they'd told themselves, rather than being underdone.

The beef was moist but not too rare. Although there were some who preferred it rare there were many who liked it quite well done, a rich brown colour with no hint of redness. And the students knew they must aim to please.

Ian and Darren's custard turned out just right despite their anxiety. Ian was pleased because his dad and Norma had opted for the plum tart and custard, knowing that Ian had had a hand in it.

There was very little time for conversation between the students who were serving the meal and their guests, apart from that which concerned the food. It so happened that Ian's guests and Darren's were seated at the same table – one that had been set for six – so there was a spare place.

Alec and Norma were a sociable couple; Alec had been much more so since meeting and marrying Norma. They had politely asked the Riley family, who seemed a friendly trio, if they could join them, rather to the surprise of Ian and Darren when they'd seen them sitting together.

It hadn't taken long for the two couples to be on first-name terms. Mr and Mrs Riley were Derek and Enid. They had discovered that Ian and Darren knew one another quite well and often worked together.

'Oh, yes, we've heard about Ian,' Mrs Riley said. 'I'm glad he and Darren are friends. Darren's a really nice lad. We're really pleased to have such a nice, well-brought-up young man staying with us, aren't we, Derek?'

Her husband nodded his agreement.

'Yes, you can always tell when they come from a good home,' she went on. 'We were hoping we might get another young man to share with him. It's a twin double room, you see, and, to be honest, it's a nice little income for us. We've been taking students for a few years now. Darren seems OK on his own, though, and I'm sure he's got a lot of friends here. He's a lively lad but very respectful, if you know what I mean, isn't he, Alison?' She turned to her daughter, who nodded.

'Yes, he's a nice lad, Mum.' She smiled to herself. There was a lot that her parents didn't know about Darren but she had no intention of telling them. She doubted that they would understand – at least, probably her mum wouldn't – and most likely they would be horrified.

'I thought that he and our Alison might have got friendly,' she said, looking coyly at her daughter. 'I know they're only young but you want them to have someone you can trust, don't you?'

'I've told you. I like him, Mum,' said Alison. 'We are friendly but he's not my boyfriend and he's not likely to be. I think there's someone where he comes from, in Bury.'

Brief introductions were made when Ian and Darren served their family members.

'Let me introduce Mr and Mrs Riley and Alison,' Darren said to Ian. 'I've told him all about the good digs I've got.'

It wasn't possible for them to shake hands because their hands were otherwise occupied, but they all said 'Hello' or 'How do you do?' and smiled at one another.

Alison saw that Ian was a good-looking lad with brown hair and thoughtful grey eyes, possibly a little reserved – Darren had hinted as much – but she liked what she saw. He might be worth a try . . .

Ian noticed that Alison was an attractive blonde girl with hazel eyes that looked at him appraisingly for a moment. Then she smiled at him in a questioning sort of way. She looked nothing like Sophie. He still tended to compare every girl he met with Sophie, who was small and dark-haired with a bubbly personality. This girl looked far more suave and sophisticated. Her hair was smooth and straight and reached almost to her shoulders. She was slim and he guessed she would be quite tall, although it was hard to tell when she was sitting down.

Ian found, to his surprise, that he was thinking about her

quite a lot as he continued to serve the meals. Maybe he should find another girlfriend or, at least, a girl to get friendly with, as Darren and other friends here had advised him to do. But it seemed to him that Alison Riley might be far out of his league. And how would he go about it? He had found it quite easy to approach Sophie, and she had met him more than halfway when he had suggested that they might go out together. But Alison looked as though she knew her way around, and he didn't want a rebuff or to be made to look stupid.

As it happened, he need not have worried. When he came to clear away the dishes after the three courses were completed, Alison stood up to speak to him. As he had guessed, she was as tall as he was, about five foot seven, quite tall for a girl. She moved a little way from the table and gently touched his arm.

'I'm glad I've met you, Ian,' she said. 'Darren has told me about you. I was wondering if you would like to meet me sometime, then we could get to know each other better? Maybe we could have a walk on the prom, or in the park. You live near there, don't you? And then perhaps have a coffee or . . . something?'

Ian was somewhat taken back but very relieved. He had no hesitation in saying, 'Yes, that would be lovely. Wait a minute, though. I'd better get these dishes moved. I'll be bringing your coffee in a little while.'

'Guess what?' he said to Darren. 'Alison asked me if I'd like to go out with her!'

'Good for you!' said Darren. 'I thought she might. She's not backward in coming forward, our Alison. You said yes, I hope?'

'Well, yes, of course. What else could I say? It would've been rude to refuse.'

'And you had no intention of refusing, had you?'

'Well . . . no. She took the wind out of my sails. I was trying to pluck up courage to ask if I could see her sometime, then I thought, perhaps not. She looks so . . . grown up, and I thought she wouldn't want to be bothered with me. Hasn't she got a boyfriend?'

'Not that I know of. Like you say, she appears a bit superior but she's not when you get talking to her. She's in the sixth form at the girls' grammar school, so I don't suppose she meets many lads. Anyway, you get in there, Ian lad, while you've got the chance.'

They gave their guests time to finish their coffee then went to clear the tables. Ian smiled at Alison, a little unsurely, and she stood up, moving away from the table again so that they could talk. Ian noticed that Norma gave a little smile, seeming well aware of what was going on. His dad was deep in conversation with Mr Riley, and Mrs Riley was looking very relaxed, enjoying a cigarette. She seemed nice, Ian thought, and so did her husband. Mrs Riley was an older edition of Alison – plumper, though, with a more rounded face and blonde, greying hair. He knew that Alison was their only child, and he guessed they must have been in their thirties when she was born.

Ian decided he had better start the conversation and not leave it to Alison, as though he was unsure of himself.

'When shall we meet then, and where?' he began. 'We finish college at the end of the week but I've got a job at a hotel on the prom, near central pier. It'll be shift work, I suppose, so I don't know what hours I'll be working yet.'

'And school finishes, too,' said Alison. 'I'm not working, though. I had a job at Marks and Spencer's during the summer holiday and I'll probably go there again this year, but I've nothing to do now except revision, if I feel like it! Mock A-levels coming up soon.'

'Oh, yes . . . What are you going to do when you finish school? Go to college?'

She shrugged. 'Haven't decided yet. I've another year in the sixth. Look . . . ring me, and perhaps we can sort something out after the Easter weekend. No doubt you'll be busy then?'

'Probably. OK, I'll do that. I'll get your phone number from Darren. He's off home to Bury at the weekend.'

'Of course.' She grinned. 'I'm glad you got friendly with Darren. He's a nice lad, although I know you're not . . . his type.'

'Er . . . no. We're good mates though,' said Ian, feeling a little nonplussed. 'OK, then, I'll ring you, Alison. I'll look forward to seeing you. Better get on now; all this clearing up to do.'

'See you soon then, Ian. I'll look forward to it as well.' She gave an almost imperceptible wink as she sat down.

'I'm glad to see that you and Ian are getting friendly,' said her mother, smiling knowingly at her. 'Norma has been telling me how hard he's working here, but he needs to get out and enjoy himself when he can.'

'You don't miss much, do you, Mum?' said Alison, but not resentfully. 'Yes, we're going to meet after Easter.' She turned to speak to Norma. 'Darren's told me a lot about Ian, so I'm pleased to meet him at last. We're about the same age, I think.'

'Ian will be eighteen in August,' said Norma.

'So I'm just a month younger,' said Alison. 'Eighteen in September.'

'Better to have someone your own age,' said her mother. 'Alison had a boyfriend last year who was a few years older,' she told Norma. 'He was in the RAF, stationed at Weeton Camp near Blackpool; then he was demobbed and I was jolly glad, I can tell you.'

'Don't talk about me as if I'm not here, Mum,' said Alison in good humour. 'I have to agree with you, though. He wasn't right for me. I soon realized that.'

'We made him welcome at our home, though,' Enid went on. 'I like to meet all of Alison's friends. But there was something a bit . . . shifty about him. You didn't realize when you first met him.'

'Well, it's all water under the bridge now, Mum. Ian's quite different; I could tell that at once.'

Alison could feel her face turning a little pink. Her mother did go on at times! Jeffrey was history now. She had been only sixteen when she'd met him at the tower ballroom and they had started going out together. She'd felt pleased with herself to have a boyfriend – her first one. She no longer felt out of it when the girls in her form boasted about their conquests. But Jeffrey had wanted to move things on too quickly for her liking. She would take things nice and steady this time.

Ian was very busy over the Easter weekend. Being a student and a part-time worker, he had to fit in whenever he was needed. Fortunately the hotel was not too far from his home and he cycled there and back each time. If he was on the early shift he started at seven o'clock. Breakfast was served from seven thirty – for the early risers – until nine thirty. After serving the breakfasts then clearing away, he was free until the evening dinnertime.

They had their own expert chefs, so he did not get any experience with the preparation of the meals. His main job was to wait on at the tables; he also gave a hand in the kitchen with dishing up and clearing away.

On Wednesday, however, he would not be required until six o'clock in the evening. Many of the visitors had been there for the Easter weekend and had returned home on Tuesday morning.

He knew he must phone Alison or she might think he had changed his mind about meeting her, which was certainly not the case. She had been very much at the centre of his thoughts since the previous week. He thought it might be better to spend a casual afternoon together at first, then, if it went well they could go out somewhere for the evening, which would be more of a 'date'.

Alison seemed pleased to hear from him, and they decided they would have a walk around Stanley Park. As Ian lived closer to the park than she did she suggested that she should walk up to his home.

He had been waiting eagerly to hear her ring the doorbell, but he greeted her casually. 'Hi there, Alison. Good to see you again. OK, then, let's go.'

It was a ten-minute walk or so along the tree-lined avenues to the imposing main gates of the park. They were both a little quiet at first, then Alison asked how he was liking the job. It broke the ice as he told her, probably in more detail than was required, about his work at the hotel.

The trees and bushes in the park were only just showing their springtime greenery, but there were crocuses and early daffodils in abundance. They wandered down to the lake where ducks and Canada geese were swimming, some wandering on to the pathway hoping for tidbits from the children who frequented the area with their parents. A visit to Stanley Park was a pleasant way for visitors to the town to spend an afternoon, and for residents who had the time.

'Do you fancy a row on the lake?' asked Ian, watching a few brave souls who were pulling away at the oars.

'Are you offering to row?' asked Alison, looking quite surprised.

'Yes, why not?' He'd tried rowing only a couple of times, with some of his schoolmates, but he was sure he would be able to cope. It might impress Alison, and they couldn't stroll around aimlessly all afternoon.

'No, I don't think so,' said Alison, somewhat to his relief. 'It looks too much like hard work to me, and you're working at the hotel later. You don't want to tire yourself out. What about a game of putting? There's a putting green just over there, and that's not a strenuous game.'

'Good idea,' said Ian. He had played there sometimes, mainly with Janice after they had come to live near Stanley Park.

They collected their putters and balls and score cards from the kiosk. It was an enjoyable way to spend the next hour. Ian felt his skill returning as they went from green to green. Alison was jolly good and he guessed that she played all kinds of sports at her school. Neither of them managed a hole in one but they both achieved a two. When they totted up their scores, Ian had won by two points. He was pleased because he felt that his honour was at stake.

'I'll beat you next time, you'll see!' said Alison, laughing.

He felt very much at ease with her now and glad that she had mentioned a next time.

'Let's go and have a cup of tea, or whatever you fancy,' he said, 'then I suppose we'll have to be heading back. I mustn't be late at the hotel.'

They went to the cafe, a rather genteel place with white cloths on the tables, china cups and saucers and an air of refinement. Only a few of the tables were occupied, by people rather older than themselves, and there were no children running around.

They ordered toasted teacakes with butter and strawberry jam, and a pot of tea. It was served by a waitress wearing a white cap and apron.

'Has Darren got a holiday job in Bury?' asked Alison.

'I shouldn't think so,' said Ian. 'He didn't say that he had and I don't imagine there are many hotels in Bury. I know he likes to go home to see his parents, and I dare say he has friends at home. I don't think there is anyone . . . special, though.'

'You know about Darren, don't you?'

'That he's, er . . . gay. Well, yes, I do. I didn't realize at first, not until he made a move towards me, so I had to put him right.'

Alison laughed. 'Whoops! He didn't tell me that. He hasn't actually told me anything, but I guessed; there was just something about him. Mum thought that he and I might get friendly, so I told her that I thought he had a girlfriend at home. I couldn't possibly tell her. She'd most likely be shocked, and my dad as well. They think he's such a nice lad, and of course he is.'

'Yes, it's not something you discuss with your parents, is it? I doubt that my dad and Norma would understand either.' Ian himself had been very green about such matters until recently.

'Anyway, never mind about Darren,' said Ian. 'What about you and me? Would you like to go out one evening? To the pictures, or . . . something?' He wasn't sure what to suggest.

'Yes, of course I'd like to,' said Alison. 'What about the palace? You get a lot for your money there.'

'Yes, so you do,' agreed Ian. 'I've been to the cinema there, and a variety show, but I've never been in the ballroom.'

'Well, now's your chance,' said Alison. 'I'm not a brilliant dancer, but I can manage a waltz and a quickstep, and they have old-time dances at the palace as well. We had dancing lessons at school; well, it was after school really, with the boys from the grammar school. All very proper, you know, organized by the teachers. I say, you were at the grammar school, weren't you? Why didn't I see you there?'

'Because I didn't fancy dancing lessons. My mates and me, we played football and chess. The only dancing I've done is jigging around at the youth club. Yes, the palace sounds like a good idea.'

The palace building, originally known as the Alhambra, had been opened at the very end of the nineteenth century. It was on the promenade, on the block next to the tower building. The palace included a cinema, a theatre and a ballroom, as well as various cafes and bars. It now belonged to the tower company.

'We'd better make the most of it while it's still there,' said Alison. 'There's a rumour – well, more than a rumour; it's probably true – that the building is going to be sold and the site used as a department store. My dad works for the council, in the borough treasurer's department, so he's heard about it. No doubt they think – whoever they are – that there are enough ballrooms in Blackpool, with the Winter Gardens and the tower, and we've umpteen theatres and cinemas.'

Ian nodded. 'Yes, let's give it a try. We'll go now, when you're ready. I'll just pay the bill.'

He felt very pleased to be paying out of his earnings, which his dad had said he must keep for himself. And Alison didn't argue about her share, which was just how he wanted it to be.

They set off walking back home, and Alison insisted that she should walk the rest of the way on her own. It made sense as Ian had to get ready to go to his place of work. He had very bravely taken hold of her hand, but he didn't try to kiss her goodbye, not in broad daylight. There would be another time.

They agreed to meet early on Saturday evening, Ian calling for Alison this time, then they would watch the first house variety show and spend some time in the ballroom.

Ian thought how attractive she looked when she opened the door to him. She was wearing a blue dress in a silky material, with a full skirt and what he thought was a heart-shaped neck-line. He knew very little about colours and fashion, but he thought the colour was like blue hyacinths. Her blonde hair, soft and shiny, was curled under in a page-boy bob.

'Hi there, Ian,' she said brightly. 'I'm ready. Come in a minute while I get my coat.' She took a white woolly jacket from the hallstand.

'Bye, Mum, Dad,' she called. 'We're off now.'

Mrs Riley appeared from the room at the back. 'Hello, Ian. Nice to see you again. Well, it's hello and goodbye, isn't it? Have a good time.'

There were no warnings about not being late home. Ian knew that Mrs Riley was concerned for her daughter but was being careful not to embarrass her, and that she would trust him to take care of her.

The palace building was already busy, early on the Saturday evening. This was the evening when many people went out to enjoy themselves at the end of the working week.

There were queues for tickets for the first house at the cinema, and at the theatre for the variety show. There was ample room, however, and they had seats in the centre stall.

'My treat,' said Ian.

He was pleased when Alison said, 'Thanks, but let me pay for a drink afterwards, OK? My dad gives me an allowance.' She laughed. 'I've decided not to call it pocket money now I'm in the sixth form. And I hope I'll get a job again in the summer holiday.'

Ian grinned. 'That's OK with me.'

The variety show followed the usual pattern of chorus girls, comedian, solo singers – a soprano and a baritone who then joined together for duets – a ventriloquist, a juggler and a comedy sketch. It was all very enjoyable, although none of the artistes were well known. During the summer season, when the town was packed with visitors, there would be more famous artistes. The really top-class acts would perform for the whole of the season at the Opera House or the Grand Theatre.

'Let's go and have that drink I promised you,' said Alison when the show came to an end.

'What do you mean by a drink?' said Ian.

'Tea or lemonade . . . or something stronger?'

'Well, I'm only seventeen, and so are you. That's not to say that I haven't broken the rules now and again, and I'm sure you have as well?'

Ian nodded. 'Darren was the first one to lead me astray! Let's play it safe, eh? We mustn't spoil the evening by getting into hot water.'

They refreshed themselves with orange juice before making their way to the ballroom.

The design of the ballroom was similar to that of the Winter Gardens or the tower, but on a smaller scale and, therefore, it had a more intimate and friendly ambience. There was a stage at one end where the band was playing, a highly polished wooden floor in a tessellated pattern of mahogany, oak and walnut, red plush seating and marble pillars soaring up to a balcony above.

The band was playing 'Que Sera, Sera' as a young woman vocalist sang the song that was made famous by Doris Day.

'What will be, will be . . .' Ian recognized it as a waltz tune and decided it was now or never.

'Shall we give it a try?' he asked.

Alison replied, 'Why not? That's why we're here, isn't it?'

They took to the floor and Ian realized this was the first time he had been so close to Alison. They were pretty much the same height. Her hair brushed against his cheek and he was aware of a floral scent, like roses and lavender, drifting around him. He tried to concentrate on his steps, dancing cautiously for fear of treading on her toes. He decided not to talk in case he went wrong. Alison was a more than adequate dancer, and it was thanks to her guidance that he did not stumble.

'Well done,' she said when the dance came to an end and they left the floor. 'Don't tell me you can't dance.'

He grinned. 'Well, I survived, and so did your feet!'

There was a lull for a few moments, then the compere announced that it was time for a change of style and rhythm. 'Our old-time session, ladies and gentlemen, starting with the Valeta.'

This was one that Ian had learnt at the youth club and, after a moment or two, when there was a fair number of couples on the floor, Ian and Alison joined them, dancing to the strains of 'I'll Be Your Sweetheart'.

Ian found he was enjoying it very much, and it seemed that Alison was, too. There followed a barn dance, a St Bernard's Waltz, a military two-step and the Gay Gordons. They took part in most of them, then it was time for the last waltz.

'I'm sorry to be a killjoy,' said Alison, 'but do you mind if we go now? Or else there will be a massive queue in the cloakroom.'

'Suits me,' said Ian. 'It's been fun, hasn't it?'

'Great!' said Alison, her eyes shining with pleasure. 'Come on, let's go.'

She collected her jacket from the cloakroom and they started walking home.

'Aren't your feet tired after all that dancing?' asked Ian, glancing at her open-toed sandals.

'No, I'm OK,' she replied. 'My sandals are not too high and they're quite comfy. Anyway, it's not worth getting on the tram for a couple of stops, is it?'

They set off walking along Church Street. This time it was Alison who took hold of Ian's hand.

'I've really enjoyed it tonight,' she said. 'I've been there with some of my friends from school but it's not the same, dancing with another girl.'

'And hasn't there been . . . anyone else?'

'No . . . Well, not for quite a while. And I hate standing by the ballroom floor like a wallflower.'

'We can go there again, if you like, or perhaps we can try the tower or the Winter Gardens?'

'The tower gets a bit rowdy sometimes at the weekend.'

'And you won't want to go out during the week, I suppose, because of school?'

Alison gave a mock shudder. 'Don't mention it! I suppose I shall have to get stuck in with exams looming, but I'm not a slave to it. And I like to enjoy myself.'

'I can see that,' said Ian. He had thought she seemed rather aloof and superior when he first met her, but he knew now that this was not so.

'And I shall have to see what's going on at college. There'll be end-of-year assessments coming up. I'll ring you, shall I? That is . . . if you'd like me to?'

'Of course I would,' she said with a laugh. 'I told you, I've really enjoyed it.'

He hesitated when they arrived at her gate. She smiled at him coyly but with a gleam in her eyes.

'Aren't you going to kiss me goodnight?' she said.

And he did so, tentatively at first, then with more confidence as he felt her respond. She broke away then kissed him playfully on the cheek.

'Night night, Ian,' she said. 'See you soon.' She scurried up the path, then turned to wave as she reached the door.

Ian walked home feeling happy and very pleased that a girl like Alison wanted to see him again. Then he thought of Sophie and felt a tiny pang of regret. But as the song went: 'Que sera, sera, whatever will be, will be . . .'

THIRTEEN

Val and Sam had settled down to a happy and peaceful family life again. Lucy seemed to have suffered no ill effects from her abduction, and Val could see that she had been well-cared-for. There was no sign of nappy rash, and the nappy she had been wearing when she came home was spotlessly white.

She had seemed a little confused at first, staring around as if unsure where she was; then, to their delight, she'd smiled at them and the words 'Da-da' and 'Ma-ma' that they had been eagerly waiting to hear started to trip from her tongue. Not just once but repeatedly, as she became familiar with the sounds she was making.

They had wondered if the improvement in Russell's behaviour would continue. A week later he was still being good, or as good as could be expected from a nearly three-year-old. He was gentle with Lucy, and Val was touched at the way he often went up to his little sister and stroked her face.

'I love Lucy, Mummy,' he said.

And Val was able to answer without hesitation, 'So do I, Russell, and I love you too, very much.' To her delight, he was now responding more readily to her cuddles.

But her thoughts were still with the poor woman who had taken Lucy, and she had been adamant that she must not be punished for her actions. Hazel, who had been their family liaison officer, had become more of a friend now, rather than a policewoman doing her duty. After a fortnight or so had passed, Val enquired again about the woman, whom she had learned was called Claire.

'She's in a much more stable frame of mind now,' said Hazel. 'The doctor is treating her for depression and her husband is at home for another week before he starts his next tour. He seems a very understanding sort of man. He must have been horrified at what she had done but he didn't go off the deep end about it.'

'Do you think I could go and see her?' asked Val, as she had asked once before at the police station. But the sergeant had told her then that it would not be a good idea.

Hazel looked at her with understanding, but then shook her head doubtfully. 'I'm . . . not sure. It's not what usually happens and it might not be a good idea. But I know you've shown great understanding and forgiveness . . .'

'That's because I've been in the same position myself. I was desperate for a child, and I know now how silly and impatient I was. Lucy was on the way when we'd not even thought about having another baby. We'd only recently adopted Russell. I suppose I'd calmed down and wasn't getting all worked up about it, and that's when it happened. I'd like to tell Claire about what happened to me, and perhaps it'll help her not to get too anxious about it all.'

'You weren't thinking of taking Lucy with you, were you?'

'No, of course not.'

'Well, it's rather irregular, but . . . would you mind if I came with you? Not in my uniform, just as a friend. I don't like the idea of you going on your own.'

'Yes, I think that's the best idea,' said Val. 'My mum will look after the children.'

Hazel said she would be free the next afternoon and they decided to go in Sam's car rather than a police vehicle. Sam occasionally walked to work, leaving the car for Val to use when she needed it.

Hazel cycled to Val's home and they set off, leaving Russell and Lucy in the care of their capable grandma.

Claire Dawson lived with her husband, Greg, in a small, semi-detached house at the far end of Queensbury. Val felt a little apprehensive as they walked up the path. It had been her idea to make the visit but she was wondering what sort of a reception she would receive.

After they had rung the bell twice and Val was beginning to think she was not there, the door opened.

Claire was a small woman, very girlish in appearance, although Val knew she was, at thirty-one, a few years her senior. She had wispy blonde hair, a pale complexion and a delicate prettiness.

'Oh . . . hello, Hazel,' she said, sounding surprised, 'I wasn't expecting . . .' She looked curiously at Val, whom she had not seen before.

'Hello, Claire,' said Hazel. 'This is Val . . . Lucy's mum. She said she'd like to come and meet you.'

'Oh . . . oh, I see.' Claire's face went a shade paler, if that were possible. She reached out to hold the doorjamb for support. 'You'd better come in, then.'

Val reached out and touched her arm reassuringly. There's nothing to worry about,' she said. 'I do understand about what happened, and you took good care of Lucy.'

'Is Lucy all right?' asked Claire, looking anxious.

'Yes, she's fine; she's with her gran – my mother – and her brother, Russell.'

'Well . . . come in, then.'

They followed Claire into the living room, which had windows at the front and the back: a combined dining room and lounge, nicely furnished with G-plan furniture from the mid-fifties.

They sat down on the two-seater settee and Claire sat opposite on a matching chair, only to jump up again immediately.

'Would you like a cup of tea?' she asked.

'That would be nice,' said Hazel, 'but I shall make it. I know my way around your kitchen. You have a chat with Val.'

Claire nodded. 'OK, then.'

She smiled nervously at Val when they were alone, then looked down at the floor for a moment before she looked at Val again.

'I'm sorry,' she began. 'Really sorry about what I did. I don't know what came over me.' She shook her head in bewilderment. 'Well, I suppose I do know really. I saw this lovely little girl; she was just waking up, and I wanted her so badly that I hardly thought about what I was doing. I just got hold of the pram and wheeled it away. Nobody took any notice of me. I knew, though – I knew all the time that I couldn't keep her. I was waiting for them to find her. And now I'm really, really sorry. I don't know how you can be so nice about it.'

'Because I've been in the same position myself,' said Val. 'No . . .' She shook her head. 'I don't mean that I took a baby, but I was desperate for a child, as I know you have been.'

'I still am,' said Claire, 'but I'm feeling a lot calmer now, more resigned to it all. The pills are helping. You say you wanted a child? But you have two now?'

'Yes; I realize now that I was getting too anxious about it. We'd been married for only two years – no time at all, really – and that's what Sam, my husband, kept telling me, but I'd convinced myself it would never happen. I'd had one or two false alarms, then I had a miscarriage at six months. I was devastated, I can tell you. Then we had the opportunity to adopt Russell when he was seven months old. And I realized soon afterwards that I really was pregnant. It seemed like a miracle. Lucy was born when Russell was not quite two years old. So, Claire, you must not give up hope. Nature has a way of knowing when it's the right time.'

'I hope so,' said Claire. 'We've been married more than three years and I've had two miscarriages. The last one was at six months, like yours. It was just before Christmas, and I suppose I never got over it. Thank you for telling me your story. The doctors say there's nothing wrong with me, but then I'm rather older than you, aren't I? I'm thirty-one, and I feel that time is running out . . .'

'But it isn't,' said Val. 'My mum was thirty-four when I was born. I can't tell you not to worry or get depressed, because I know how I felt myself. But I went back to work after I'd lost the baby. I work in the office at Walker's mill; it's my husband's family firm. And that helped me a lot, stopped me from dwelling on my problems all the time. Then, as I said, we adopted Russell.'

'Which you might not have done if you'd known you'd soon have a baby of your own?'

Val smiled. 'That's impossible to answer because we can't see into the future. Who knows? Maybe it was fate; maybe it was what we had to do. I know that we wouldn't want to be without Russell now. He's part of our family, just as Lucy is.'

Val was realizing more and more that this was true. She had – almost – forgotten the times when she had wondered whether they had made a mistake in taking Russell into their family, the times when she had despaired of his bad behaviour. She knew now that she could not bear to be without him.

'I think that caring for Russell may have intensified my maternal feelings,' she said, 'and perhaps that's why I got pregnant with Lucy so soon. I can't be sure, of course, but Sam and I are very thankful that it happened. And I do hope, so very much, Claire, that it will happen for you.'

'Thank you,' said Claire. 'You've helped me a lot. You were talking about going back to work and Greg has been trying to persuade me to do that when I'm feeling strong enough. I was a shorthand typist; I worked for a solicitor but I gave my job up when I was pregnant. It shouldn't be difficult to find something, though, even if it's only a temporary post.'

Hazel had returned while they were talking and was handing round mugs of tea. 'And I've found some shortbread biscuits in a tin,' she said. 'Hope you don't mind me making myself at home!'

Claire smiled. 'You're very welcome; it's so nice to have some company.' She was looking much more cheerful and relaxed. 'Actually, I can't go back to work just yet,' she said, 'because we're going away on holiday. You know that my husband drives for a travel firm? Well, they are allowed to take their wives, now and again, if there's room on the coach. So I'm going with Greg on his next trip. It's to Austria and Germany. I've never been to either place, and Greg has told me how beautiful it is around there, all the mountains and lakes and lovely towns and villages.'

'That will do you a world of good,' said Hazel. 'You are already looking a good deal better than the last time I saw you.'

'And I'm so glad you came, both of you,' said Claire. 'Yes, I am feeling much better now about everything. I was still feeling terribly guilty about what I'd done. I know it was a dreadful thing to do and you've been so understanding.'

'Don't worry any more about Lucy,' said Val. 'She's fine, and we've all settled down happily again. In fact, Russell's much kinder to his little sister now. I know he missed her and couldn't understand why she wasn't there. He could be a little demon at times, you know, and now . . . well, it's hard to believe he's so much better. I'm not saying it will last, but it's more peaceful at the moment.'

They finished their tea, then Hazel nodded to Val, signalling that she thought it was time to go. Val gave Claire a hug as they said goodbye. 'Now, remember what I said. Don't worry any more. I hope you have a lovely holiday.'

'I think you made the right decision,' said Hazel as they drove away. 'She looked scared stiff at first, but you were so nice with her.'

'I hope she gets what she wants,' said Val. 'I think she might, eventually. Look at me! I got far more than I bargained for, but it's turned out for the best.'

'I'm glad that Val and Sam are OK again,' Janice remarked to Phil. Her friend had phoned to say that all was well, and that they were looking forward to visiting Harrogate before too long.

'Val says that Russell is behaving well but she's keeping her fingers crossed, wondering how long it will last . . . Do you think we should include children, Phil, when we have our opening ceremony? Well, not exactly a ceremony, but you know what I mean.'

'A "bit of a do", said Phil. 'That's perhaps the best way to describe it. Maybe it should be just adults if we put on a three-course meal. Let's cross that bridge when we come to it, eh? We can't fix a date yet, until we see how things go.'

The work was progressing well upstairs, the workmen trying to make as little disruption as possible to the family as they constructed the extra bedrooms. The noise of banging and hammering was taking place in what had been the upstairs of the florist's shop, so it was not disturbing the customers at Grundy's overmuch. And for the evening diners there was no disturbance at all.

Phil had given a good deal of thought to the details of their new venture, and Janice had left the planning mainly to him as he would be the one largely responsible for the restaurant meals in the evening, while she would be in charge of the daytime sessions. When the wall between the two shops was eventually knocked down there would be a much larger dining area.

They decided they would continue as they were doing now during the daytime, serving morning coffee, midday snacks and afternoon tea. Three-course meals would be served in the evenings; these would not need to be pre-booked as they were at present, although bookings would be taken if required.

'Very ambitious, Phil,' said his father. 'Don't bite off more than you can chew, lad.'

Ralph Grundy and his wife, Patience, ran a successful country pub and restaurant, the Coach and Horses, near to Ilkley, which was where Phil had worked as an assistant chef before starting out on his own.

'I know that, Dad,' said Phil, 'but nothing ventured, nothing gained. I like to think we've built up a good reputation and we'll take on extra staff if necessary.'

The business was known just as Grundy's but they intended in future to have two different names for the daytime and evening sessions. During the daytime it would be known as the Coffee Pot and in the evening as Changing Seasons.

Phil planned to change the menu along with the different seasons. They would concentrate on salads, light grilled meals and a variety of fish dishes for the spring and summer, with many kinds of fruit served as a starter or dessert, and a selection of gateaux and meringue dishes and ice cream for puddings. The traditional roasts, casseroles and steak or chicken pies and hearty soups would be the main items on the autumn and winter menus, with specials for such times as Christmas, Halloween or Bonfire Night.

This meant that the menu would not be too extensive, and therefore easier to cope with, rather than serving a vast variety of dishes all year round.

When Grundy's had opened three years before, Janice had wanted a light-hearted, summery feel which had been evident in the floral curtains, displays of seasonal flowers and the floral cups, saucers and plates. As they had been watching the cost at the start, they had bought oddments of china from market stalls and second-hand shops, in many different floral patterns. It had not mattered that the cup and saucer might not match as it all added to the gaiety of the place. For the lunchtime and evening sessions they had used more traditional plain crockery.

On the walls there were pictures of summery and springtime scenes from all parts of the country, taken from calendars and mounted in plain wooden frames.

By now some of the oddments of floral china had been broken, so they decided that maybe it was time for a complete change.

'We can't go mad, though,' said Janice. 'We can't afford Shelley or Rockingham but I think we should stick to china, rather than earthenware, for the mornings and teatimes.'

'All the same design, though, this time?' suggested Phil. 'A floral design, but maybe something more abstract, one that would be suitable for all times of the year. That's your province, though, so you must decide what you want.'

'And we'll need new plates and dishes for Changing Seasons, won't we?' said Janice. 'That should be your choice.'

'Yes . . . Something traditional but not plain white. Perhaps a rich cream shade. We'll ask my dad about the wholesaler he deals with. We were highly satisfied last time and he's not too expensive. We'll need to watch the pennies!'

They were feeling excited but also a little apprehensive as the weeks went by. They still planned to open at the end of May if all went according to plan.

'What about the first Monday in June?' said Phil. 'The Coffee Pot will be the same as before, just a new name. But I want Changing Seasons to be a really new venture.'

'And what about our own private party?' said Janice. 'Shall we have that on the Saturday, the third of June? Just for family and friends. They're all eager to see what we're doing. And, like I mentioned before, shall we invite the children . . . or not?'

'I rather think not, this time,' said Phil. 'Changing Seasons is an evening venue, so I suggest we put on a typical evening meal just for the adults. Some of them could stay with us – we'll have four bedrooms by then – and there are plenty of hotels nearby, although I dare say our friends from Halifax would drive back the same evening; it's not all that far. I don't suppose they'll have any problems getting babysitters.'

'What about our parents?' said Janice. 'I mean . . . your parents, and my dad and Norma?'

'My mum and dad will drive back the same evening,' said Phil. 'They'll be able to leave the inn for a few hours; they have very good staff. Your dad and Norma will have to stay overnight. And do you think Ian will be able to come?'

'I don't see why not. He's not at college on Saturday or Sunday unless there's something special going on. We'll ring up and ask them.'

To their surprise, Ian asked if he could bring Alison as well. Alec said they would love to stay overnight. He and Norma were longing to see the new premises.

'That's a turn up for the book!' said Phil. 'Ian must still be seeing Alison. Do you think they will want to share a room?'

Janice looked at him in amazement. 'Don't be ridiculous, Phil! Of course not! They're only seventeen. And certainly not when Dad and Norma are there. You know how naive Ian is, or used to be. There was all that to-do when he overheard my dad and Norma having sex.'

'Well, he's probably grown up a lot by now. I see what you mean, though. There'll be plenty of room, and Ian won't mind kipping on the sofa if necessary.'

'It will be nice for Ian to be waited on for a change,' said Janice, 'and not have to help with the cooking and clearing up. I wonder if he'll come and work for us in the summer again?'

'I hope so,' said Phil. 'He's shaping up very well and we'd be glad of his help. But I suppose it all depends on . . . well . . . a few things, really. Sophie might want a holiday job and it could be awkward if Ian was here. On the other hand, maybe not. They've both got new partners; well, new . . . friends, or whatever. And there'll probably be several more, for both of them, before they settle down.'

'Yes . . . maybe,' said Janice. She was thinking, though, that Phil had been her first real boyfriend and she had known very soon that he was the one she wanted. She knew there could never be anyone else.

FOURTEEN

'It'll be great to have a night on our own, won't it?' said Cissie to Walter. 'It's real good of your mam to say she'll have the children. And Val's mam is going to look after Russell and Lucy.'

The four of them – Val and Sam, Cissie and Walter – were going to Harrogate for the opening of Changing Seasons on the third of June. They would be travelling in Sam's car as it was more spacious than Walter's, and Sam had booked rooms at a hotel overlooking the Stray, not far from Phil and Janice's place.

Cissie was still enjoying her job at the cafe in the market, and had managed to juggle her hours so that she would be free on Saturday afternoon.

Val, also, was looking forward to the short break. She had felt, since Lucy's return, that she hardly dared to let her out of her sight, but she knew it would be a pleasant change for her and Sam, and that the children would be well looked after by their grandparents.

It was Lucy's first birthday on the first of June. She was not yet old enough to understand what was happening, so they had just a simple tea party for the four of them to mark the occasion. Val made a cake, more for Russell, really, as he said he would blow the candle out for his little sister. He did not understand about making a wish at the same time, so Val made a wish for all the family: that they would continue to live peacefully and happily together, with no more traumas.

She had been rather worried, though, about Sam. She knew that something was troubling him, and had thought at first that Lucy's disappearance was still affecting him, even after her safe return.

It was the evening before their trip to Harrogate, when both children were in bed and asleep, that he told her the reason for his preoccupation and his bouts of silence, which were not like him at all. They were not getting the orders at the mill that they had depended on for so long. It seemed as though, very soon, workers might have to be laid off. This was something that his father, Joshua, was trying to avoid at all costs; he had always been a fair and responsible boss.

'One thing is certain, though,' Sam told his wife now. 'There isn't room any more for three bosses. And it seems to me that I am the one who will have to go.'

Val stared at him in astonishment, almost horror. 'You mean . . . your father wants you to leave?'

'No.' He shook his head. 'That's not what I meant at all. This is my idea. Father hasn't suggested it; he may not even have thought of it. But I feel it's time that I made a break. I'm the younger son and, as I said, I don't think there's room for three of us now.'

'But surely . . . your father is near retiring age, isn't he? He'll have to let go of the reins sometime.'

'He's only in his early sixties, and as far as I can see he has no intention of giving up just yet. Can you imagine him, honestly, wanting to retire and live a life of ease? It would drive him mad, and probably drive Mother mad as well, having him there all the time. He's never really had many interests outside of the mill, only the things he does in the evening, like his Rotary Club and the Masons.'

Val looked worried. 'How serious is it, then, the situation at the mill?' she asked. 'And what about Walter? He isn't in danger of losing his job, is he?'

'No, Walter's in charge of pretty much all the working side of things now, and the three of us, Father and Jonathan and I, see to the administration. But it doesn't need all three of us. You know the root problem, of course. It's the way all these new synthetic fibres are taking over. There isn't the same demand for wool any more. It's the same in Lancashire with the cotton industry – they're starting to feel the pinch with all the longer-lasting fibres, the nylons and terylenes and crimplenes.'

'Couldn't you change over? Adapt some of the looms to make the new fabrics?'

Sam smiled wryly. 'No, it would be a colossal task; it's not possible at all. Nothing is going to happen overnight, though. I'm sure there'll always be a demand for wool but not as much as there has been in the past. There is no substitute for wool in the long run. I feel sure of that, but we have to look ahead. At the moment, it means that we don't employ anyone else if someone retires or leaves. Women are leaving all the time, as you know. And some of the women have asked if they can do part time, so that has eased the situation a little.'

'Have you said anything to your father about leaving?'

'No, I'm just mulling it over . . . with Colin, actually.'

'Colin? What does he have to do with it?'

'Well, he's ready for a change, just as I am. He's been in the same job with the insurance firm since he left school. He's had a promotion, of course, but it's not the most exciting of jobs. He and I have been wondering – it's only an idea at the moment – if we could start up in business together.'

'What sort of business?'

'Well . . . possibly a sports shop or something of the sort, selling sports gear like golfing equipment . . .'

Val smiled. 'Yes, I thought golf might come into it.'

Sam still played golf occasionally with his two oldest friends, Colin and Jeff. They had been at school together and had never lost touch with one another. Val recalled how the three young men had been on a golfing holiday in Blackpool – enjoying the other delights the town had to offer as well – when she and Sam had met at the Winter Gardens ballroom.

'But you don't know anything about the retail trade, do you, either of you?' said Val, feeling quite bewildered.

'No, but we could learn and take advice. We're both pretty good businessmen. I've dealt with facts and figures and so has Colin. My father made sure that I knew all that there was to know about the mill. I started right at the bottom and worked my way up, just like other trainees do, so I feel now that I could turn my hand to anything.'

'You've taken the wind out of my sails,' said Val. 'I can't quite take it in at the moment. Does Colin's wife know about it, I wonder?'

'I don't think so, not yet. It's just an idea at the moment. We know there'll be a lot to consider.'

'You would need to find suitable premises. And were you thinking of staying here, in Halifax?'

'I can't give you any answers at the moment because I just don't know,' replied Sam. He sounded a little on edge, perhaps wishing he had kept his mouth shut. 'I don't suppose something will suddenly turn up out of the blue. We'll have to make enquiries at estate agencies. And I don't know whether it would be in Halifax. Most probably not . . . Let's not talk about it any more tonight. I had to tell you, though; I couldn't keep it to myself any longer.'

'Well, I'm very glad you did,' said Val. 'Goodness me! Look at the time: half past eleven! Well past our bedtime. And tomorrow we're off to Harrogate. So we'll have to put it out of our minds for now and enjoy the weekend.'

'Well, we've done it,' said Janice on the Friday evening when Sarah was tucked up in bed in her new bedroom.

'As near as done it, anyway,' said Phil. 'Just a few finishing touches tomorrow before our guests arrive, then we'll have all day Sunday to make sure we're ready for the grand opening on Monday.'

'Do you think it will be?' said Janice, a little nervously. 'A grand opening, I mean? We've been closed for more than a week. I hope our customers will come back.'

'Of course they will, in droves,' replied Phil with a great show of enthusiasm which Janice did not think was feigned. Phil was ever the optimist. 'It's been well advertised and our regulars will be dying to see what changes we've made. Don't worry; they'll come back all right.'

They had been closed for ten days while the restaurant was being enlarged, which had involved knocking down the central wall then painting and decorating the area that had been the florist's shop in a matching neutral shade. They had invested in a new carpet for the whole of the floor space, in a design of autumn leaves – brown, orange and gold – and tie-back curtains in a golden, silky rayon fabric for the large windows. There were new signs hanging in the windows, one saying Grundy's, the Coffee Pot, and the other, Grundy's, Changing Seasons. There were menus by the door showing the range of choices for both of them.

The pictures which were already on the walls showed

landscapes from many parts of the country, in spring, summer and autumn. These were now interspersed with winter scenes, which Janice had avoided in their original venture but were necessary now to depict all the changing seasons. Scenes of the snow-covered Yorkshire Dales and the Scottish Highlands, and the city of York at Christmastime. Janice had also bought some inexpensive reproductions of Monet's floral scenes and winter scenes by Brueghel. There would be something to appeal to all tastes in their new environment, to the eye as well as, more importantly, to the palate.

Phil knew that they had reached their limit as far as bank loans were concerned, but he was confident that they would quite soon recoup what they had borrowed and start to show a profit again.

They had been fortunate with their staff. Phil had a very good chef, Toby, who had been there from the start, working with him. Toby was as keen as Phil to work hard and make Changing Seasons a success.

Janice, also, had an excellent co-worker, Marjorie: a middle-aged lady, now a widow, who had been in the catering business for many years. They worked together on the fancy cakes and gateaux and all kinds of pastry. Janice had managed to cope reasonably well with her work at Grundy's as well as looking after her baby daughter, although it had not been easy. Now that Sarah was nearly two years old and walking and talking, it was difficult to watch her all the time. They had become friendly, though, with Martin and Chloe, a young married couple of similar age to them, who also had a two-year-old daughter. Along with Martin's parents, Mr and Mrs Banks, they ran the post office and newsagent's shop at the other end of the terrace from Grundy's. Chloe now took charge of Sarah for a couple of hours each day, along with her own little daughter, at a time convenient to both of them.

The waitresses, Brenda and Jessie, had also been with them from the start and were willing to carry on with the new arrangement. Phil and Janice had found all along that they had little difficulty in employing part-time waiters and wait-resses, and had extra help in the kitchen as and when it was required. During the school holidays there were always sixth-form students, such as Sophie and her friends, looking for a holiday job.

There would be eighteen guests at the private party on Saturday; twenty sitting down for the meal, including Phil and Janice. Phil would be involved in its preparation, along with Toby. He would then leave Toby in charge and act as host to their guests.

Marjorie, who was Janice's assistant and did not usually have anything to do with the evening meals, had agreed to come and help with the finishing touches to the meal, and Brenda and Jessie, their very capable waitresses, would wait on at the tables. There would be other waiters and waitresses who would work on a part-time basis when the restaurant opened the following Monday.

The guests had been invited to a pre-dinner drink in the new bar area at six thirty, followed by the meal at seven o'clock.

'Our relations will probably be the first to arrive,' said Phil. 'Your dad and Norma and Alison will want time to settle into their rooms; I'm looking forward to meeting Alison. You've told Ian he'll be kipping on the settee, haven't you?'

'Yes; he doesn't mind. He seemed quite relieved actually. I expect the ones from Halifax will go to their hotel first and book in; we probably won't see them till the evening. And the others are local. Oh . . . and there's Bella and her sister, of course. They're staying at a hotel because Dorothy didn't want to drive back late at night.'

Bella Tarrant, the previous owner of the florist's shop, had been invited, with her sister, Dorothy, with whom she now lived, close to Thirsk. It was not a great distance away but they had decided to make the most of their short break. Their friends and neighbours from the newsagent's shop were invited, as well as Lynette, who owned the hairdresser's salon next door, with her husband, Bernard.

As they had expected, the quartet from Blackpool arrived in the middle of the afternoon. Alec and Norma were very impressed as they looked around the new premises.

'By heck, you've worked wonders here,' said Alec. 'I'm really impressed.'

'It all depends on whether the food is as good as the decor,' said Ian, winking at his brother-in-law. 'As I'm quite sure it will be,' he added. 'Do you need any help tonight, Phil? I'm willing and able.'

'No, of course not,' said Phil. 'Thanks all the same. We're all sorted. I shall be dining with our guests and leaving Toby in charge. But we're hoping you'll be with us in the summer, unless you are otherwise occupied in Blackpool?'

'I haven't decided yet,' said Ian, glancing at Alison. She shrugged and gave a non-committal smile. 'It will be up to you,' she said. 'I shall probably be working at Marks and Spencer's again.'

Janice made a cup of tea for them, a 'must' after a long car drive, then, when they had sorted out their small amount of luggage and made a big fuss of Sarah, who, understandably, was overawed at all the attention, they set out on foot to explore the town.

'You two go on ahead,' said Norma, knowing that the younger couple would not want to stay with them all afternoon. 'Your dad and I will have a leisurely stroll. We'll see you later.'

'Your sister's very nice and friendly,' said Alison. 'She's a pretty girl, and Sarah's a little love.'

'Yes, so she is,' said Ian. 'I'd never had much to do with babies but I was thrilled to bits when they asked me to be her godfather.'

'Gosh! I didn't know that. They've done very well, haven't they, to have a business like that at their age?'

'Yes. They were lucky in the beginning, though, because Phil's aunt left him a lot of money in her will and that helped them to get started. But they've worked hard as well, of course.'

'You and Janice get on very well together, don't you? A lot of brothers and sisters don't.'

'Yes, we do. We've always been good friends, even though she's six years older than me. I missed her when she moved over here, especially as Dad had married Norma, and I didn't like that very much at first. We're OK now, though; I've got used to Norma.'

'Yes, she seems a good sort; quite easy-going.' Alison smiled.

'I thought your sister might have put us in the same room but no such luck!'

Ian turned to look at her in amazement. 'What! With Dad and Norma there! Don't be daft! Anyway, we're OK as we are.'

Alison laughed. 'If you say so, and don't look so horrified. I was only joking, you know. I'd guessed we'd be kept well apart. But you'll know where I am . . .'

'Don't be stupid, Alison! You know we can't.' Ian was starting to get hot under the collar.

'Spoilsport!' said Alison, laughing. She grabbed hold of his arm. 'Come on, now. Where are you taking me? I've never been to Harrogate before.'

'We'll go down to the Valley Gardens. They're just at the bottom of this hill. And that's Betty's at the corner, the famous tea shop. But Janice's cakes are just as good . . .

Phil's parents arrived soon after their first lot of visitors had gone out. They, too, were very impressed with all the changes that had been made, especially the extra space that had been created in the restaurant.

'We don't expect to be full all the time,' said Phil, 'especially during the day, but we were rather cramped before. There's plenty of room now to spread out and leave a good space between the tables.'

'Well, I hope you get off to a cracking start on Monday,' said Ralph. 'Have you had some bookings in advance for Monday evening?'

'Yes, quite a few,' said Phil, 'and probably others will turn up on spec. We don't ask them to choose their menu in advance now, unless it's a large number for a wedding or some special occasion.'

'It's a good selection for us to choose from tonight,' said Phil's mother. 'All very nice and summery. It's a good idea to change the menu according to the seasons.'

'And we've got a good range of appropriate music as well,' said Janice. 'We had to have Vivaldi, of course – "The Four Seasons" – but there's a lot of other stuff as well; some popular, some classical, but not too highbrow, and music from the shows.'

'Well, I'm sure it's going to be a rip-roaring success,' said

Ralph. 'I'm real proud of you, lad, and you as well, Janice. You're a grand team.'

Alec and Norma arrived back from their sortie round the town, followed soon afterwards by Ian and Alison. Between them they looked after Sarah while Janice and Phil were busy in the kitchen. Sarah soon lost her shyness and enjoyed all the attention until Janice came to whisk her away for an early bedtime.

Then the other guests started to arrive; the neighbours from the shops, the four from Halifax, and Bella and Dorothy from Thirsk. By six thirty they were all assembled in the new bar area. As he had done two years previously when Grundy's first opened, Ralph Grundy proposed the toast to Phil and Janice and the success of Changing Seasons.

They all raised their glasses of Bristol Cream sherry. 'The Changing Seasons,' they repeated wholeheartedly, some adding, 'good luck', 'all the best,' and 'good health and happiness'.

Phil and Janice looked at one another, smiling in delight and not without some pride. Then they sat down with their guests, knowing that all would be well left in the capable hands of their staff.

Everyone agreed that the meal was a great success and boded well for the future of Changing Seasons. It was a delicious summery meal: homemade pâté, seafood cocktail or melon, followed by poached salmon, chicken breasts in white wine sauce or home-baked gammon with salad. The desserts were Janice's specialities: coffee and hazelnut gateau, strawberry pavlova or chocolate profiteroles with cream. There was a choice of white or rosé wine, followed by fragrant coffee and chocolate mints.

During the meal, Phil was responsible for the taped music: a selection of songs from *Salad Days*, 'Summertime' from *Porgy and Bess* and Mozart's *'Eine Kleine Nachtmusik'*.

When the meal ended the guests mingled, moving from one table to another to talk with someone different, or gravitating to the small bar area where Phil served drinks as required. As it was a private party, there was no restriction. On the other hand, no one wanted to abuse Phil and Janice's hospitality. Some had to drive home that night and others were just content to sit and chat. Phil and Janice, after making sure they had spoken with everyone and thanked them for coming, sat down to chat with Sam and Valerie.

'So you're having a night away from the children,' said Janice. 'Your mum's in charge, is she, Val?'

'Yes, so she is,' replied Val. 'She loves having them. Lucy has never been much trouble, and as for Russell, well, you'd hardly believe it was the same child. He has his moments, of course – don't they all? But the scare we had with Lucy really shook him up.'

'Yes, that must have been a dreadful time for you,' said Janice, 'but at least some good has come out of it.'

'Lucy was none the worse, thank goodness, and we really think that Russell has grown up and become more of a little boy than a baby. You know the pantomime we had with him at the playgroup? But we think we might try him there again in September; he'll be three by then. And he keeps asking when he can go back, much to our surprise!'

'He'll probably be fine next time,' said Val. 'We were sorry we didn't see Sarah when we arrived.'

'I decided to get her to bed early,' said Janice, 'and once she's asleep she's no trouble. We've been up to check on her; her bedroom's a bit further away now, but she's settled there very well and she loves her new bed. Perhaps you could call and see her before you set off back in the morning?'

'Of course we will,' said Val. 'I'm dying to see my little goddaughter again and I know Cissie will be as well. They grow up so quickly, don't they? Cissie's two are both at school now; well, Holly's at playgroup, but she'll be starting proper school before long.'

'And Cissie's enjoying her job at the market, is she?'

'Oh, yes, she loves it. No doubt she'll tell you all about it when she's finished chatting to your dad and Norma.'

Cissie and Walter were at one of the other tables with Janice's father and Norma. Cissie, who was far more gregarious than her husband, was talking animatedly to Norma. Walter, also, was chatting quietly to Alec.

'So how are things at the mill, Sam?' asked Phil. 'I've heard there's something of a slowdown in the woollen industry. Is Walker's being affected?'

'Not all that much, yet, but the writing's on the wall,' replied Sam. 'We know there will have to be changes. As a matter of fact . . .' He paused and looked at Val with a questioning smile. 'Shall I tell them or do you think it's too soon?'

'No, you tell them if you want to,' said Val. 'I know you're dying to share it with someone and you can trust Phil and Janice to keep it to themselves, not that there's anything much to tell at the moment.'

'I don't intend saying anything to Cissie and Walter, though,' said Sam. 'You know what a chatterbox she is! She wouldn't be able to resist telling someone.'

'That's true,' said Val. 'She's a good friend but I know what she's like. Go on, tell them while she's busy talking over there.'

'What's all this?' said Phil. 'It all sounds very intriguing.'

'The thing is . . . I'm thinking of leaving the mill and doing something completely different,' said Sam. 'And while we were in Harrogate this afternoon we saw something that was of great interest to us. Well, of great interest to me, I should say . . .'

'And to me as well,' added Val. 'I wasn't sure at first but I'm coming round now to your way of thinking, Sam . . .'

FIFTEEN

The hotel where the four from Halifax were staying on Saturday night was very close to the centre of the town, facing the Stray. Sam parked the car outside the hotel, and when they had booked in and taken their small amount of luggage to their rooms, they set off on foot to explore the town.

'Look, that's Betty's on the corner,' said Cissie, pointing across to the famous tea shop. 'Shall we go and have a cup of tea and one of their gorgeous cakes?'

'No!' said Walter firmly. 'They're far too expensive, from what I've heard, and it's too early in the afternoon.'

They had all had a sandwich lunch before setting off and had arrived in Harrogate soon after two o'clock.

'Maybe we could have something later,' suggested Val. 'We won't want much, though. We don't want to spoil our appetites for the evening meal. I know Phil and Janice will be putting on something quite special. Anyway, like Walter said, Betty's is rather pricey and I'm sure that the cakes that Janice makes are just as good.'

'I tell you what,' said Sam, 'let's go our separate ways. We'll probably want to look at different things and we don't want to keep one another waiting. We'll go and see the Valley Gardens, shall we, Val? Then we can walk back to the town later.'

'Suits me fine,' said Val. She knew that a little of Cissie went a long way with Sam, even though he had grown quite fond of his wife's oldest friend since their marriage. Cissie had chattered almost incessantly on the journey from Halifax while Sam was trying to concentrate on his driving.

'Happen we'll come across you later then,' said Cissie. 'I want to go and look at the shops. Is that OK, Walter?'

'I suppose it will have to be,' said Walter, with a look at his wife that was half smile, half frown. 'If we don't meet up later we'll see you back at the hotel, shall we?'

'Yes, we'll have to leave time to get dressed up for the "do" tonight,' said Cissie. 'See you later, you two.'

She waved cheerily as she and Walter headed for the shops, and Val and Sam walked down the steep road that led down to the valley.

'Peace at last!' said Sam. 'She can't half talk.'

'She's excited,' said Val. 'It's a nice change for Cissie to go out for the evening to what she calls a "posh do". Although I know it will be quite informal and friendly.'

The Valley Gardens in their early summer flowering were a peaceful haven away from the bustle of the town. The trees still showed the bright green hues of springtime before turning to the darker shades they wore in late summer. The rose bushes were still in bud, but the flower beds and borders were bright with begonias and wallflowers, tall lupins and yellow and orange marigolds.

The did a circuit of the gardens, then, despite Val's warning about spoiling their appetites, stopped for tea, with just a small piece of shortbread, at the outdoor cafe. Then they strolled through the colonnades, where wisteria and vines climbed up the trelliswork and along the veranda overhead, the path leading them back to the main gate and the town.

It was a steep climb back to the shopping area but, living in Halifax, they were used to the hilly terrain of most Yorkshire towns. Val enjoyed the elegant shops of Harrogate, which were rather grander than those in their home town, just as much as Cissie did.

'Now, what would you like?' said Sam. 'I think you deserve a treat.'

'But it's not my birthday,' she replied, 'and there's nothing I need, not really.'

'Well, that doesn't matter, does it? Don't refuse when I'm feeling generous. It might not last.'

'You spoil me, Sam,' she replied, squeezing his arm. 'Actually . . . it would be nice to have a little clutch bag to go with the dress I'm wearing tonight. I've brought this shoulder bag but it's rather clumsy.'

Her dress was a simple shift dress in a silky rayon material, the new shorter knee length in a deep raspberry pink. The fashions were changing and girls no longer wore the full skirted summer dresses of a few years ago.

They went to a well-known department store, which was a delight to Val as there was not a branch in their home town. It was impossible to match the pink shade, so she chose a small, dainty-looking bag in soft fawn suede with a golden clasp and chain strap. It would go well with her sandal-type shoes that were a similar colour.

Val was pleased with their purchases and tried to persuade Sam to buy something for himself: a colourful tie or a new shirt, a striped one rather than the coloured ones he usually wore. For a young man – well, youngish – he was very conservative in his choice of clothing.

He shrugged. 'It's as you say, Val; I don't really need anything so why spend the money?' Like most Yorkshire men, he had that innate thriftiness, but could be generous when that way inclined.

They had wandered to the outskirts of the town. 'Oh, look, there's a sports shop,' he said, pointing across the road. 'Come to think of it, I could do with some more golf balls.'

'I'm not surprised at the rate you lose them,' said Val with a smile. As they crossed the road, she noticed the sign in the window. 'Look, Sam; there's a closing-down sale. You'd better stock up with them. Better to lose half-price ones, don't you think?'

He laughed. 'Oh, come on! I don't lose all that many. Anyway, it's an occupational hazard.'

They stopped by the window. The sign above read *Bateson's Sports Emporium, established 1910.* There was a wide variety of goods in the window, all at reduced prices, covering a range of sports. Clothing for golfers, hikers, cricketers, tennis players; golf clubs, cricket bats, tennis racquets and, of course, golf balls of the make that Sam used, at half price.

Sam stood still, staring at the display. 'I wonder why they're closing down?' he said thoughtfully. 'And why sell the stock? I would have thought . . .'

'What, Sam?' asked Val. 'What are you thinking?' Although she did have an idea what it might be.

'Well, it's usual to sell a business as a going concern, stock and all, and the goodwill.'

'I'm sure they have their reasons. I know what you're thinking, Sam. Let's go in and you can make some tentative enquiries.'

'Shall we?' She could see the light of optimism and enthusiasm in his eyes. 'It might be just what we were looking for, Colin and me, although we haven't really looked anywhere yet. It doesn't say the business is for sale, though . . .'

'Well, you won't know until you ask. Come on, let's go in.'

Sam pushed open the door which gave a jingle as they entered. It was a roomy shop with two long counters at either side and stands in the middle with the display of goods.

A man was being served at one of the counters. A middle-aged man at the other one looked across, saying politely, 'Good afternoon, sir, madam. How can I help you?'

Sam started by saying that he wanted a dozen golf balls.

'A good price, sir,' said the salesman. 'They're going very quickly. We haven't many left now.'

He seemed a friendly, approachable man, formally dressed in a dark suit with a white shirt and a tie. Sam guessed that he might be the owner.

'I hope you won't mind me asking,' Sam went on, 'but I was wondering . . . are you by any chance selling the business or just the stock? I'm not just being nosey. A friend and I are looking for a business such as this, and it seems too good an opportunity to miss, that is . . . if you're thinking of selling?'

'We are but it's not yet with an estate agent,' the man replied. 'It was my father's idea to sell the stock. He thought it might be better to sell an empty shop, then it could be used however the buyer wanted. I'm Thomas Bateson, by the way.' He shook hands with Sam, then with Val.

'How do you do?' replied Sam. 'I'm Sam Walker and this is my wife, Valerie. We're from Halifax. My father owns Walker's mill.' He decided it would do no harm to reveal his credentials. 'We're here for the weekend, visiting friends.'

'Well, I'm certainly very pleased to meet you, Mr Walker . . . Do sit down, Mrs Walker.' There was a chair next to the counter. 'It seems to me that we might be able to do a business deal. This is a family business, run jointly by my father and myself.'

He went on to explain that his father, William, was now

nearly eighty and thought it was time he retired. He had been coming into the shop most days until recently, but had finally decided that enough was enough. He and his wife were still active and wanted to spend their remaining years in a leisurely fashion. The business had been started by William's father and handed down from father to son.

'I'm fifty-five now,' said Thomas, 'and my wife and I have decided to go and live in Devon where our only daughter and family live. We've done well out of this place but family comes first. We might even persuade my parents to join us down there . . . But it seems to me that you and I, and Father, of course, might be able to do a deal.'

Sam shook his head, not in negation but rather in bewilderment. 'This is all happening so suddenly,' he said. 'I didn't think for one minute that it might be so simple. Of course, I would have to talk it over with my friend. We had only recently started to think about making a change of employment. Colin feels that he wants to do something more interesting than working for an insurance firm. And, as I said, I'm a manager at the mill along with my father and elder brother. I think we all realize that one of us is expendable in the present climate but Father would never want to suggest it. So I need to tell him what's in my mind, as well as seeing how Colin feels about it.'

'And my father needs to be put in the picture,' said Thomas Bateson. 'We would need a solicitor, of course, but we should be able to do a private deal, if we're all agreed, and manage without an agent.'

'We'll leave it at that then, shall we?' said Sam. He turned to Val. 'How do you feel about it, love?' he asked. 'Do you think we should go ahead if everyone is agreeable?'

'It's up to you, Sam,' she replied, 'but if it's what you want, then so do I. You go for it.'

The two men exchanged addresses and telephone numbers, shook hands and promised to be in touch as soon as the other people concerned had been contacted.

'My head's in a whirl,' said Sam as they walked back to their hotel. 'It seems too good to be true.'

'Let's not count our chickens,' said Val, 'but I have a feeling it might well work out right for us.'

'Not a word to anyone yet, though,' said Sam.

But, later that evening, he could not resist telling Janice and Phil. 'It's all very hush hush at the moment. I have to talk it over with Colin and my father. And then Thomas Bateson will set the wheels in motion, providing his father agrees.'

'So you'll be coming to live in Harrogate,' said Janice. 'How lovely! Is there living accommodation over the shop?'

'I don't think so,' said Sam. 'If there is, they don't live there and neither would we. Yes, we'll be looking for a house if all goes according to plan. But not a word to anyone; you understand, don't you? And we won't be telling Walter and Cissie – not just yet.'

'We understand,' said Phil. 'Our lips are sealed.'

Cissie and Walter moved across to join them at that moment. The conversation centred mainly around the children, about school and playgroup and how the younger girls, Lucy and Sarah, were progressing with their walking and talking. They agreed to meet the following morning so that the five children could play together before the Walker and Clarkson families drove back home.

Two by two, the guests drifted away, all of them saying what a lovely occasion it had been and wishing Janice and Phil every success in the coming months.

'And now it's up to us,' said Phil when the last guests had departed. 'I know it's going to be a great success. You and me, we're a great team, Mrs Grundy.'

SIXTEEN

'**A**re you absolutely sure that this is what you want to do?' said Joshua Walker.

Sam had told him as soon as they arrived at the mill on Monday morning about his decision to leave Walker's mill and go into partnership within Colin Wyatt.

'Very sure, Father,' said Sam. 'I went to see Colin yesterday and he is just as keen as I am. But it all depends on what Mr Bateson thinks about it; if he's willing to negotiate with us, and with a solicitor, of course.'

'But sports equipment,' said Joshua, looking bewildered, 'and the retail trade? You've no experience of anything like that.'

'I know about sales techniques; we do a lot of that here; and Colin is used to dealing with money matters. We're both keen sportsmen – golfing in particular – so it'll be good to be involved in something we both enjoy.'

'Aye, I know you're a keen golfer – summat I never fancied taking up myself. But this is work, lad, not play. And . . . there was no need for you to be so hasty, you know. I'd never even thought of you or Jonathan leaving. We're still ticking over quite nicely. I know the boom days are probably over; it's the same for all t'mill owners round here, but I reckon we'll be here for a good while yet. There's no substitute for proper wool, whatever they say about their fancy nylons and terylenes and all that stuff.'

'But it will help not to have to pay my salary, won't it? There's no need for three bosses. You and Jonathan can cope very well without me, and there's Walter Clarkson, of course. Walter's job is safe, isn't it, Father?'

'Oh aye, young Walter's shaping up very nicely. And when – if – you go we can give him more responsibility and put his wages up a bit. But we'll miss you, there's no doubt about that. You'll be going to live in Harrogate, I suppose?'

'Well, yes, of course. But it's not far, only thirty miles or so. It'll be nice for you and Mother to drive over on a Sunday. That's all in the future, but not too far ahead, I hope. Colin and I will be going to Harrogate later this week to discuss matters further. By the way, Father, not a word to anyone else yet, apart from Jonathan and Mother, of course. We want to be certain it's all going ahead before we spread the news around.'

It all went according to plan, so smoothly and easily that Sam and Colin were amazed to soon find themselves co-owners of a business that was far removed from anything they had done before. A price agreeable to both sides had been agreed upon. Joshua was generous to his son, giving him a lump sum, a goodly share of the profits that the mill had made, which amounted to what would have been his salary for the following year.

Colin also received a good handout from his firm. Both men had been thrifty over the years and were able to take on the business with not too much of an overdraft.

The Batesons agreed to close the store immediately, the remaining stock to be sold at the reduced price when the shop reopened. New stock would need to be ordered and Thomas introduced them to the wholesalers they had used. Sam and Colin, however, intended to make certain changes, concentrating, maybe, on fewer sports with a different range of goods.

A notice appeared in the window of the store. *Closed for business. Reopening shortly under new management.* They decided, tentatively, on early August, which would give them a couple of months to ensure that everything was ready.

And, of course, time to find new homes in Harrogate. Val and Sam tried, whenever possible, to leave the children behind, usually with Val's parents, to give them a chance to concentrate more fully on the task in hand.

The news gradually became known, via the grapevine, that Sam and Val were leaving for pastures new and that Sam would no longer be working for the family firm. Val had made a point of telling Cissie before she heard from someone else. As Val had expected, her friend was sorry and rather disgruntled at the news. They had been friends for such a long time and, although they didn't see one another quite as often now, Val's departure would leave a big gap in her life.

'I won't half miss you,' she moaned. 'Who will I be able to tell my troubles to? You've always been there to listen to me.'

'Well, we'll be able to phone one another,' said Val, 'but I'm hoping you won't have any troubles. You're not in trouble now, are you?'

'No, of course not, but you never know. And you'll be near to Janice, won't you, not to me? Do you want to get a house round there, near to the Stray? I wish Walter and me could move somewhere a bit posher. I'd like a bigger garden and more room for the kids to play in.'

Cissie was somewhat mollified, however, when Joshua Walker spoke to Walter, telling him that when Sam had gone he intended to give him more responsibility. Sam had been in charge of personnel, dealing with any complaints that might arise with the workforce. These, fortunately, were very few. Joshua felt that Walter could be relied on to be as diplomatic as Sam had been. The young man had changed since his marriage to Cissie, becoming more likable and less aloof in his manner.

After a couple of weekends of house hunting, Val and Sam found one that they both thought would be ideal. The house was in an avenue close to the Stray and, therefore, quite close to Janice and Phil. In many respects, it was similar to the three-bedroomed semi they were leaving. They needed to sell their own house, however, before anything could be settled with the new property. They had had a few enquiries and a few couples had viewed the house, but there was no deal so far.

On the following Monday morning, Walter approached Sam while they were at work. 'Is your house still for sale,' he asked, 'or have you found a buyer?'

'No, I'm afraid we haven't,' Sam replied. 'There's been a few enquiries but no takers. We can't understand it; it's what the estate agents call a "desirable residence". Why? Do you know someone who might be interested?'

'Yes, I do. It's me. That is to say, it's Cissie and me.'

Sam was surprised but tried not to show his feelings. After all, why shouldn't Walter be interested? He suspected, though, that Cissie might have had a lot to do with it.

'We'd like more room,' Walter went on. 'We're rather cramped now the kids are getting older and I've decided we're in a position to make you an offer. Thanks to your father, of course. The extra pay will make all the difference, and I've been careful with my brass over the years. So . . . what do you think?'

'I think that's great,' said Sam. He didn't want to embarrass or patronize Walter by asking if he was sure he could afford it. He knew that Walter was astute and would have done his sums. 'You'll need to see our estate agent, and I'm sure that, together, we'll be able to come to an agreement. Good for you, Walter! Val will be pleased when I tell her.'

Walter did not say that Cissie had been pestering him and trying to persuade him that they could afford it. Cissie had tried not to be envious of her friend, who lived in the more salubrious suburb of Queensbury, but she could not help feeling, deep down, somewhat peeved that Val had always been a step or two higher on the social ladder.

They had little difficulty in finding a buyer for their rather more modest house. Very soon plans were being made for their move to the Walkers' residence, which was to coincide with Val and Sam's move to Harrogate.

Cissie felt pleased with herself and a trifle smug. She had started off as a mill girl and had then been promoted to the burling and mending room, but had still been regarded as a mill girl. Now, her husband was shortly to become one of the bosses at Walker's mill – or so she saw it – and they would live in the affluent district of Queensbury.

SEVENTEEN

'Ian says he'd like to come and work for us again this summer,' said Janice to her husband. It was an evening in July and she had phoned her brother, quite expecting him to say that he would be staying in Blackpool and working at one of the promenade hotels in what would be their busiest time of the year.

'I'm pleased to hear that, but rather surprised,' said Phil. 'I thought he had other interests in Blackpool as well as work. He seemed to be getting rather keen on that girl, Alison. Did he say anything about her?'

'I didn't ask; I didn't mention her name at all. I just said we would be pleased to have him here if he hadn't made other plans. I sort of hinted that there might be other attractions for him in Blackpool but he was very cagey about it. 'Not any more,' he said, so I didn't enquire further. I said we'd look forward to seeing him again.'

'And when will that be?'

'The end of July, soon after he finishes at college. Just in time for the August bank holiday weekend. Not that that will make much difference to our business here; in fact, a lot of the local people may be away on holiday.'

The clientele consisted mainly of local people, many of whom had come out of curiosity to see how Grundy's was faring with its new names. And, having come once, they came again and told their friends how much they liked the changes that had been made. The menu at the present time consisted of a good selection of light, summery meals that no longer needed to be ordered in advance. The service was prompt and friendly, as it had always been, and there was a happy ambience to the place.

Although some local people would be away on holiday, there were others from different parts of the country who visited Harrogate as a holiday resort. It had once been a famous spa town but was still popular for its pleasant surroundings, its nearness to the Yorkshire Dales, the moors and the ancient city of York. Changing Seasons was well advertised and visitors to the town, especially those staying at guest houses that provided only bed and breakfast, found it an ideal place for an evening meal. The food was appetizing and, most importantly, not too expensive. Phil had decided at the outset to charge prices that were within the budget of most people and would encourage them to come again.

The morning following Ian's phone call, Sophie called at Grundy's just before the Coffee Pot was due to open for its early customers. Janice was pleased to see her and rather hoped that she might be offering her services for the month of August. She was not disappointed.

'I was wondering if I could come and help out here again?' she asked. 'I shall understand if you're fully staffed, but I enjoy working here. That's not the only reason I've come, though. I wanted to see you and to wish you well with your new venture. Mum told me you're doing splendidly. She and Graham have had an evening meal here and she sometimes pops in for coffee.'

'Yes, so she does,' said Janice, 'and of course, we'd be delighted if you can come and work for us again. We have a few part-time students from the school, like you used to be, but there's certainly room for one more, especially somebody who knows the ropes like you do.'

Janice hesitated before she went on to say, 'Ian will be working here as well. I phoned him last night and he said he'd be pleased to come again. Does that make any difference to your plans?'

'No, why should it?' said Sophie. 'Ian and I parted on friendly terms and I'll be pleased to see him again. Actually . . . I'm no longer seeing the young man I was friendly with at college, but that doesn't really matter. I know Ian has a girlfriend in Blackpool but there's no reason why we can't work together amicably. He'll be in the kitchen most of the time, won't he, and working mainly in the evenings?'

'Phil hasn't decided yet exactly what he wants Ian to do.' Janice didn't say that there was no longer a girlfriend. Ian hadn't said that in so many words, but that was what she had surmised from his caginess. Janice thought it best to keep out if it and let Ian and Sophie sort it out for themselves.

'So, when would you like to start, Sophie?' she asked. 'You can come as soon as you like but I expect you'll want some time at home first?'

'Yes, that's right. I need a little time to recuperate after my teaching practice and exams. And I want to spend some time with Mum; we like to go shopping together. We thought we'd go to York for a day, as though we're tourists.' She laughed. 'It's been ages since either of us was there and there's so much to see. You don't really appreciate places as you should, do you, when they're almost on your doorstep?'

'That's true,' agreed Janice. 'Of course, Yorkshire was all new to me till I married Phil, and I was surprised at the variety of the scenery: the dales and the moors, and the quaint villages and seaside towns. We don't have much time now, though, to go touring around.'

'And I've some school friends I want to catch up with,' Sophie went on. 'Gail and Dawn are at different colleges and Jean's doing a nursing course. We'll all get together and have a natter. So . . . what about a fortnight from now? Would that be OK?'

'That's fine, Sophie. And would it be for about six weeks or so?'

'Yes, thereabouts; maybe a little longer if you still need me. We don't go back until nearly the end of September.'

'And that will be your last year, will it?'

'Oh, no, it's a three-year course now. It used to be two but they changed it in nineteen-sixty, so I just missed out on that. It seems a long time but no doubt it will pass quickly – we're kept very busy. Ian's course is two years, isn't it?'

'Yes; he has one more year to do but Phil thinks he's pretty competent already.'

'Well, he learnt a lot from you and Phil, didn't he?'

'I suppose he did; particularly from Phil, of course. That was what made him decide he would like to be a chef. He had never considered it until he started seeing Phil at work.'

'I'd better leave you to get on now,' said Sophie, glancing at her watch. 'It's getting on for opening time.'

'Yes, so it is, but I doubt there'll be a rush just yet, especially on a Monday morning. So shall we say a fortnight today? We'll sort out your hours together, you and me. I know you won't want to work full time.'

'Great,' said Sophie. 'Thanks ever so much, Janice. I'll look forward to it. Bye for now . . .'

Sophie was settled into her routine at Grundy's by the time Ian arrived. He would be employed mainly in the Changing Seasons restaurant, assisting with the preparation of the meals and then waiting at the tables.

Sophie was simply a waitress, helping in the Coffee Pot, which was open for morning coffee, snack lunches and afternoon tea. All in all, it was a busy establishment, but with ample staff so that no one was overworked.

Ian and Sophie met again when he arrived on a Friday afternoon near the end of July. Phil had met him at the station following his rail journey from Blackpool. The cafe was closing following the afternoon tea session, and Sophie was just removing her apron before walking back home.

'Hello, Sophie.'

'Hello, Ian . . .' Their greeting was a little restrained, neither of them making a move towards the other.

'Good journey?' she asked.

'Yes, not bad. Changed at Leeds and the station there was crowded. Holiday time, of course. I had to stand part of the way on the first train. Anyway . . . how are you?'

'Very well, thanks. Just recovering after a busy term, as no doubt you are.'

They looked at one another uncertainly; it was Sophie who broke the ice. Janice had tactfully left the room, leaving them on their own.

'Look, Ian . . . We'll be seeing one another here from time to time. It's unavoidable and, anyway, I don't want to avoid you. I know you've got a girlfriend in Blackpool but we decided, didn't we, that we could still be friends?'

'I haven't, not now,' said Ian briefly.

'Oh . . . oh, I see. I'm sorry to hear that.' Although Sophie was not sorry at all.

'Don't be. I'm not! What about you? Are you still friendly with the fellow you met at college?'

She shook her head. 'No, we called it a day. At least . . . I did.'

'Oh, I see . . .' They were still regarding one another intently, then Sophie laughed and so did Ian.

'This is daft, isn't it?' she said. 'Shall we get together and have a chat? That is, if you'd like to. Just as friends, I mean?'

'Yes, of course. I'd like that. I'll walk back home with you now, shall I?'

'No, you've only just arrived. You must be weary after your journey, and you'll want to unpack and have a chat with Janice and Phil. I'll be busy tomorrow; Saturdays are always busy here.'

'What about Sunday then?' suggested Ian. 'We could go for a stroll on Sunday afternoon, perhaps?'

Grundy's were still keeping to their policy of closing on a Sunday. Gradually, more and more places were opening on what used to be called the Sabbath Day. Times were changing, and so was the outlook of many people regarding Sundays. Some still adhered to the religious principle of not working on a Sunday. Janice and Phil had decided to close because Sunday was their only free day; a day in which they could spend precious time with their little daughter, or visit Phil's parents, or just enjoy one another's company.

Phil and Ian discussed Ian's timetable for the coming weeks over the next two days, a flexible one according to whether the restaurant was busy or not.

'And you will want some evenings off,' said Phil, 'if you want to go out, to the cinema or . . . wherever.'

Phil did not mention Sophie, although he had heard from Janice that both the teenagers appeared to be 'fancy free' again.

Ian didn't mention her either. He nodded and gave a wry grin. 'We'll have to see how it goes . . . How is Changing Seasons going on? You've been open for about seven or eight weeks now, haven't you?'

'Yes, that's right,' replied Phil. 'It's early days and we can't grumble. As a matter of fact, we're quite pleased, but we can't afford to be complacent. Some folk will have come to give us a try because it's somewhere new, but it's encouraging when we see familiar faces appearing again. Our regulars have been faithful to us and they like being able to choose from the menu when they arrive and not have to book the meal in advance.'

'Do you find there's a lot of wastage with the new system?'

'No, it's working out quite well. We don't keep a huge amount in stock, especially the perishable items like fruit and veg. We have a good supplier who comes regularly. We still take bookings in advance, as we did before, if it's for a special occasion, say a birthday or anniversary, and then we do like them to choose the menu. There hasn't been an evening so far when we haven't had any customers. Sometimes there may be only six or eight; other times, especially Fridays and Saturdays, we might be almost full. They don't all come at once, of course. We're open from seven o'clock and we take the last orders at eight thirty. We're usually finished by half past ten.'

'And are there just you and Toby doing the cooking and preparation? You must be working flat out.'

'We have an assistant now, Jason. He's sixteen and just left school. He's not had any experience or training but he's keen to learn, so I suggested he might go to college a couple of days a week. At the moment he's preparing the veg and clearing up; doing the donkey work, I suppose, but he seems to like the environment. And we'll have you starting on Monday; that will make things easier.'

'I hope so,' said Ian. 'I want to earn my keep.'

'Don't worry; I shall make sure you do that!' said Phil, grinning at him. 'And then there's the lunchtime snacks. You could help out there if needed, but we're never too busy midday. We have a couple of part-time women who help out there. So, all in all, I believe we're coping pretty well.'

Ian phoned Sophie and they agreed to meet and go for a walk on Sunday afternoon.

'I'll meet you outside Grundy's at two o'clock,' she said. 'There's no need for you to come out of your way to meet me; it's only a few minutes' walk.'

She arrived almost on the dot as Ian was coming out of the door. They both smiled as though they were very pleased to see one another again. Ian felt happiness bubbling up inside him and realized how much he had missed her. For a while, he had been contented with Alison; at least, he had convinced himself that he was growing fond of her and that they were good together, until things started to go wrong.

He stole a sideways glance at Sophie as they strolled along the pathway through the Stray, thinking what an attractive girl she was – not only pretty but with a lovely personality as well. She had a freshness and an honesty about her which was very appealing, and he had always known that he could trust her. She was not what you would call worldly-wise but neither was she naive.

She and Alison were very different, both in looks and in personality. Ian had felt from the start, deep down, that he could not entirely trust Alison, and this had proved to be so. She had appeared mature and sophisticated but that was largely a veneer. Underneath, she was, in fact, insecure and hid behind the facade of a devil-may-care attitude.

Sophie looked most attractive today in a bright pink dress with polka dot spots which Ian thought was now called a shift dress. Her dark hair curled gently around her face. She wore very little make-up apart from a touch of coral lipstick, and she sported a healthy tan.

She glanced back at Ian and smiled. 'Penny for them,' she said, 'or have I got a smut on my nose?'

'No . . . sorry,' he said. 'I was just thinking that you've caught the sun. You're very brown, but nicely so. You look . . . very nice.'

'We made the most of the sun the last week of term when exams had finished. We played quite a lot of tennis and I've been playing with my old school friends since I came home. I've not been sitting out in it; I was never one for lounging in the sun.'

'Yes, I remember that you played tennis. You told me that you were in the school team.'

'The second team; I was only a reserve for the first team.'

'Very good, though. Tennis is a sport I never learnt. We played cricket at school, which was OK, but I had no experience of tennis. It was football, of course, that was my passion, although we had to play rugby at school.'

'Yes, I know you were a football fanatic. You still are, I suppose?'

'Yes, I have a kick around with the mates I had at school, when we can get together. There's no time for sports, though, at the catering college. They don't go in for that sort of thing.'

'I should imagine it's jolly hard work in this weather, working in a red-hot kitchen?'

'You get used to it; you have to if you intend to be a chef. But it's good to feel the warmth of the sun for a change after working at a boiling hot range.'

They were quiet for a few moments, then Ian plucked up courage to ask what he wanted to know.

'So . . . it's all over, is it, with you and . . . whoever he was, at college?'

'He was called Patrick . . . Yes, it's all over. He's left now anyway, because he was a year above me, but I doubt that it would have continued after he left. I decided that he was too much for me, if you know what I mean?' She looked at him keenly, raising her eyebrows.

He nodded. 'Yes, I think I do,' he replied.

'I've another two years to do at college,' said Sophie, 'and I want to get to the end of my course without having to leave under a cloud. Actually, that was what happened to a girl who was in the same hall as me, and on the same course as well, so we'd become quite friendly. We knew she had a boyfriend – not one of the college chaps; he was in the RAF, stationed quite nearby, and she went off at the weekends to meet him. Anyway Pamela – that was her name – didn't come back at the end of the second term, after the Easter break. Her mother wrote a letter to the college principle saying that Pamela was getting married and she wouldn't be returning to college. The news trickled round on the grapevine, of course, and we all guessed the reason. Then Pamela wrote to me and said that she was three months' pregnant and they were getting married. She said her parents were quite complacent about it because they knew it was serious between her and Victor. I can't understand why she started the course at all. And I knew that if it happened to me my mother would certainly not be complacent about it! Anyway, I shall make sure that it doesn't.'

'So I take it that this . . . Patrick wanted rather more than you were prepared for?'

'A lot more! The girls and the men do get friendly; it's inevitable at a co-ed college. We have separate halls of residence, at either side of the campus, as far away as possible, and it's a strict rule that never the twain shall meet, except for dances and social occasions. But there are ways of getting round this, as you can imagine. I've heard of girls who've been smuggled into the men's hostels and vice versa. Goodness knows why none of them have been caught, at least not so far.'

'And I suppose this Patrick wanted you to . . .?'

'You've got it. He wanted me to stay the night, or part of it. I refused, of course. Rules are there for a very good reason and it's a most foolhardy thing to do. Besides, I didn't feel that way about him and I don't think I ever would have done. He was just a chap I got friendly with; good fun at first but not somebody I could feel really close to. So that was that.'

'Yes . . . I see. I'm glad you didn't get too involved. He sounds a bit of a bounder, as they used to say in the olden days!'

Ian remembered very well a conversation that he and Sophie had had when they were going out together. They knew they were getting closer to each other; their kisses and embraces were becoming more ardent. Ian was quite an innocent lad but he knew very well where it could have led and he knew that he was not ready for that. And neither was Sophie. They had agreed that they were young, with all their lives ahead of them, and it was not time for their tentative lovemaking to go any further. There was far too much to lose.

Sophie had told him how some of the girls at school boasted about what they got up to with their boyfriends. She wasn't sure that she believed them, but, even if she did, she thought it was foolish. She knew she had to wait until the time was right, and she felt that she would know when that time came.

Ian told her now that the same sort of thing had happened between him and Alison – that she had wanted more than he was prepared to give. He did not want, however, to tell Sophie the full story. He often thought about it, though, and he realized that it had not been a good idea to get involved with Alison in the first place. But he had lost Sophie and thought that Alison was a very attractive girl.

He had soon realized that she was given quite a lot of freedom at home. Her parents' guest house was small and they did not take many visitors, just couples for bed and breakfast. Ian's student friend, Darren, had a room there, which was a sort of study-cum-bedroom, and Alison's room was similar. She entertained her friends up there, where they chatted and played records. She even had her own small television set. As the only daughter she was inclined to be indulged, if not spoiled. Ian was surprised that she was allowed to invite him up to her room as well.

They had indulged in kisses and embraces, but Ian was always aware that Alison's parents were not far away. Later in the evening, her mother would knock on the door, bringing them tea and biscuits on a tray. It was all very cosy and Ian was content to go along with it.

Then, one night in mid-June, Alison had told him that her parents had gone out for the evening to a dinner and dance at her father's Masonic lodge and would not be back until about one o'clock in the morning.

'She won't be disturbing us at ten o'clock,' Alison had said with a knowing grin. 'So you can stay longer; not all night, of course, but . . . well . . . we can make the most of it, can't we?'

She'd sat on the bed and patted the candlewick cover next to her. 'Come on, Ian. What are we waiting for?' She'd begun to unbutton her blouse. 'I know you want to, just as much as I do.'

Ian had felt himself going red and was completely at a loss as to what to say. He'd blurted out the first thing that came into his head.

'No, Alison, we can't. That's not what I want at all. You've got it all wrong. We can't do . . . that. It's not right, not for us.'

'But why not?' She'd pouted, then looked at him provocatively. 'I thought you liked me . . . a lot.'

'I do like you, Alison,' he'd replied, 'but not like that. I'm not ready for all that and neither are you. I'm sorry, I don't want to upset you, but I can't . . . do what you want. And I can't stay any longer now.'

He'd grabbed his jacket from the back of a chair, bolted out of the door and down the stairs.

She'd jumped off the bed and ran after him. 'Ian . . . don't go. I'm sorry. I really thought you . . .'

But he'd already been out of the front door and dashing along the street. Fortunately, she hadn't followed him. He'd leaned against a wall to get his breath back, then walked slowly home. If his dad or Norma asked why he was home early he'd say that Alison was not feeling very well. As it happened, they had not enquired. And neither had they asked the why and wherefore when he told them, a few days later, that he would not be seeing Alison again.

She'd phoned him, though, at home, a couple of days after the incident.

'I'm sorry Ian. I know now that I shouldn't have suggested . . . what I did, and I understand that you didn't want to.' She hadn't sounded as though she was laughing at him or thinking he was prudish. 'And . . . please, can I see you again? I don't want it to end like this.'

But Ian knew that he didn't want to see her again. 'I'm sorry, Alison,' he'd said. 'I don't think it's right with you and me. It just wouldn't work.'

'I'm sorry,' she'd said again. 'It was the girls at school, you see. They're always on about . . . what they do, and they keep asking if I've done it yet. And so I thought . . .'

'I don't care what you thought, Alison,' he'd replied, trying not to shout, because he was really angry. The fact that she had been talking about him to the girls at school, comparing notes, made it worse. 'You'd better find someone else to . . . do what you want, not me. And I don't think the girls sound like very good friends.' He'd been aware he sounded a bit stuffy and pompous but he hadn't cared. 'Goodbye, Alison. It's best if we call it a day. I'm sure you know that.' He'd put the phone down.

He had not seen her since then, nor had he heard much about her. He had not told Darren what had happened, only that he was not seeing Alison any more. Darren had not asked for any details. He'd told Ian that she seemed cheerful enough and had not said anything to him about their separation.

'She doesn't seem to be eating her heart out,' he'd said. 'Maybe she wasn't right for you. I never really thought she was, you know. Is there anyone else in the picture?'

Ian and Darren were good mates, and the mistake that Darren
had made regarding Ian's sexual preferences was never referred
to. Darren was inquisitive, though, and liked to know what was
going on in the love lives of his friends, even though they were
not of his persuasion.

'No . . .' Ian had replied, '. . . although I still keep thinking
about Sophie. I've never really forgotten her but I know I should
try to put her out of my mind. She had a fellow at college and
still has, as far as I know. I shall no doubt see her when I go
to Harrogate . . . unless she's doing something else, of course.'

'Well, there are other fish in the sea for a good-looking lad
like you.'

'Maybe so . . . What about you? You've not . . . met anyone?'

'No, not yet, but I'm OK. I've enjoyed my first year here
and I've got some good mates, like you. Maybe next year;
there'll be a new bunch of students in September. I'm still
waiting for someone to share my digs, but I don't want to make
a mistake.'

'No, of course not,' Ian had replied. He'd reflected that some
lads might not be as understanding as he had been about Darren's
faux pas. Darren might well have ended up with a bloody nose.

Ian and Sophie's stroll had taken them along the Strand down
the hill leading to the Valley Gardens. As they walked, he told her
he had realized that he and Alison were not right together. He
did not want to tell her the full story. Sometimes he felt hat he
had behaved like an idiot, running off as he had done as though
he was scared out of his wits. He had acted on the spur of the
moment, surprised – shocked, even – at what she was suggesting
so early in their friendship. The possible outcome of such an
encounter was too awful to even think about.

'Alison was too hot to handle,' he said now with a laugh. 'I
didn't think it was right to . . . you know what I mean, and
I told her so. I think she had been egged on, though. I remember
you telling me about the girls at your school and I rather think
it was the same with her. She didn't want to be the only one
who hadn't . . . but I had no intention of being used as a sort
of trophy.'

'She sounds quite immature,' said Sophie, 'and it's stupid to
take any notice of what the girls at school say. A lot of it is

only in their minds; wishful thinking, you might say. I'm glad
we've met up again, Ian . . . I've missed you, you know,' she
added, smiling at him warmly and not at all shyly.

He took hold of her hand, the first time he had done so
that evening. 'And I've missed you as well,' he told her. 'Would
you like to come out again, perhaps to the cinema, or a coffee
bar, or . . . somewhere? I won't be working every evening and
I'm here for a few weeks.'

'Yes, I would love to,' Sophie replied. She looked at him
squarely. 'I know where I am with you, Ian. We think the same
way, don't we?'

'Yes, I think we do,' he agreed.

They stopped for a moment on their walk through the colonnades, below a canopy of wisteria and trailing vine leaves. There
was no one else in sight as Ian kissed her gently on the lips.

'It's good to be together again, Sophie,' he whispered as she
responded to his kiss.

EIGHTEEN

It was a hectic time for the Walkers and the Clarksons during the last two weeks in August as they prepared to move to their new homes.

Sam Walker was the busiest of all as he, together with his friend and partner, Colin Wyatt, dealt with the organization of the business they were taking over from the Bateson family.

There was a notice in the shop window. *Opening soon under new management: Walker and Wyatt's Sports Gear. We promise you the same excellent service as before and look forward to your custom.*

The windows were now empty, but there was the remainder of the old stock, to be sold at reduced prices, in the stockroom, and new stock was already arriving daily. Thomas Bateson was proving to be a great help in every way he could to make the changeover as trouble free as possible. His assistant, Desmond, a young man about the same age as Sam, was staying on as chief sales assistant with Thomas's firm recommendation. They were also advertising for a junior sales assistant, either male or female, not necessarily with experience, as Thomas assured them that Desmond would be a very good tutor, with all the patience and diplomacy needed in a salesperson.

As both Sam and Colin were keen golfers, they had decided to concentrate largely on what they knew and stock a wider range of golfing equipment than the shop had held in the past. The other sports were not neglected. There would be equipment for hikers and climbers, as the Yorkshire Dales were not far distant, as well as gear for tennis and cricket enthusiasts. Neither would indoor sports be overlooked: badminton, squash and table tennis, even darts and chess.

Val was very busy with all the household side of the removal. With the help of her mother and her sister-in-law, Thelma, taking down curtains, emptying cupboards and bookshelves, then packing everything carefully in tea chests – provided by the removal firm – and labelling each box accordingly: kitchen utensils, crockery and china, books, ornaments, household linen, etc.

Some of the curtains could be used again in their new home, while others would not fit the windows. After taking the measurements at the new house, Val had ordered fresh curtains to be made by a firm in Halifax market that she knew to be reliable and not too pricey.

Cissie was equally busy preparing for the move. Her mother had agreed to help but Hannah Foster did not do so with the same grace and willingness that Val's mother had shown.

'I hope you're not getting ideas above your station, you and Walter,' she told her daughter, not just once but repeatedly. 'Going to live up there among the posh folk.'

Cissie knew that her mother was probably a little envious. ''Course we're not, Mam,' she replied. 'Walter's earning good money now, you know. He's almost one of the bosses at Walker's.'

Hannah sniffed. 'Aye, he is. I know Walter's a good lad.' She had always had a soft spot for her son-in-law, and if anything went wrong between them she would always say that Cissie must be the one to blame.

'I suppose you'll be giving up your job at the market now,' she went on, 'seeing you'll be living among the toffs.'

But Cissie had no intention of giving up her job. She loved working at the market, meeting different people each day, and it was pocket money for her, without having to rely on Walter to give her an allowance. She knew, though, that the move to Queensbury would involve some changes. A change of school for Paul, for instance, although she was sure that he would soon settle down in a new environment. He was a bright lad and seemed to be learning things very quickly. He was five years old and could already read the books about Janet and John that he brought home from school. A change of playgroup, too, for Holly – probably the one from where Russell had been banned, Cissie reflected – although she would be starting proper school before very long.

Cissie would also have further to travel to the market in the centre of Halifax, but she would deal with that problem in due course.

Before the move was due to take place, however, Val had a phone call from Hazel, the policewoman who had been involved when Lucy was missing. It was one evening during the second week in August.

'Hello there, Val,' she began. 'It's Hazel, your friendly police-woman. Do you remember me?'

'Yes, of course I do,' replied Val. 'There's nothing wrong, is there?'

She knew, though, that there couldn't be. Sam was at home, both children were tucked up in bed and Hazel sounded cheerful enough.

'No, nothing wrong,' said Hazel. She laughed. 'Why does everyone assume it's bad news when they get a call from the police? No, far from it. Do you remember Claire Dawson?' she asked. Then went on to say, 'Silly question! Of course you remember her. How could you forget her?'

'Yes, I remember . . .' said Val thoughtfully. 'As you say, I could hardly forget her.' Claire Dawson was the woman who had absconded with baby Lucy in her pram, causing a lot of worry and heartache but, fortunately, the problem had been resolved quite quickly.

'How is Claire?' Val asked. 'Much more contented now, I hope?'

'Yes, she was thrilled to bits when she rang me to say she had some good news. You can probably guess what it is. She's expecting a baby – not till early next year, but she's very excited and I thought you would like to know. I remember you were so kind and understanding with her, Val, and you did such a lot to help her get things into perspective.'

'Well, I hope so, and it's certainly good news.'

'I think she would like to see you and tell you about it herself, but she feels rather hesitant about asking you to go round again. Do you think you might . . .?'

'Yes, of course I'll go and see her and tell her how pleased I am. Actually, I'm very busy at the moment but I'll try and make time. We're moving, you see, to Harrogate. My husband is going into business with a friend; they're taking over a sports shop.'

'You mean . . . he's leaving the mill?'

Val explained that the time seemed to be right for a change of career because of the way things were going in the woollen industry. 'So it will be a big change for all of us. We're moving at the end of August and the shop will be reopening soon afterwards.'

'Well, I wish you all the very best,' said Hazel. 'I'm sure your husband will make a success of it. He's a very go-ahead sort of fellow, isn't he? Now, shall I give you Claire's phone number? You don't want to call and find that she's not at home, especially when you're so busy. I know she'll be delighted to see you.'

Val wrote down the number and said she would see Claire later in the week.

'Who was that?' asked Sam when she returned to the living room.

'It was Hazel, the policewoman . . .'

'What did she want?' he asked, looking concerned. 'There's nothing wrong, is there?'

'No, not at all. She rang to tell me some news about Claire . . . Claire Dawson. You know who I mean?'

'Yes, indeed I do – the woman who ran off with our Lucy. So . . . what about her?'

Val knew that Sam had not been so magnanimous in his attitude towards Claire as she had been. And who could blame him?

'She's expecting a baby now,' said Val, 'and she's thrilled to bits, of course . . . I said that I'd go round and see her,' she added tentatively, guessing what Sam's reaction might be.

'Why?' he asked. 'So she's having a baby, and I hope it goes well for her, but I don't see what it has to do with us.'

'Claire was pleased when I went to see her before,' Val explained patiently. 'She'd had a miscarriage and that was what led her to . . . do what she did. I told her that I'd had a miscarriage – more than one – and that it all worked out OK in the end. She's rather an insecure sort of person, Sam. I just want to go and tell her how pleased I am.'

Sam smiled at her lovingly. 'Yes, I see. You go ahead, darling. I don't mean to be as heartless as I might sound but I can't be as forgiving and understanding as you are. You're such a kind and thoughtful person, Val. That's one of the reasons I married you; that and the fact that I fancied you like mad! Don't ever change, will you?'

'Oh, come off it, Sam! I'm not all that wonderful. Come to think of it, you're not so bad yourself . . . You don't mind me going, then?'

'No, I don't mind. But you won't take Lucy, will you?'

'Of course not – don't be silly! It would be embarrassing all round. And Lucy might possibly remember her. Who knows what children retain in their memories? I won't take Russell either. He behaves a lot better now but he won't sit quietly while ladies are talking.'

'I don't blame him!'

'I'll leave them with my mum. She always enjoys having them. She'll miss them, Sam, when we move, and so will my dad.'

'I know that,' said Sam, 'and that's another thing, Val, that I love about you. You've agreed to this move and everything it involves with scarcely a murmur of complaint, although I know it will be a wrench for you, leaving your home town.'

'It's not as though we're emigrating to Australia!' said Val. 'It's the same county, not far away at all and Mum and Dad will be able to come and visit us, possibly stay for a few days. It will be a nice change for them. Anyway, you're my husband, aren't you? And where you go, I go!'

Val phoned Claire, and it was agreed that she should visit her on the following Friday afternoon. She was welcomed as though she were royalty and shown into the living room. It was very clean and tidy, as though Claire had made a special effort for her guest. Val mused that it would not be so tidy when the baby arrived.

Claire seemed a little ill at ease at first; no doubt the memory of her misdemeanour still lingered at the back of her mind. Val soon put her at her ease.

'I'm so pleased to hear your good news,' she told her. 'You are looking very well; positively radiant. When is the baby due?'

'The end of January,' said Claire. 'I'm only about three and a half months but I knew straight away that I was pregnant. I was usually so regular, you see,' she said in a confidential tone. 'Anyway, we went to see the doctor and he confirmed that it was so. I'm crossing my fingers and praying that all will go well this time.'

'There's no reason why not if you take care, especially for the first few months, and I know you will.'

'Yes, I felt ill right from the start the last time but this time I feel fine.' She smiled a little coyly. 'Do you remember I told you that Greg was taking me with him on the trip to Austria? That's when it must have happened. It was a wonderful holiday; well, a holiday for me, although Greg was working. I felt so relaxed and carefree and . . . here we are!' She smiled happily.

'I'm sure Greg must be pleased,' said Val. 'Is he away at the moment?'

'Yes, he's on a week's tour to the Cotswolds. He'll be back on Sunday. It's all coming and going with that job, but he's asked if he can do just the British tours from now on instead of the Continental ones.'

There was a pause in the conversation. 'How is Lucy?' Claire asked, a little diffidently, as though she had been plucking up courage to mention the little girl. 'I expect she's growing quickly, isn't she?'

'Yes, they don't stay tiny babies for long. She was one in June; she's walking now and trying to talk.'

Claire looked pensive but Val had no intention of bringing the little girl to see her. Enough was enough. She guessed that Claire was a shy young woman who probably did not find it easy to make friends and, having found a sympathetic person, she might be inclined to cling and become dependent. She was obviously pleased at Val's visit but that must be as far as it could go. Besides, they were moving away so there was no possibility of an ongoing friendship. She knew she must tell Claire what was in store for them.

'Actually, there are big changes ahead for us,' she began. 'We're moving soon, to Harrogate. Sam and I, and the children.'

Claire looked bewildered. 'But your husband is a manager at the mill, isn't he?'

'Yes, so he is, but it's time for a change of direction.'

'Oh, I'm sorry you're leaving . . . I'll just go and make a pot of tea, then you can tell me all about it.'

She arrived back in a little while with a tray laden with china cups and saucers in a design of pink roses, no doubt her best tea set, and a matching teapot, milk jug and sugar basin. She placed the tray on an occasional table.

'Just a mo . . .' she said excitedly. 'I'll get the cakes.'

She returned with two plates, one holding almond tarts, which Val's mother always called maids of honour, and another with a large cake decorated with frosted icing and cherries. She placed them on the second of the nest of tables then placed the smallest table in front of Val. She poured the tea like a perfect hostess and invited Val to help herself to cake. Neither had she forgotten the napkins – freshly laundered damask ones rather than paper serviettes.

'My goodness!' said Val. 'You've been busy. 'Homemade, aren't they?'

'Yes, I make all my own cakes,' said Claire with a hint of pride. 'I know I won't have as much time to bake when the baby arrives . . . Now, tell me about your move. When are you going?'

Val explained again, as she had done several times to different people, that Sam had decided it was time to leave the mill because of a slight downturn in the woollen industry, and the opportunity to take over the sports shop had come at just the right moment.

'So you'll be leaving all your friends and your family,' said Claire. 'You must feel rather sad about that?'

'We're not going very far away and we have some friends in Harrogate already. They have a restaurant there and we'll be living quite near to them. Plus there are always new friends to be made wherever you go.'

'Yes . . . and I'm sure you make friends easily,' said Claire wistfully. 'I've never found it all that easy, and since I gave up my job – when I was pregnant before – I've felt very much on my own.'

'The last time I saw you, you were thinking of going back to work, weren't you?'

'Yes, but then this happened . . .' she patted her stomach, '. . . so there would be no point, would there?'

'No, none at all,' agreed Val, 'but you don't need to feel that you're on your own when the baby arrives. You'll be able to meet other young mothers at the clinic. And before the baby arrives you'll be going to the clinic quite regularly for check-ups, won't you? I know they try to make it a sort of social occasion at some places.'

'Yes, I shall be going there,' said Claire. 'They want to keep an eye on me because of what happened last time. Yes, I've a lot to look forward to, and a lot to be thankful for . . . I suppose.'

'Indeed you have,' said Val. It passed through her mind that Claire was the sort of person to whom the glass was always half empty rather than half full, a tendency towards pessimism rather than looking on the bright side. She had seemed on top of the world when Val arrived, but now, on hearing of her departure, she was becoming a little introspective again, even though she and Val were not close friends.

'I really must congratulate you on your baking,' said Val, changing the subject. 'These almond tarts are delicious, as nice as any I've tasted, and may I try just a tiny piece of your iced cake? Never mind my waistline! I can't resist it.'

This was not idle flattery; Val meant every word. The cakes compared admirably with the ones that Janice Grundy made, and she was regarded as a professional.

'Thank you,' said Claire, looking pleased. 'I've always enjoyed baking and cooking.'

They chatted for a while about the move to Harrogate; Val told her about the house and Sam's plans for the shop. 'It will be a big change for us all but worthwhile in the end, I'm sure.'

Claire asked for her address, saying that she would send a card at Christmas and inform her when the baby arrived. It was a pleasant afternoon and they promised to keep in touch. But when all was said and done, Claire was only an acquaintance, not a close friend, and Val knew that she would never be able to regard her as one. The circumstances of their first meeting could never be entirely forgotten.

There was little time to think of anything over the next couple of weeks as they prepared for the removal. During her odd reflective moments, Val pondered that it would be a great upheaval for her, even though they were moving only a short distance away. She had never been away from her home town for more than a couple of weeks at a time, whereas Sam had done his two years of National Service. Val had always been close to her parents, especially since her twin brothers had moved away, and she had several good friends in the town.

There was Cissie, of course, and she knew that Cissie would miss her very much, although the separation would be somewhat mollified for her friend because they would be moving into the house that she and Sam were vacating. Val smiled to herself, knowing that her friend was looking on this as a step up the social ladder. And Cissie had other friends in the town as well as the job that she enjoyed so much.

Val would miss her, and the girls in the office with whom she still kept in touch, and her sister-in-law, Thelma, who had become a bosom friend. But there would be Janice and Phil not far away, and new friends to meet in a new neighbourhood.

She and Sam sat in the lounge on the evening before the removal day, surrounded by stacked-up furniture and packing cases.

'Well, we're almost there,' said Sam. 'Only one more night in our first home, and I know we're going to be just as happy in the next one.'

'Yes, fresh fields and pastures new,' said Val, musingly.

'It's woods, actually,' said Sam.

'What is?'

'It's fresh woods, not fields,' he replied, 'although it's often misquoted. I know because we studied Milton for our School Certificate. It's from a poem called "Lycidas". "Tomorrow to fresh woods and pastures new".'

'My goodness!' said Val with a laugh. 'How lucky I am to be married to a grammar school boy! I bow to your superior knowledge.'

'Well, whatever they are – fields or woods, mountains or valleys, we'll travel them together,' said Sam. 'Come along, Mrs Walker. It's time for bed. It's a big day tomorrow.'

NINETEEN

They moved on a Friday morning. After watching all their possessions loaded into the removal van and seeing it drive away, they locked the door and set off in their own car in the wake of the van.

'New house, new house,' chanted Russell excitedly. He had been with them to the house in Harrogate a couple of times and was looking forward to living in his new home. Now he was a big boy he would no longer be sharing a room with Lucy. He would sleep in the back bedroom where he would have lots of room to spread out his toy cars and garage, and his railway track with the wooden engine and coaches. Sam was looking forward to the time when Russell would be old enough to appreciate the tinplate Hornby trains that he had played with as a boy and had kept in good condition for such time as he would have a son of his own.

Lucy would sleep in the small room, often called the box room, but it was quite a good size. It would all seem strange to her at first, but Val knew that she would soon settle down with the people she knew around her – her loving parents and her big brother, who now regarded her as his nice little sister, not the nuisance and the interloper he had once thought of her as.

They would have the weekend in which to get the house reasonably shipshape, although it would take ages to make it completely to their liking. Sam's greatest sorrow was leaving his garden. It had been something of a wilderness when they'd moved in, and he had spent long and enjoyable hours getting it to its present state, with a smooth lawn, a rockery, well-tended bushes, flower beds and shady trees. Now he would have to start again, although the new garden was in pretty good shape.

They had had a summer house in Queensbury, which had been a fad of Val's at the time. There was a small greenhouse at the new house with flourishing tomato plants and cucumbers, and other lesser known hot house vegetables. Val was contemplating taking this up as a new hobby. It was doubtful that Sam would have time to attend to it with everything else he had to do at home and at the store.

When they arrived late on Friday morning, Sam supervised the removal of the furniture while Val kept the children in the garden away from any possible danger. Fortunately it was a sunny day.

Everything in the kitchen was in working order, so they had a quick lunch of beans on toast before tackling the unloading of the packing cases. Lucy was ready for a sleep and Russell 'helped' by carrying unbreakable items such as kitchen utensils, but not knives or scissors – books, cushions and his own toys to their allotted places.

'A place for everything, and everything in its place,' was a favourite saying of Val's mother. Val, had always tried to keep to it, but she reflected now on the amount of stuff – what other word was there to describe it? – that one accumulated in just a few years. And who was it who said that there should be nothing in your home that was not useful or beautiful? Or, as her own mother might have said, 'Neither use nor ornament.'

Val thought about this as she looked at the teddy bear with one eye and a loose leg that had been a childhood favourite, and a pot cat with a red bow round its neck, a birthday present from Cissie many years ago. Surely there was such a thing as sentimental value as well?

They were exhausted by the time Friday came to an end. On Saturday, Sam was obliged to divide his time between his home and the store, which would be opening on Monday.

On Sunday, though, their good friends Janice and Phil came to help as their business was closed on that day. Russell was left 'in charge' of the two little girls, his own sister and Sarah, now almost two years old.

'We can trust him now,' Val assured Janice, sensing her friend's slightly troubled air. 'We couldn't have done at one time but his behaviour really has improved such a lot.'

The three children played in Russell's bedroom with his cars and Lucy's dolls and cuddly animals, an adult popping in every five minutes or so to see that all was well.

Val made time during the afternoon to prepare a casserole – beef, potatoes and vegetables all in one large dish which cooked slowly in the oven. And at six o'clock, when the work was more or less completed and they were too tired to do any more, they all sat down to a a a tasty 'hot pot', followed by an apple pie which Janice and Phil had contributed from their freezer.

Sam brought out a bottle of sherry after the meal, then it was Phil who proposed a toast.

'To Sam and the success of Walker and Wyatt's Sports Gear. And to Sam and Val in their new home. Good luck, good health and happiness.'

The children drank from beakers of orange juice, even Lucy in her high chair. They seemed to sense the air of excitement, although it was bedtime and the two little girls were yawning.

'Thank you for your good wishes and all your help today,' said Sam. 'It is much appreciated, I assure you.'

'And all the best for the grand opening tomorrow,' added Phil. 'I'm sure you'll have lots of customers.'

'I hope so,' said Sam, but there's no grand opening ceremony – we've not invited the mayor and the town council! We're just going to open – well, reopen with new owners and a new name – and hope for the best.'

Sam could not help feeling, at the heart of him, a little anxious that it would all go well for himself and for Colin. He had given up a great deal – and so had Colin – to take a step into the unknown. Val, also, was leaving behind so much that was familiar and loved. He knew that the success of the new venture was in the hands of himself and Colin, but they were both ready for the challenge and looking forward to working together as partners as well as longtime friends.

'Let's go and see Daddy in his new shop, shall we?' said Val to Russell on Monday morning.

Sam had set off bright and early while Val and the children were still having their breakfast. He had seemed cheerful and optimistic. Val had been aware of his air of preoccupation, which he had been trying to hide, the previous evening, but that seemed to have vanished. She had kissed him and wished him luck, and said that she would have a walk round later. Her thoughts had been with him all morning. It was now almost eleven o'clock, by which time they should have found their feet after the opening of the store at nine o'clock.

Val doubted that there would have been a rush of customers. It was not like a newly opened bakery or a butcher's shop with fresh produce on sale. She guessed that most of the customers that day, or even that week, would come out of curiosity to see what changes had been made. It was, also, a specialized shop, of interest mainly to those who played a sport of some kind. If she were honest, it was not the sort of shop that would normally be of great interest to her. She had learnt to play tennis at school but had not kept it up, and had played table tennis at the youth club she had attended in her early teens, but that, also, was a thing of the past.

Golf was Sam's 'thing'; she could not imagine ever playing it herself, nor had Sam ever suggested it. He had always regarded it as his recreation, something apart from his home and family and his job, and she had never objected to his absences. She knew how the sport relaxed him, and she had never been what one could call a 'golf widow'. Now, though, Sam's hobby would be part of his work as well as being his hobby.

Russell was excited. 'Daddy's shop!' he shouted. 'Daddy's shop!' He had been there once or twice and it was something else to interest him, as well as the new house and new friends, like Auntie Janice and Uncle Phil, and Sarah, another little girl for him to play with, although she was rather small.

It was a good walk along the Stray and then through the streets to the other side of the town. Russell trotted along manfully at the side of the pram, with Lucy sitting up and staring around curiously at everything they passed, especially the dogs on leads. Val had noticed before how she smiled and pointed to them, and she had wondered if it might be a good idea to get a dog as a pet for the children, and for her and Sam, of course. Or had she quite enough do with Russell and Lucy? It would be something to consider when they were more settled in their new home.

She could see as they drew near to the town that Russell was flagging a little.

'Tired, Mummy,' he said. 'Ride on Lucy's pram?'

'All right then. Up you go.' She lifted him on to the seat that was fastened to the front of the pram. He grinned and gave a chuckle.

'See Daddy soon. Daddy's got a new shop.'

Val was as anxious as anyone to see the display in the windows. She had seen the shop gradually taking shape but had not seen the final result. When she did she stood and stared in admiration.

Colin's wife, Carol, had been an art student, and a very talented one. She had worked as a window dresser but there had not been much scope in Halifax. Then she had worked for a department store in Bradford but that had come to an end when their son, Seamus, was born two years ago. She now worked from home, designing greetings cards, and had a few outlets for her work. She had been delighted at the idea of designing a backdrop for the windows of the new store, and when she had taken the measurements she had set to work at home.

It was a double-fronted shop with one window concentrating mainly on golf and the other on hiking and climbing. One scene depicted a golf course, with men playing the game and others walking with trolleys or carrying golf bags. There were trees in the background and a blue sky above with fluffy white clouds.

The other was a scene of rugged hills, such as one might see in Swaledale or Coverdale. On the peaks there were climbers with ropes. Sheep grazed on the lower pastures and a rippling stream flowed through the bottom of the valley. Walking along its banks were hikers with colourful clothing and rucksacks.

One window held golfing equipment: bags, clubs, a specimen trolley and a pyramid of boxes of balls. Clothing, too: anoraks, waterproof jackets and trousers, gaily patterned Aran jumpers, caps and sturdy shoes.

The hiking window displayed rucksacks, climbing boots, ice axes, ropes, a small tent, maps of Yorkshire and clothing for all weather. A small section of each window was devoted to other sports. There were tennis racquets and balls, cricket bats and balls but not the appropriate clothing. Sam had explained that different sports would be highlighted as the seasons changed, but golfing and hiking enthusiasts did not stop because the weather was inclement.

In another section were darts and dartboards, table tennis bats and balls, chess sets, even Scrabble and Monopoly. Something to suit almost everyone, for outdoor activities or the more leisurely indoor pursuits.

Val stood for a few moments, very impressed with the eye-catching display. It should certainly be an incentive to would-be shoppers. 'Come along, Russell,' she said. 'Let's go and see Daddy.'

He was hopping on one leg then the other with impatience. He had looked in the window but there was nothing of particular interest to a little boy.

'Yes, yes!' he cried. 'And Lucy.'

'Oh, yes, we won't forget Lucy,' said Val. Never again would she leave Lucy outside in her pram after the frightening experience they had all endured. She didn't mention it to Russell, though; possibly he had forgotten as he never mentioned it now, but his tolerance of his little sister had improved from that moment on.

Val lifted the little girl out of the pram, thinking that she felt heavier each time she picked her up. She pushed open the door and Russell laughed at the strange jangling sound that the old-fashioned bell made.

The shop was not crowded, but she had not expected it to be. There was a customer at each counter, one woman being served by Colin, who smiled and raised his hand in greeting as he saw Val come in. Desmond was serving the other man, and two people were browsing, but Sam was nowhere in sight just then.

The lay-out was the same as it had been when they first saw the store. Russell made a beeline for the central display where things were near enough to touch, not out of reach behind glass.

'Now, don't touch, Russell,' said Val, imagining a pyramid of boxes crashing to the floor.

But Russell was staring at a row of footballs on a carpet of artificial grass.

'Footballs, Mummy,' he said. 'Like the men on the telly.'

He did not understand the game, of course, but he enjoyed watching a match – or part of it, until he got bored – with his daddy. He gave one of them a gentle kick, seeming to know that he mustn't be too boisterous. It didn't move very far and Val didn't scold him. Balls were meant to be kicked and it was very tempting.

Sam appeared at that moment. 'Sorry, I didn't see you come in. I was busy in the stockroom. So . . . what's your verdict?'

'It's great!' replied Val. 'The window displays are superb. I'm most impressed.'

'Football, Daddy,' said Russell. 'I like that big football.'

'I'm sure you do, but that one is too big and heavy for you, Russell. We have some smaller ones. Look – over here.'

Russell followed him to the other side where there was a basket of smaller white and black balls, much lighter and not liable to make as much damage to windows and greenhouses.

'I'll bring one home tonight,' said Sam, 'then we can have a game in the garden before you go to bed.'

'And Lucy?' said Russell.

'I don't think Lucy's big enough to play football yet,' said Val. She had put her down as she was too heavy to carry.

Lucy toddled round the display stand, holding her big brother's hand.

'Don't touch, Lucy,' he said.

Sam and Val laughed. 'It's very tempting,' said Val, 'for grown-ups as well, I imagine. Have you had many customers?'

'Quite a few. Not too bad,' replied Sam, 'considering it's Monday morning and not a good day for shopping. A few came out of curiosity, I suppose, but they all bought something. The cut-price golf balls have nearly all gone but I think all our goods are reasonably priced. And we will take orders if the item is not in stock. Thomas said they did a lot of trade that way.'

'Has Thomas been in today?'

'No. A wise decision, I think. He's been a great help getting us started but now it's up to us. And Desmond has all the facts at his fingertips . . . Are you walking back home now?'

'Of course – what else can I do?'

'I meant . . . are you doing any shopping while you're here in the town?'

'No, not today. We've just come to see you. I know it's quite a long way to walk but I've not much else to do. I'll go and have a word with Colin, then we'll set off for home.'

'Good to see you, Colin,' said Val. 'I hope it all works out well for you and Sam. You've taken a great leap into the unknown but you've both got what it takes to succeed. And will you please tell Carol how I love the window display? It will certainly bring the customers in. What a talented lady she is.'

'Yes, I must agree with that,' said Colin. 'You must come round and see her. She was asking about you. You can bring Russell to play with Seamus. He's a bit younger than Russell but he's been a bit lonely since we moved here. Carol's sister and her husband and children lived near us in Halifax. I know we'll miss them but I'm sure we've made the right decision. Carol's busy with her greetings cards, so it might be better if you ring and arrange a meeting.'

'Yes, I'll do that. Bye for now, Colin,' she said as another customer approached.

Sam said goodbye to them all, then went to talk to a customer who was needing help.

Val was thoughtful as she walked back home. It had occurred to her that she was the only one of her close associates who was not working. Carol, who, like herself, must have found it a great upheaval moving to another town, was happily engrossed in her art work, which she enjoyed and which earned her some money.

Janice was busy in the Coffee Pot for a large part of each day, and Cissie, back in Halifax, was still enjoying her job at the market. Whereas what was she, Val, doing?

Snap out of it! she told herself. She was looking after her children and supporting her husband – wasn't that what she had always wanted to do? She remembered how she had been so depressed when she had wanted a baby and there had been no sign of one. They had adopted Russell and then, miraculously, Lucy had come along. What more could she want?

The store closed at five thirty and Sam was home by six o'clock. He had deposited the day's takings at the nearby bank just before it closed, bringing the remainder of the money, taken later in the day, home for safe keeping. He and Colin would take it in turns to do the banking. They were quite satisfied with the turnover for the day. Desmond, who had been in the shop with the previous owners, said that the amount compared favourably – slightly up if anything – for a Monday.

So far so good, Sam and Colin agreed, and were confident that it would improve.

Russell was waiting for his daddy to come home with the new football and insisted on a game straight away. The children had had tea, and Val was preparing the evening meal for her and Sam to enjoy in peace when they had gone to bed.

Sam complimented Val on the braised steak and onions with fluffy mashed potato, followed by apple tart and cream.

'Homemade, isn't it?' he said. 'I can tell the difference; it's delicious, darling.'

'Yes, a treat for your first day at the store,' she replied. 'It passed the afternoon nicely, doing some baking, and it's a change from sorting out our belongings.'

Sam looked at her, a little concerned. 'Do I detect a hint of dissatisfaction or sadness, maybe? I know it's been a big upheaval for you moving here and I do appreciate it that you've done it for me. Cheer up, darling. I know it's all new and different but we're all here together, you and me and Russell and Lucy.'

'I am trying to be cheerful,' said Val, 'and I've told myself that I'm being silly. I've got you and the children, and a lovely new home . . .'

'But you miss the old one? Is that it?'

'Partly . . . I feel a bit lonely with only the children for company. There were lots of people to see in Halifax. Mum and Dad, of course, and your family, especially Thelma. And Cissie – we used to meet sometimes when she'd finished at the market, and there were the girls at the office. I don't know anyone here.'

'You know Janice and Phil . . .'

'Yes, but Janice is busy. She works jolly hard at the cafe and she doesn't get much time for socializing. And Carol's busy, too. Colin suggested I should go and see her, but she's so engrossed in her art work that I would have to arrange a time; I can't just pop round.'

'You'll soon make new friends. You're that sort of person, aren't you? You don't find it hard to get on with new people.

Didn't you say you would try Russell at playgroup again when he's turned three? You'll get to meet the other mothers there, won't you?'

'Yes, no doubt I will. But I feel as though I should be doing something else as well as looking after the children. Janice is working, and Cissie, and Carol works at home. I know I can't go out to work, nor do I want to, but I want to feel . . . useful. Oh, dear! It's your first day at the shop and I'm doing nothing but moan! I'm sorry, darling.'

'Don't worry, I understand. But you're such a good mother, and what would I do without you? We're very happy, aren't we?'

'Of course we are. I've told you; I'm being silly. I'll try to snap out of it.'

Sam was thoughtful for a moment. Then, 'How about you doing the bookkeeping for us,' he said, 'and being in charge of the orders? Thomas said his father used to take care of all that, especially when he got older and didn't come into the shop as much. We really need someone to take it on. I suppose we thought we'd do it between us, but it would be great if you could do it. What do you think?'

'I could try,' said Val. 'Maths is not my strong point but I did OK with it at school and I'm used to office work. Yes, why not?' She found she was smiling with pleasure.

'We'll need an accountant, possibly a couple of times a year, to make sure that everything is in order. And we will pay you; we won't expect you to do it for nothing.'

'Don't be daft, Sam! I don't want paying. It's a family business – well, ours and Colin's – and I'd like to think I'm a part of it.'

'A small allowance then, so you can treat yourself to a new dress or something when you feel like it.'

Val laughed. 'OK, if you insist.' She had been used to having a wage when she worked at the mill and hadn't liked being dependent on Sam for everything, although he was very generous.

'I'll get started whenever you like,' she said. 'And, to change the subject, I've been wondering about Russell's birthday. He'll be three in a couple of weeks and I think we should have a little party . . .'

TWENTY

Cissie also found that she was missing her best friend. She and Val had not seen one another quite as much after they had both married and had their children, but Cissie had known that Val was always there, ready to listen and to offer advice if she was in trouble or anxious about something.

They had been friends since they were four years old. They had lived in the same street of terraced houses near the centre of the town and had started school together. It had soon become clear that Val was the cleverer of the two, probably because she applied herself more to her school work and was keen to learn.

When they were eleven years old they moved to the secondary school; there was no possibility of either of them going to the grammar school. They were put into different forms, being graded according to ability. Cissie had feared that Val would make new friends and not want her any more, but her fears were unfounded. They had both made new friends in their different classes. Cissie was popular because of her devil-may-care attitude and her cheerfulness, but at the heart of her there was insecurity and she and Val remained as close to one another as ever.

They both left school at fifteen and found employment at Walker's mill. Val, after passing the required test, was offered a post in the office as a junior clerk. She soon proved that she was a conscientious worker and was not the one who always made the tea and ran errands for long.

Cissie worked in the weaving shed and proved to be competent at the job, so much so that she was offered a place in the 'burling and mending' room. This was where a team of women examined the finished cloth for faults and mended the mistakes as invisibly as possible.

When their shifts coincided the two girls would walk home

together and go out in the evenings, usually to the local cinemas a couple of times a week.

In the August of 1955 they spent a holiday together in Blackpool. It had proved to be an eventful week. They had made a new friend, Janice Butler, who had been helping out as a waitress at the family hotel which was run by her mother. And Val had met Samuel Walker in the Winter Gardens ballroom.

Sam had not realized, until Val had told him, that she worked in the office at his father's mill. But that had not concerned him at all, and it had been, more or less, love at first sight for the pair of them.

Cissie, though, had been anxious about the budding friendship, and, if she were honest, a little jealous and peeved at her friend hobnobbing with one of the bosses. She had warned Val that no good could come of it and it would never work.

She had been forced to eat her words, however, when the couple became engaged and then married. Cissie, in the end, had been happy for her friend. The four of them, Val and Sam, and Cissie and Walter, had become firm friends. The girls had been bridesmaids for one another and godmother to the children that had followed.

And then, suddenly, Val was no longer there. Admittedly she was not a thousand miles away and they could keep in touch by phone. They were close enough to visit, too; they could easily travel there and back in a day, and that would be happening very soon. Val had phoned and invited them all to Russell's third birthday party.

One great thing, of course, had come out of Val and Sam's move to Harrogate: they had sold their house to Cissie and Walter. Never in a million years would Cissie have imagined she would ever live in the salubrious residential district of Queensbury. But here they were, she and Walter, living in a lovely semi-detached house at the top of the hill which led up from the town centre. There were wonderful views all around, and the air was fresher and cleaner up there.

Sam had worked hard in the garden. Cissie knew he was regretful at leaving it, but Walter had promised to carry on the good work to the best of his ability. It was far larger than the garden they were leaving, which was more of a backyard with a tiny lawn and a simple flower bed. Here there were trees and shrubs, rose bushes and what Val called an herbaceous border. There was even a summerhouse, which delighted the children as well as Cissie.

She thought to herself, however, that their new home was in keeping with Walter's position at the mill. Since Sam's departure he had been given more responsibility and a rise in pay. He was – almost – one of the bosses now, and Cissie was pleased and proud to tell people how well he was doing.

So there were good things to counteract the sadness at losing her best friend. Cissie had other friends, of course. There was Megan, who had lived in the same street. Their little girls, Holly and Kelly, were good friends and went to playgroup together. Cissie had thought that this might have to end when they moved, and that Holly would go to a different playgroup nearer to their home, but Megan had agreed to take Holly and collect her each day as she had always done. So Cissie travelled down to the town by bus each morning, left Holly at Megan's home and collected her when she had finished her work at the market cafe.

Cissie loved her job and had no thought of giving it up and becoming a lady of leisure, even though her husband had become rather more than a mill hand. She had made new friends while working at the market and had many a good laugh with the other waitresses; they helped to prepare the food and wash up as well as waiting at the tables. And most of the customers were friendly and easy to please. Some of them came in each day at the same time, and Cissie had a good rapport with several of the regulars.

But Cissie knew she would always think of Val as her special friend. She was looking forward to the coming Sunday when they would be going to Harrogate for Russell's birthday party. Sunday was the only day on which the adults were free. It would be good to see Janice and Phil Grundy again as well. Val and Sam's new home was not too far from Grundy's, and Cissie guessed that Val and Janice would be able to see one another quite regularly.

She could not help but feel rather jealous at the thought of the two of them becoming more friendly. No, maybe jealous was too strong a word. So . . . what exactly did she feel? She recalled the time when she and Val had moved to the secondary school and been put into different classes. Cissie had worried then that these new girls Val was meeting – cleverer girls than Cissie was – might lure Val away from her. But this had not happened.

Nor would it happen now. Cissie told herself not to be silly, and to look forward to Sunday when she would be seeing both her friends again.

Val had suggested that they should have just a small party to celebrate Russell's third birthday, but she ended up with what amounted to a houseful. Sam had reminded her that it could not be just for the children; their parents would need to be invited as well.

'Yes, I know that,' she'd replied. 'Obviously the children can't come on their own, but we don't need to invite your parents or mine. It would not be your mother's cup of tea at all to be in the midst of so many children, and my mother would prefer to be just with her own grandchildren. They can come another time. But we must invite Jonathan and Thelma, and Rosemary. The ones from Halifax won't need to stay overnight. It will be just a teatime party . . .'

When they counted up there would be seventeen in all; more adults than children. Colin and Carol and two-year-old Seamus were invited. Russell and Seamus had met and had got along as well as little boys could be expected to do.

'Can you cope with so many?' asked Sam.

'Of course I can,' Val replied. 'It will only be a bun fight. Well, not literally, I hope! But you know what I mean: sand-wiches and buns, and jelly and ice cream; things that kiddies like. I'm not doing a special meal for the parents but there'll be beer and wine if they want it. It won't be up to Janice and Phil's standard but I don't think anyone will mind.'

They had decided on a Sunday, not Russell's actual birthdate but a day that was more convenient for the parents, especially Janice and Phil, who would have a rest from catering.

It turned out to be a jolly occasion, with all the children, even Russell, behaving well. The children sat around the tea table, with cushions on chairs if necessary, and Lucy, the youngest, in her high chair. The adults balanced their cups and plates on their knees, getting up when they were needed to lend a hand.

It was the sort of party any three-year-old could wish for. Salmon paste, egg and potted meat sandwiches (minus the crusts for a special occasion), sausage rolls, crisps, iced buns and jelly – red, of course – with ice cream. There was a birthday cake with three candles and 'Happy Birthday, Russell' piped in red icing sugar, and if it was a trifle wobbly no one commented. Russell seemed to know what was expected of him and puffed out his cheeks for a good blow at the candles while everyone sang 'Happy birthday to you'.

Only three of the children, Paul, Holly and Rosemary, who went to school or playgroup, were old enough to understand party games, so they sang songs instead; nursery rhymes and jingles that the older ones had learnt at school.

The men then volunteered to amuse the children in the garden with a game of football. This was Russell's latest craze since his daddy had brought the football home. For his birthday, Val and Sam had bought him a red jersey and white shorts, like the men on the television wore, and a pair of 'football boots' – not heavy enough to do any damage – all of which he had insisted on wearing for his party.

The two younger girls, Sarah and Lucy, stayed inside with the women who were tackling the washing up. The shouts of delight coming from the garden indicated that the men and the older children were having a good time.

The five women enjoyed chatting together. Carol was the only one who was a comparative stranger to everyone but Val. She was soon joining in the general chatter, though, about husbands and children and the problems of settling into a new home.

Val overheard a conversation between Cissie and Carol and smiled to herself.

'Of course, Val and I have known one another for ever,' Cissie told her new acquaintance, 'ever since we started school together. And now we've bought the house they had up at

Queensbury. My husband, Walter, has taken over a lot of the work that Sam used to do at the mill . . .'

'Yes, I go out to work as well,' she went on in answer to one of Carol's questions. 'I don't really need to but I have a nice little job at the market cafe and I love it.'

She heard Thelma confiding to Janice something that she and Sam already knew. 'Jonathan and I are expecting another baby in February. Rosemary is five now so it's about time, really, isn't it?'

And Janice remarked to Cissie that she didn't really see all that much of Val. 'No, we don't meet very often even though we live quite near. I'm working at the cafe a lot of the time and Val's kept busy with Russell and Lucy and the work she's doing for the shop. But it's good that the three of us are all together again today. That was a smashing week we had together in Blackpool, wasn't it? I'm sure it was fate, you know, the way we all met. I often think about it, how I met Phil and Val met Sam, and you went back and married Walter . . .'

TWENTY-ONE

Cissie was reminded forcibly of that week in Blackpool a few days later. It was around eleven o'clock on Wednesday morning, one of their busiest times of day, although there was scarcely a time when they were really quiet. Women who were shopping often stopped for a cup of tea or coffee and maybe a bun, mid-morning, before walking or taking the bus home. It wasn't often that men were there at that time. Workmen came later for a spot of lunch before starting their afternoon shift.

There was a young man sitting on his own at a corner table now, though. Cissie glanced in his direction as he studied the menu. She was just making her way to his table when he looked up, and she stopped dead in her tracks. Was it . . . him? No, surely not, after all this time. How long was it? Six years! But there was no mistaking that shock of unruly fair hair and round face.

At that moment he looked across at her and their eyes met. Her heart gave a jolt . . . Those bright blue eyes that she remembered so well, although she hadn't given him a thought for a long time. But there was no doubt about it. It was Jack Broadbent, the young man she had met in Blackpool in 1955.

She could see the look of puzzlement in his eyes change to one of recognition, and what else could she do but walk towards him?

'Hello, Jack,' she said quietly and in a matter-of-fact tone, not smiling at him.

'Cissie? It is Cissie, isn't it?'

She nodded. 'Yes . . . Long time no see, Jack.'

'Yes . . . yes, I meant to get in touch but then . . . well . . . all kinds of things happened. You're working here, then?'

'Yes, just a part-time job. What can I get for you?'

'A cup of tea, please, and a scone with butter and jam.'

'OK, coming up . . .' She walked away feeling strangely

light-headed, remembering the last time they had met and what had happened on the promenade before she had left him to go back to her boarding house in a taxi. At least he had given her the fare, she recalled. She was soon back with his order.

'Stay and chat to me,' he said, pointing to the chair next to him.

'I can't, Jack. I'm working. We're not supposed to sit and chat to the customers.'

'What time do you finish, then?'

'One o'clock, but I have to go and collect my little girl.'

'Oh . . . You've got a daughter?'

'Yes, and a son . . . It's been a long time, Jack.'

'Will you meet me when you finish tomorrow then? I'll come in a bit later, then we can have a cup of tea together and . . . catch up, eh? I'm in this area all week.'

She didn't ask what his job was; a driver of some sort, she supposed, although he had used to work in a mill in Bradford.

'OK, then,' she said, but not with a great show of enthusiasm. Then she saw his blue eyes twinkle and the lop-sided grin that she now recalled so well. He had been such a charmer and she had been unable to resist him. She had no intention of getting involved with him again, though, but he did owe her an explanation for not getting in touch as he had said he would.

'Tomorrow then,' she said, as casually as she could. 'One o'clock, when I finish. OK?'

'OK. See you then, Cissie.'

There were other customers waiting to be served and she did not go near his table again. Then she saw him pay his bill and walk away.

She felt jittery and unsettled for the rest of the day, so much so that Walter asked her that evening if there was anything troubling her.

'No, 'course not,' she replied. 'We were busy at the cafe today and I was a bit harassed because I kept wondering how Paul was going on at school.'

It would not have been practical for Paul to continue at his former school in Halifax, so he had started on Monday at the one in Queensbury, which was not very far from where they

now lived. Walter dropped him off on his way to work each
day and Cissie collected him at the end of the afternoon.

What Cissie had said was partly true. Paul had not been too
happy for the first couple of days. Although he was an adapt-
able little boy and made friends easily, it had all been new and
strange to him. He missed his old friends, and the children at
the new school all knew one another.

Today, though, when she had met him, he had seemed happier.
The boy he sat next to in class had invited him to join in their
game at playtime; just kicking a football around with no
particular rules, but he had enjoyed it. The way they did sums,
though, was different, and he hadn't quite got the hang of it.
The reading books were also different from the ones he had
had before.

'He's settling down fine,' Walter said now. 'Don't worry
about him; he'll soon get used to it all. Didn't he tell you he's
got a new friend, Lee, who sits next to him?'

'Yes . . . yes, he did tell me. I'm OK, Walter, honest I am.
It's all different, though, isn't it? And we've still not got the
house straight, have we?'

'Never mind, it'll get done sometime. You want to carry on
with your job at the market, do you? You don't have to, you
know.'

'No, I want to do it, Walter. I really enjoy it and I've got a
lot of friends there.'

'That's OK then . . .' He settled down again behind the
evening paper.

Cissie pretended to read her *Woman's Own* but her mind was
wandering. And a little later, when Walter switched on the
television for their favourite police drama, she was only half
watching. Ever since that morning she had been remembering
her first meeting with Jack Broadbent . . .

She had not met him at the Winter Gardens on the night that
Val had met Sam and Janice had met Phil. It had been a few
days later at the tower ballroom. Jack had asked her to dance,
and they soon discovered that they had quite a lot in common,
including their happy-go-lucky approach to life.

They'd realized at once, of course, that they were both from
Yorkshire. He'd told her that he worked at a mill, as she did,

in his home town of Bradford. Cissie had felt pleased that she had met someone, as both of her friends had done, and had not hesitated to spend the rest of the evening with him, enjoying the delights that the tower had to offer.

There'd been a lot to do as well as dancing in the ballroom to the music of Reginald Dixon on the organ. They'd had a drink at one of the many bars, went to see the animals in the small menagerie and the fish in the aquarium. Jack had then seen her back to her hotel, when she'd realized she must put a stop to his over-amorous caresses; after all, they had only just met. She did agree, however, to meet him again later in the week and spend the day with him.

She remembered that they had gone to the fishing port of Fleetwood along the coast from Blackpool. It had been a pleasant ride on a tramcar past the rows and rows of hotels and the manmade cliffs that reached down to the sea. There had been an aroma of fish in the air at Fleetwood and a brisk breeze blowing in from the sea as they strolled along the promenade.

They had enjoyed a hearty meal of crispy battered fish and chips at a cafe, then had a trip on the ferry boat across the estuary of the River Wyre to a little place called Knott End. There had been nothing to do there. It really was like the end of the world, but she had been happy and relaxed in Jack's company.

When they'd arrived back in Blackpool they went their separate ways for their evening meal at their respective boarding houses. Jack had begged her to spend the evening with him as well, and after only a moment's hesitation she had agreed. She'd hoped that Val might be seeing Sam that evening as she had already spent the day with him. Yes, it turned out that it was so, and Cissie did not need to feel guilty about making her own plans. She remembered how Val had warned her to watch herself with Jack; and she, Cissie, had replied that she could take care of herself and there was no need to worry.

She had met Jack later that evening by North Pier, and they had gone to the Tivoli cinema to see Marilyn Monroe in *Gentlemen Prefer Blondes*. Afterwards, they went to the nearby Yates's Wine Lodge.

Cissie had been in a mellow mood after her first gin and lime, and after two more of the same she'd felt so carefree that she'd scarcely known what was happening. Nor had she cared; she was with Jack, he was jolly good company and she was enjoying herself.

They'd strolled across the tram track, then wandered down to the lower promenade. There had been a series of secluded colonnades away from the busy main promenade, although the clang of the trams could be heard in the distance.

Jack had been surprisingly gentle with her, so much so that she had gone along with his lovemaking without demur. It all seemed unreal, almost like a dream, and it was only later that she began to realize what had happened.

'I must be getting back,' she'd said eventually, and Jack saw her into a taxi at Talbot Square, with instructions to the driver to see her safely back to her boarding house. He'd given the driver some money, then kissed her cheek and said, 'I'll be seeing you soon.'

They had already exchanged details of one another's whereabouts earlier in the evening; at least, she had scribbled her address on a scrap of paper and Jack had shoved it into his pocket. He had given her a phone number, explaining that they had a phone not because they were posh, but because his father was an odd-job man and people had to be able to get in touch with him.

The next morning, Cissie had woken up to reality. What on earth had she done? How could she have been such a silly little fool? She had felt ashamed but knew she could not keep it to herself. She had to tell Val. It had been later that morning, when they were on the sands sunbathing – or trying to, in the fitful sunshine – that she'd told her friend what had happened.

She'd been able to tell that Val was surprised, even shocked, but she had not condemned her. She hadn't said, 'I told you to watch him!' or told her that she'd been stupid. Val had tried to make light of it, saying that it wasn't possible to get pregnant the first time it happened, something that they both knew was not strictly true but more of a common fallacy.

'But supposing I am?' Cissie had said. 'I might not know for ages; you know what I'm like with my periods.'

Yes, Val remembered that her friend was very irregular. She could go two months or more without a period, but her doctor had said not to worry; it would sort itself out in time.

'And I had one just before we came away, so it might be too late before I find out.' Cissie had been worried. 'Oh, crikey! What am I going to do?'

'Will you be seeing him again, this . . . Jack?'

'Yes, he's got my address and he gave me a phone number,' Cissie had said without much conviction.

'Well, there you are then. Don't let it spoil the rest of your holiday. We're having a smashing time, aren't we?'

It had cast a shadow over the rest of the week, though, for Cissie at least.

They had come back to reality on the Monday when they were home again and starting work. Val had her budding friendship with Sam to look forward to, but Cissie had been frantic with worry.

After a few days, when there had been no word from Jack – and she'd known, deep down, that it wasn't likely – she'd decided to ring the number he had given her. It had not been a great surprise to her when she'd found there was no such number. Things had sorted themselves out in time, however . . .

She met Jack, as arranged, in the cafe the following day. She had been in two minds whether or not to agree to see him, but he had seemed keen to meet her and he did owe her an explanation.

He was there at the same corner table at ten minutes to one, and when she had finished her shift she sat down opposite him.

'What are you having?' he asked. 'My treat. I'm having a ham sandwich and a cup of tea.'

'I'll have the same then,' she replied. 'They're as good as anything we do. I won't need to have anything when I get home. My friend's giving my little girl her lunch 'cause I said I'd be a bit later today.'

'How old is your daughter, then?'

'She'll be four at Christmas. She's called Holly. She goes to playgroup and I collect her when I've finished here.'

'Jolly good . . . Did you say you had a boy an' all?'

'Yes, a little boy called Paul. He's . . . five and a bit.'

'Gosh! You didn't waste much time then. I see you're married,' he added, looking at her wedding ring.

'Of course . . . And you?'

'No . . . no, not me. I'm still as free as a bird.' He motioned to the waitress and gave her their order. Daphne winked at Cissie, who had felt obliged to tell her fellow waitress that she was meeting a friend.

'A mate of Walter's,' she had lied, not wanting her friend to think she was up to something.

There was a short silence before Jack spoke again. 'I'm sorry, like, that I didn't get in touch with you. To be honest, I lost yer address. It were on a bit of paper an' it must have come out of me pocket with me hanky or summat. And you weren't on the phone.'

'No, but you said you were, Jack, or your dad was, anyroad. I rang but there was no answer. It made a funny noise as though it wasn't a proper number.'

'Well, it was, I can tell you. Happen you dialled it wrong.'

'I don't think so.'

'Well, happen I wrote it down wrong. One digit can make all the difference an' I wrote it in a hurry. Well, ne'er mind, eh? You're here now. It's good to see you again, Cissie.'

She did not say, 'And you too,' unsure of how she was feeling. She didn't think she believed his story.

'So you're not in the same job, Jack?' she asked as they started to eat their sandwiches. 'You used to work at the mill, didn't you?'

'Aye, so I did, but I were made redundant about a year ago. A sign of the times; things are not what they were in the woollen trade. But I reckon you know that. You worked at the mill an' all, didn't you?'

'Yes, but I finished when . . . when I got married. It's the same at Walker's now; the orders are not coming in like they used to. But it worked out quite well for my husband and me. Walter – that's my husband – was the chief overseer, but he's been promoted an' he's one of the managers now.' Cissie knew this was not strictly true but it sounded good, and Walter was thought so highly of now that it was quite possible that he would be, one day.

'You probably remember Sam?' she went on. 'The mill owner's son; he got friendly with my friend, Val when we were in Blackpool. Well, Val and Sam got married and went to live in Queensbury. But Sam decided, not so long ago, to get out and do something else. Like you said, the times are changing. Sam's got a sports shop in Harrogate now and Walter has stepped into his shoes at the mill.'

'I see. You've done well for yerself, haven't you?'

'Yes, I suppose I have.' Cissie could not help her smile of satisfaction. 'We live up at Queensbury now; we bought Sam and Val's house. There's a lot more room there and a big garden.'

'So you're not exactly working to make ends meet, not if you're married to one of the bosses?'

'No, I do it because I enjoy it. Both the kids are at school – well, playgroup for Holly – like I said . . . I've not seen you in here before, Jack. What brings you to this neck of the woods?'

'I'm a driver for one of them mills that's gone on to synthetic fibres. I've only been with 'em for three weeks an' it's the first time I've been in this area. I go all over Yorkshire and Lancashire, and into Cheshire an' all. I was with a haulage firm before but I didn't care for the long distances. I like to get back to me own bed at night.'

Cissie had already learnt that he was not married; whether he shared his bed or not was another matter.

He was looking at her keenly, half smiling, and, somewhat discomfited, she looked away.

'I must say you're looking well, Cissie,' he remarked. 'Married life must suit you. You didn't say 'owt about having a feller, though, when I met you in Blackpool.'

'Well, I didn't tell you everything, did I? But Walter was my . . . boyfriend.'

'When did you get married then?'

'Oh . . . later that year, November.'

'And yer little lad's five? When were he born?'

'What's it got to do with you? OK, so Walter and me might have jumped the gun a bit. So what? It's not a crime, is it? We're very happy, me and Walter.'

'I'm glad to hear it. It's just that you didn't say 'owt about him.'

'No . . . Well, I was on holiday with a friend and he'd gone off cycling with his club. But we'd been going out for ages and it was time we got married.'

'These sandwiches are good,' said Jack, adding a little more mustard. 'I shall come here again. Like I was saying, I'm in this area all week. How about meeting me again, eh?'

'Oh, I don't know about that, Jack . . .'

'Why not? Just for a friendly chat, like. We could drive a bit further out and have a drink. I'm really sorry I couldn't get in touch with you. I want to make up for it.'

'I told you, I have to pick up my little girl.'

'Just for an hour or so. Your friend won't mind, will she?'

'Er . . . no. She sometimes has her a bit longer when I go shopping.'

Jack was smiling at her, and she found herself remembering the fun they had had that time they went to Fleetwood. Walter wasn't much fun lately; he was taking his new responsibilities very seriously. And what harm could it do? She would make it clear that it was just for a drink together and nothing else.

'OK, then,' she said. 'That would be nice.'

'Jolly good! Shall we say next Friday? I'll meet you outside the market at one o'clock. I'll be off now; I've a few more calls to do before I head back home. 'Bye for now, Cissie . . .'

Was she being a fool? she asked herself. Perhaps she was, but it would be the very last time she saw him. Cissie hated lying; it was not one of her failings but this time it was necessary. When she collected Holly she told her friend, Megan, that she had a dental appointment on Friday that she had only just remembered. She wouldn't breathe a word to anyone about Jack, not even Val. She could imagine what Val would say . . .

TWENTY-TWO

As Jack Broadbent drove back to his poky flat in Bradford at the end of the day, his mind was buzzing with all that Cissie had told him. It had been good to see her again, although he had not thought about her for years. He remembered she had been a jolly, good-natured girl, and she was still a good looker. They'd had fun together, but it had only been a holiday fling and he'd had no intention of seeing her again, despite what he had said. He had hoped that she would forget about him and carry on with the life she had in Halifax.

He knew he might have gone a bit too far but they had both had too much to drink, she was a pretty lass and she had not seemed unwilling. It had come as a shock to him, though, that it must have been the first time for her. He had thought, rather, that she might have been around quite a bit. He had felt somewhat guilty afterwards and had seen her into a taxi and safely on her way home.

His mind was busy now, though. She had a little lad, five years old, and she said she'd got married in November, three months after their meeting in Blackpool. And the kid had been born . . . when? She hadn't said exactly, only that he was five. She'd been flustered, though, and had admitted that she and Walter might have jumped the gun.

But what if the child had been his, Jack's? And what did her husband know about it? Nowt at all, he suspected, and she wouldn't want him to know, either. He liked Cissie and might have wanted to get friendly with her again if the circumstances were right. But they weren't; she had a husband. Happen he could scare her a bit, though; get her to part with some of that dosh she and her husband were earning. Big posh house in Queensbury, manager at the mill . . . She could afford a bob or two.

He'd told her that he was not married – at least, he had given that impression. But he had been married. He was divorced now and his ex-wife was hounding him for maintenance for his three-year-old son. He was a few weeks behind and living from week to week, almost from day to day. Yes, it was worth a try, and he was seeing her again on Friday.

She was waiting for him outside the market, as they had arranged, looking very fetching in a bright red coat with lipstick to match. He would have to go gently with her at first and not let her suspect anything. She was a nice lass and he didn't want to do her any harm, but it was too good a chance to miss.

She seemed pleased to see him, anxious to get in the van, though, and on their way. He drove out of the town and along the road towards Hebden Bridge, then stopped at a little wayside pub that he knew. She said she'd have a shandy, a sausage roll and a packet of crisps when he insisted she must have something to eat. He had his usual pint of bitter and a meat pie.

They were quite relaxed and chatted together as though they were friends, not as though there had been a period of six years since they last met. She told him about Janice, her other friend who had worked at the Blackpool hotel and now ran a thriving restaurant with her husband.

'She met Phil that week an' all, when Val met Sam.'

Jack grinned at her. 'And you met me.'

'Yes . . . so I did.'

'And you went back home and married your boyfriend.'

'Yes, I did. I told you; Walter and me had been going together for ages.'

'But he didn't know you got friendly with me in Blackpool, did he?'

'No . . . why should he? You keep quiet about some things, don't you, then nobody gets hurt?'

Cissie was starting to feel alarmed. Jack had been nice and friendly, but there was a calculating gleam in his eye now that she didn't like.

'I've been doing some sums in me head,' he said. 'That little lad of yours; when did you say his birthday was?'

'I didn't say, but it was the first of June. Like I said, it were a bit too soon, but these things happen, don't they?'

'He could be mine, couldn't he?'

Cissie's heart started to beat faster and there was a panicky sensation in her chest.

'Of course he's not yours!' She tried to laugh, but it sounded forced. 'He's the image of Walter. I've got a photo of him; I'll show you. Paul looks like Walter and Holly looks like me.'

She rummaged in her bag and handed him a snapshot. It had been taken in the garden of the old house and showed a blonde-haired, chubby little girl and a dark-haired boy with rather more sharp features.

'Bonny kids,' said Jack. 'But that doesn't mean a thing. Kids are sometimes a throwback to a previous generation.'

Cissie shook her head vehemently. 'He's Walter's. There's no doubt about it. Everybody says he's like his daddy.'

'Maybe they do, but "Daddy" wouldn't be pleased to know that his girlfriend had been playing around not long before they were wed, would he? And that his little lad might not be his?'

'Stop it, Jack!' she said. 'I know . . . what we did, but it was wrong and . . . and I want to forget about it.'

'I'm sure you do.' He gave a wolfish grin. 'But what is it worth? Happen a few quid, eh? I'm hard up, Cissie. I don't like to admit it, but I am, and you're living in the lap of luxury. Come on now, how about a tenner? That's not much.'

'Ten pounds! I haven't got ten pounds, Jack. I don't carry much money around with me, an' I don't earn all that much either.'

'No, but your hubby does an' I'm sure he doesn't leave you short. I don't mind waiting. I'll be round here again next Friday. That'll give you plenty of time.'

Cissie could feel tears threatening and she tried to blink them back. 'I can't, Jack,' she said, the words catching in her throat. 'Anyroad, why d'you need it? You've got a steady job and you said you weren't married.'

'Aye, but I was, an' I've got an ex-wife an' a little lad. She'll have me up in court soon if I don't cough up with what I owe her. Come on, now, Cissie; it's just between you and me an' I won't say 'owt.'

She could feel her hands trembling and she clenched them tightly together. Walter must never find out what she'd done, how she'd tricked him into marrying her. He'd never forgive her. She knew she had to give Jack the money to keep him off her back.

'I'll have to go now, Jack,' she said, as composed as she could manage. 'I've to pick Holly up and then collect Paul from school.'

'Okey-doke,' he said cheerfully. 'Let's get going then.'

They spoke very little on the way back as Jack sped along the country road. He stopped near the market where he had picked her up.

'Same time next Friday, then?' he said. 'Remember what I've said. I'll say nowt if you do as I say. You've a hell of a lot to lose, Cissie.'

'All right, Jack; I'll see you then.' She opened the van door and stepped out on to the pavement.

He grinned. 'Good girl! You know it makes sense. Ta-ra, Cissie.'

He drove off at top speed as she stood forlornly staring at the disappearing van. She remembered then that she was supposed to have been to the dentist and she hurried off to Megan's house.

'You look a bit worse for wear,' said her friend. 'Was it awful?'

'Not too bad really, I suppose,' lied Cissie. 'Only a filling but I hate going to the dentist. Come on, Holly, love. Say bye-bye to Kelly. Thanks for looking after her, Megan.'

They took a bus back home, then it was time to collect Paul. Cissie tried to calm down, helped by a cigarette and a tot of brandy, before Walter came home.

But what on earth was she to do? She decided almost straight away that she would do what she always did when she was in a dilemma – she would ring her best friend. And there was no time like the present. She would ring Val at once.

Paul and Holly were watching a children's programme on the television. It would be almost two hours before Walter came home.

She crossed her fingers that Val would be there as she picked up the phone in the hall and dialled the number. Val answered almost at once.

'Hello, Val. It's me, Cissie. Have you time to talk?'

'Of course I have. What's the matter, Cissie? You sound a bit strange. What is it?'

'Oh, Val, I'm in the most awful trouble! D'you remember Jack Broadbent?'

There was a pause, then Val said, 'Do you mean the lad you met in Blackpool? Oh, Cissie, don't say . . .'

'Yes, he's turned up again. I never thought I'd see him again. I'd forgotten all about him – well, nearly – and then there he was in the market.'

'Go on,' said Val. 'Tell me what's happened.'

So Cissie told her friend how they'd got chatting and she'd had a cup of tea with him and he'd seemed OK, quite friendly, like. And how she'd agreed to go for a drink with him today . . .

'He turned nasty, Val. Not violent or 'owt like that, but he's been putting two and two together and he asked if Paul was his child. I told him no, of course he isn't. He's Walter's; he's the image of him an' I showed him a photo. But he still said that Walter wouldn't want to know what I'd been up to in Blackpool.'

'So he's blackmailing you?'

'Well, I suppose he is really. He says I have to give him ten pounds next week or else he'll tell Walter that Paul might not be his son. But he is Walter's! I know that, Val, and so do you, and so does everybody.'

'Yes, we do now, but you remember the time when you were not sure who the father of your child might be? You didn't know until he was born, did you?'

Cissie, indeed, had been in a quandary following her escapade in Blackpool. Her periods were irregular and she hadn't known for ages that she was pregnant. And Walter had been there, still wanting her to do what she had refused to go along with so many times. But she had known then that this was the solution to her problem. If she did what he wanted then she would be able to say that the child was his if she did happen to be pregnant.

Walter could scarcely believe her change of heart, and in due course Cissie knew that she was, indeed, pregnant. They had married in haste and she had waited on tenterhooks to see who the child resembled. When Paul was born there was no doubt about it; he was Walter's. The same nose, the same dark hair, the image of his daddy. And Walter had known nothing about her misdemeanour.

'You mustn't give in to Jack,' said Val. 'This wouldn't be

the last of it, believe me. The next time he'd want more money – that's what blackmailers do. You must tell Walter what has happened.'

'Tell Walter!' cried Cissie. 'Tell him that I tricked him into getting married? He'd never forgive me. He'd leave me; he'd take the children . . .'

'Don't start panicking, Cissie,' said her friend. 'I don't think for one moment that that would happen. Maybe you don't need to tell Walter . . . everything.'

'What do you mean?'

'Well, when you met Jack in Blackpool you weren't engaged to Walter, were you?'

'No, I couldn't make up my mind about him. I was getting a bit fed up, I suppose, an' he was going off cycling with his mates so we decided to go on holiday, didn't we, just you and me?'

'Well, then, I don't suppose you were doing much wrong, were you, spending some time with Jack? It wasn't as if you'd promised to marry Walter.'

'No, I see what you mean. Happen I could tell Walter that I'd met this lad in Blackpool, and we got friendly, like – I shan't tell him what happened, though – and now he's turned up again. I'll tell Walter that he's threatening me, that he'll tell him we got . . . friendly, like, if I don't give him some money. D'you think Walter might swallow that? I don't want to say 'owt about Jack thinking Paul might be his.'

'No, don't mention that, but you have to tell him something. Like you said, though, there was no understanding between you and Walter – you'd just had a bit of a fling in Blackpool. You know that Walter loves you . . . And he's not always been a saint, has he? You remember that little incident with the girl in the cycling club?'

'Oh, yes, 'course I do. And that was after we'd had the children. It would be the pot calling the kettle black, wouldn't it, if he started making a fuss?'

'Make him a nice tea, Cissie, then tell him you've got a problem . . . And try to keep calm.'

'OK, I'll try. I'll tell him tonight before I have time to change my mind. Thanks for listening, Val. I don't know what I'd do without you. I do miss you, you know.'

'And I miss you, too. We'll meet up again soon.'

'Bye then, Val. I'll let you know what happens. Keep yer fingers crossed for me!'

'Will do. Bye, Cissie . . .'

A nice meal for Walter. She hadn't done any shopping because she'd been too worried about the meeting with Jack. What had she got in the fridge? There was bacon, sausages and eggs and a tin of beans in the cupboard. Walter liked a fry-up and she could make some chips. And there was a couple of small apple tarts from the market cafe. She would get the kids' teas sorted out earlier, then she could spend some time with Walter on his own.

He was home soon after six and the meal was ready.

'Something smells good,' he said, sounding in a good mood.

'Just a fry-up,' said Cissie. 'I know you like that.'

'So long as you've got some HP sauce!'

He tucked into his meal and did not seem to notice that she had a small portion. When he had drunk a second cup of tea, Cissie decided she could not wait any longer.

'Walter . . .' she began, '. . . I've got summat to tell you.'

He looked at her serious face. 'What is it, love? Not bad news?'

'No not really, just summat bothering me.'

'You're not pregnant, are you?' He looked surprised, possibly a little alarmed, before going on, 'Well, that's nothing to worry about, is it?'

'No, Walter, I'm not pregnant. It's . . . summat that happened a good while ago. D'you remember that time when me and Val went to Blackpool?'

'And she got friendly with Sam. Yes, I remember that.'

'Well, I met a young chap an' all, a lad from Bradford. He was called Jack . . . and we got friendly. It was only a holiday thing, Walter, 'cause Val was with Sam and I was on my own.' That wasn't strictly true, but it might make it sound more understandable.

Walter was regarding her steadily, not smiling as she went on: 'So I danced with him, like, at the tower, and then I went to Fleetwood with him one day, and to the pictures . . . An' that was all. I never thought I'd see him again. We never said we'd meet, an' it's six years ago, Walter . . .'

'So what are you trying to tell me, Cissie?'

'Well, he came into the market the other day. He didn't know I worked there an' I'd forgotten all about him, but we knew one another an' we got talking . . .' She paused, looking at him speculatively. He was very quiet.

'Go on, Cissie,' he said.

She decided not to tell him that she'd gone for a drink with him. 'Well, we were chatting, like, an' I suppose I might've been showing off a bit. I said that you'd got a good job at Walker's. I might've hinted that you're one of the bosses . . .' She saw Walter give a wry smile.

'An' I said how we lived in a posh house at Queensbury. I wanted him to see how well we've done, Walter. An' then . . . he told me he was hard up, that he's got an ex-wife an' a kid an' he owes her some money an' she'll have him up in court. I suppose he thought it was too good a chance to miss, meeting me. He said I've got to give him some money – ten pounds, he said – or else he'll tell you about us being friendly, like, in Blackpool. He knows we're happy, y'see, Walter, an' he wants to spoil it all. So I thought I'd better tell you myself . . .' Her voice petered out.

'Did you give him any money, Cissie?'

'No, of course I didn't! He wants me to meet him next Friday.'

'Don't worry; we'll sort it out.' Walter looked thoughtful. 'And you never saw him again after you'd met in Blackpool, not till just now?'

'No, I swear I didn't, Walter. D'you remember, you'd gone off cycling that week an' I'd gone on holiday with Val? I didn't really know what I wanted, then when I got back home I realized I'd been messing you about for too long and that we should be together properly, like you wanted. It was good fun in Blackpool but I didn't like it when I was standing around in the ballroom waiting for somebody to ask me to dance. That's why I got friendly with Jack. Then . . . then I knew I wanted a steady boyfriend. I wanted you, Walter.'

He remained quiet for a moment, recalling how it had been when Cissie returned from the holiday. He had been surprised and delighted when she agreed that it was time that they cemented their relationship. He had loved her for ages, waiting for her to make up her mind, but she had seemed so lukewarm. Had she told him the full story? She had had a very sudden change of heart . . . It didn't matter, though. Their marriage was as solid as a rock now and he didn't intend to let it be spoiled by some no-good scrounger.

'What's this fellow called?' he asked. 'Jack . . .?'

'Jack Broadbent,' replied Cissie.

'What does he look like?'

'He's about as tall as you and about the same age. Fair hair, sort of scruffy . . . not dirty, just needing a comb. Round face and . . . oh, I don't know, just an ordinary chap.'

'And where did you say you'd meet him?'

'I didn't say I would. I never promised, but he said he'd be outside the market, the main entrance, next Friday at one o'clock.'

'Right, I shall be there then. He'll get a shock when he sees me, won't he?'

'Oh no, Walter! I don't want any trouble.'

'What else can we do? If you don't turn up and he does what he's threatening, I don't want him looking for me at the mill, do I? This is our business, Cissie, just yours and mine, and I'm going to deal with it.'

Cissie realized it was pointless to say any more. At least Walter had taken it quite well, much better than she had feared.

As for Walter, he was a mite suspicious but he wanted to give Cissie the benefit of the doubt. Val would know what had gone on. She and his wife were as thick as thieves so there was no point in him quizzing her. He would turn up next Friday and scare the pants off this bloke.

They said no more about it over the next week. Cissie was subdued, unlike her normal self, and Walter knew she was worried.

Cissie, indeed, was wondering what might happen if Jack turned up. It would be dreadful if it turned into a fight, but she knew that Walter was not aggressive, and neither, she believed, was Jack. She guessed that he was really all bluff and bluster.

When Walter arrived at the appointed place he was rather surprised to see that the fellow was there; he had thought it might be an idle threat.

Walter approached him. 'Are you Jack Broadbent?'

Jack looked at him, a grin on his face and a curious look in his eyes. Walter could tell that he might be quite a charmer.

'The very same,' he replied. 'And you are . . .?'

'I'm Walter Clarkson, Cissie's husband. She couldn't make it today so I'm here instead, and all I have to say to you is get the hell out of here or I'll tell the police about your little game.'

'Hey, steady on now,' said Jack, raising his hands. 'I never meant no harm. I'm a bit hard up, that's all, an' I thought there were one of two things that your lovely wife might not want you to know.'

'Cissie's told me everything,' said Walter, 'and I trust her. So you'd best clear off, Jack Broadbent.' Walter felt in his pocket, brought out a ten-pound note and handed it to him. 'This is what you came for, and this is the last you'll get. I'm sorry for your problems and I realize how lucky I am. I've got a good job and a nice house, and I've got Cissie. So just leave my wife alone.'

Jack grinned. 'Well, it was worth a try. Thanks, mate.' He pocketed the money and made to walk away, then he turned back.

'But have you never thought that that little lad of yours might be mine?'

Walter laughed out loud. 'No way; he's the image of me. Now . . . scram!'

Jack shrugged his shoulders and walked away.

That was one thing of which Walter was very sure. Paul was his son, a real chip off the old block. He recalled, though, that he and Cissie had got married in a hurry, and what a fuss Cissie's mother had made, insisting that her daughter must be married in pale blue and not virginal white.

Had she tricked him, or had she really decided that she loved him and that it was he, Walter, that she wanted? He could question her, try to get to the truth, but was it worth it? As he had told Jack, they had a nice home and enough money to be very comfortable. They had two lovely children and he knew that Cissie loved him as much as he loved her. What more could he want?

TWENTY-THREE

Val was feeling much more contented now as summer changed gradually to autumn. She was happily occupied with the work she was doing for the store: bookkeeping and ordering and helping Sam with new ideas.

The shop was doing well, and Sam and Colin had no reason to think that they might have taken on too much. It had been a leap into the unknown but all seemed to be going according to plan. Christmas was not all that far away, and stores of all kinds had to start thinking early of new ideas to attract the customers.

'It will soon be time to think about changing the window displays,' Sam told Val, 'but that's largely Carol's province. We thought we might have a snowy scene as the background; not just yet, though – better to wait until Halloween and Bonfire Night are out of the way.'

'It's difficult to play games in the snow, though,' said Val, not very helpfully. 'It's a nice idea and Carol will make a lovely background, but . . . to what?'

'A bit of snow and ice doesn't put hikers and climbers off,' said Sam. 'We'll order more winter clothing and a range of bright woollen caps and scarves. It'll be time for winter sports as well – skiing and skating. Some of the more affluent folk fly off to Switzerland or Austria. I'm not suggesting we stock skis or skates – I know they often hire them – but a backdrop of snow-clad mountains will be a talking point. Lots of people have commented on our window displays.'

'And it's the football season as well,' said Val. 'I've got an idea . . . You know how Russell loves his little jersey and shorts? He'd wear them all the time if I'd let him. Well, what about a range of football shirts for children of all ages, from Russell's age up to, say . . . eleven or twelve? And they could be red or blue, or black and white, depending on which team they support. I know you can buy that sort of thing at the chain stores but this might be more authentic.'

'Brilliant idea,' said Sam, 'catering for children as well as adults. And what about a range of supporters' scarves in the various colours? Could you take charge of all that, Val, love? Ring round a few suppliers and see what they come up with?'

'Yes, I'd love to,' she replied.

Things were going well for Val. Russell had started at another playgroup, not very far from their home, and this time it was proving to be a success. She realized he might have been too young the first time, but now he had settled down very well and was enjoying it immensely. When she collected him he was always full of tales of what they had been doing.

There was a dressing-up box and they could play at being fairies or witches – for the girls – or postmen, policemen, firemen or engine drivers. There was an engine big enough to sit in, building blocks, water and a sand tray. Val hoped he had learned to behave himself in the sand! He was now drinking his milk without making a fuss and the helpers said he was no trouble at all.

They listened to stories and learned lots of rhymes and jingles. He could count up to ten and loved reciting the jingles about five little froggies or ten little mice. There was a toy telephone for imaginative play and to help them to learn the numbers. He became fascinated by the telephone at home, and Val explained to him that it was not a toy and he mustn't play around with it. She did allow him, however, to dial his gran's number – her own mother, not Sam's! – and speak to her.

'You dial nine three times – nine-nine-nine – to ring the policeman, Mummy,' he told her, 'or to get an ambulance if somebody is poorly.'

'Yes, that's right, love,' she said, 'but don't do it here, there's a good boy. We don't need a policeman and nobody's poorly.'

She was pleased, though, at the way he was learning basic facts, like saying his address and birth date and recognizing his own name from a card. He seemed to have a very good memory.

Val had been relieved when Cissie phoned to say that the problem with Jack had been solved, that Walter had gone to meet him instead of Cissie and sent him packing.

'Walter was really nice about it,' Cissie told her friend. 'I thought he'd go mad and want to know what I'd got up to in

Blackpool. I don't know if he suspected that I'd . . . you know
. . . done that with Jack, but he didn't ask, thank goodness.
Anyroad, from what I can gather he sent him off with a flea in
his ear. He gave him the ten pounds, though, to get rid of him.
He said – Walter, I mean – that he felt sorry for him, seeing
that he was down on his luck, and we've got everything we
want, a nice home and a family, and we're very happy an' all.'

'You're lucky you came out of it so well,' said Val. 'You'd
better be on your best behaviour now – mind your P's and Q's.'

'Oh, I shall; don't worry. I've learnt my lesson. Now, tell
me how you're going on with the shop, and Russell and little
Lucy . . .'

Cissie was certainly being a model wife. Walter could
scarcely believe the change in her. She was even-tempered and
agreeable, doing all she could to please him. He knew that a
great weight had been lifted from her mind. He told himself
that there was no point in worrying about what had gone on
in Blackpool. He had ended up with Cissie, whom he had
always loved, despite her frivolity and occasional truculence.
She was a handful at times but she was his wife, for better or
worse and, as far as he was concerned, life at that moment
could not be better.

The nights were longer, the days shorter and the weather was
turning colder. Curtains were drawn by five o'clock as families
settled down for a cosy evening by the fire with the radio or
television or a good book.

It was also the time for partying and merry-making for those
who were so inclined, and the Changing Seasons venue at
Grundy's was doing well, better than Phil and Janice had dared
to hope.

They put on special meals for Halloween and Bonfire Night
including pumpkin soup, Lancashire hot pot with tender lamb
chops, traditional roast beef and Yorkshire pudding, bangers
and mash, toad-in-the-hole, treacle tart, ginger pudding and
parkin served as a pudding with fresh cream.

They were planning a special Christmas meal for each evening
of the week before Christmas, and by the beginning of December
this was booking up quickly. Christmas Day would be on a

Monday, and as they always closed on Sunday they intended to take a longish break and reopen on 28 December. They knew they would be glad of a rest when they closed on 23 December and began preparing for their own Christmas celebrations.

All was going well at Walker and Wyatt's Sports Gear. The scene of snow-clad mountains with fir trees and skiers was a draw for window shoppers from early December. And not just for window shoppers. Many came in to choose items of clothing for husbands and wives, sons and daughters who were keen fell walkers or climbers. Or there were those who just liked something bright to wear during the winter. Fleecy lined jackets, colourful anoraks, striped scarves, gaily patterned woolly hats and sweaters; there was something to suit every taste and every pocket.

The football supporters' scarves were going well, as were the range of children's football strips. There was a run on boxed games, too: Monopoly, Scrabble, draughts and chess sets, ranging from reasonably priced ones to more exclusive and expensive. (Janice had bought one of these for her brother who would be coming to help out again at Christmas.) There were the ever-popular Snakes and Ladders, Ludo and Tiddly Winks, sets of playing cards, dartboards and dominoes. Val was a little concerned that they might be encroaching on the toyshops or the department stores who sold similar products, but Sam assured her that all was fair in the retail trade, especially at Christmas.

They would stay open quite late on Saturday, 23 December, the last shopping day, and then take three days' break.

'It's my parents' turn to entertain us on Christmas Day,' Val told her husband one evening in mid-December. 'Mum would like us to stay overnight if possible. Or would that cause trouble with your parents – well, your mother, I mean – if we don't stay with them?'

'I don't see why it should,' said Sam. 'Anyway, you know that a little of Russell goes a long way with my mother, although I think she's mellowing slightly towards him now. And they'll be busy entertaining Jonathan and Thelma and Rosemary on Christmas Day.'

'Yes, so they will. Thelma says she's feeling very tired with this pregnancy, far more than she was with Rosemary. Do you think she might be having twins?'

'How should I know?' Sam laughed. 'We can pop over and see them, and my parents, the Sunday before Christmas if you like. Just a flying visit to take the presents. Then we'll have a quiet Christmas Eve before we go to your parents' on Christmas Day. OK?'

'Yes, that sounds fine. Perhaps we could call and see Cissie and Walter as well . . . And how do you feel about having your mum and dad here for New Year's Day, and to stay overnight maybe? They've only been for the day so far, and I really think we should make the effort. Or . . . will the shop be open?'

'No, not on New Year's Day. Colin and I have decided to have two days' break. Neither of us is keen on all this sales fever, though we have to go along with it to a certain extent. There's so much to learn about the retail trade; all sorts of things we knew very little about. For instance, as soon we're into the New Year we shall have to start thinking about spring and summer sports. Tennis and cricket, and then there's bowls for those who are rather more mature, women as well as men . . .'

'Let's get Christmas over first!' said Val. 'But I must admit, I love thinking up new ideas. I get really engrossed in those sports catalogues, Sam. I never thought it would be so interesting.'

'And you're doing a grand job,' said Sam. 'I'm sure we made the right decision in coming here . . . Now, are you sure you want to cope with my mother and father at New Year?'

'Of course I am, especially as we won't be seeing them on Christmas Day. I don't think we'll have a turkey, though. Everyone will have had enough turkey by New Year. I'll think of something different, possibly a nice piece of pork loin . . .'

'Dad likes roast beef and Yorkshire pudding,' said Sam.

'I know, he's a true Yorkshireman! But I think I'll do pork and sage and onion and apple sauce. And what about the pudding?'

Sam laughed. 'Don't worry about it now. You've plenty of time to sort it all out.'

'Yes, so I have, but I want to get it just right. You know how critical your mother is. I always feel as though she's giving me marks out of twenty!'

'She's not as bad as she was. The last time I spoke to her on the phone she said how much she was missing us all.'

'Well, we'll make them very welcome. They'd better have our bedroom, and we'll share with the children. We really could do with a bigger house, Sam, then we'd have a guest room . . .'

'All in good time, love,' he said. 'We had to find somewhere quite quickly, you know, and this will do for us for a while.'

Val imagined the same sort of conversation going on in households all over the country. Which parents do we see on Christmas Day this year? Yours or mine? And what about Auntie Ethel? We can't leave her on her own . . . What shall we buy for your mother? We bought her a cashmere scarf last year and I don't think she liked the colour . . . We must think of something different for the menfolk; not socks and hankies again . . .

Val found it all exciting, though. She loved to see the first Christmas trees appearing in front windows, in shops and in the town square, the coloured lights along the Stray shining out into the darkness and the shop windows with tempting gifts for youngsters and for those who were older. The window at Walker and Wyatt's was as attractive as any in the town, and Val was happy to be sharing in this new venture.

Cissie and Walter were also discussing whose turn it was this year.

'We were with your parents last year, Walter,' she told him. 'Don't you remember the remark my mother made about the stuffing? Was it homemade, indeed!'

'No, I can't say I do,' replied Walter, 'but I agree that it's your parents' turn this year.'

Cissie grimaced. 'I shall have to lend a hand in the kitchen or else Mam will play at being a martyr. And I bet her stuffing will be out of a packet an' all!'

Walter laughed. 'What a palaver it all is! Why don't we all go out to a restaurant and let somebody else do the cooking?'

'Because Christmas is the time for families to be together, or so they say,' replied Cissie. 'You stay at home and cook an enormous meal: turkey and sprouts and pudding, and there's crackers and fancy hats, and the queen's speech, then the men fall asleep in front of the telly and the women do the washing-up. Nobody ever thinks of going out on Christmas Day. The restaurants are closed, anyroad. Janice and Phil wouldn't dream of opening on Christmas Day.'

'Yes, I suppose so,' said Walter, 'and I reckon that's the way it'll always be. Frayed tempers and screaming kids, and you wish everybody'd clear off home and leave you alone. But it's all jolly good fun, isn't it?' Walter raised his eyebrows and looked heavenwards.

'Of course it is,' said Cissie. 'The kids enjoy it an' I suppose that's all that matters. It's Holly's birthday an' all. Can you believe she'll be four this year? Paul will be reminding us that it's Jesus's birthday on Christmas Day. He's a shepherd this year, our Paul . . .'

As Cissie had said, Grundy's was closed for the Christmas period. They reopened for a couple of days and evenings midweek before closing again for the New Year period. There were plenty of hotels and bars in the vicinity where folks could do their merry-making. Families such as theirs with children to consider usually celebrated the coming of the new year more quietly in their own homes.

And so it was with Janice and Phil. On New Year's Eve, however, they were pleased to have Val and Sam with them to enjoy supper together and to see in the new year.

Sam's parents had travelled from Halifax on the last day of the old year, and said they would be willing to babysit if Val and Sam wanted to go out. So they were able to accept their friends' invitation to join them for a quiet celebration.

'So how was your Christmas?' Val asked Janice and Phil when they were all seated round the fire with a glass of sherry. 'I expect you would be glad of the rest when the restaurant closed?'

'We certainly were. We had a quiet Christmas Day on our own, as we did last year, then we went to see Phil's parents on Boxing Day. My dad and Norma came on Wednesday and stayed overnight. We opened as usual on Thursday, and they had a good day looking round the shops and the gardens before they drove back. It was good to see them again.'

'And what about Ian? Is he here helping out as usual?'

'Yes, he's a great help,' replied Phil. 'He's getting very proficient at his job. He came almost as soon as the college finished and he'll go back the middle of next week.'

'Of course, we are not the only attraction,' said Janice with a smile. 'Sophie has been helping here as well and they've spent most of their spare time together. They're out tonight with a group of Sophie's old school friends and their boyfriends.'

'So it's all on again with Sophie?' asked Val.

'Very much so,' replied Janice. 'They split up for a while – she had someone at college and Ian was friendly with Alison, that girl from Blackpool that I told you about. But it didn't last very long. We didn't ask any questions – Ian's quite secretive about his private life! But I rather think she was too hot to handle. We like Sophie, don't we, Phil? They seem right together, somehow.'

'Yes, she's a nice lass,' said Phil, 'but I keep telling you, Janice, it's too soon for them to make up their minds. They're very young, and Sophie has another year and a half to do at college.'

'And I keep telling you, Phil, that I was very sure when I met you that you were the one I wanted.'

'And you finally caught me, didn't you?' Phil laughed. 'Only joking, love! I was pretty sure as well about you. I would be pleased if Ian and Sophie stayed together but we'll just have to wait and see.'

'It was the same with Val and me,' said Sam. 'We knew, didn't we, love?'

Val nodded happily. 'I was worried about what Sam's family would say, though, with me being just an office girl. But they finally accepted me, didn't they, Sam?'

'I should say so! Nobody knows better than I do what a tyrant my mother can be. But Val's got round her. She even offered to babysit tonight.'

'Only when they're both tucked up in bed,' added Val. 'I can't imagine Beatrice changing a nappy.'

'Beatrice, is that what you call her?' asked Janice.

'Good heavens, no! I wouldn't dare. I never knew what to call her, but I call her Gran now we've got the children.'

'And how is Cissie?' asked Janice. 'Have you seen her lately?'

'Yes, we called to see them just before Christmas when we took the presents to everyone. She and Walter seem very happy together after their little crisis.'

Val had never been one to gossip, but she had told Janice about the reappearance of Jack Broadbent and the trauma it had caused Cissie.

'Yes, I always thought she changed her mind very quickly about Walter,' said Janice. 'I hadn't realized it had gone so far with that Jack fellow she met.'

'She didn't want to be the odd one out,' said Val. 'I'd met Sam and you'd met Phil . . . and then Jack came along and I suppose Cissie just got carried away. She's rather insecure, you know. She was really upset at first about us moving here and I know she'd love to be with us tonight.'

'Let's ring her, then,' said Janice, 'and wish them a happy new year. Do you think they'll be at home?'

'I should imagine so,' said Val. 'It's worth a try, isn't it?'

'We'll have our supper first,' said Janice. 'It's all ready, then we'll give them a ring.'

Val helped Janice to bring in the food from the kitchen. Fresh salmon sandwiches, vol-au-vents – one of Janice's specialities – and the inevitable Christmas cake. This was Janice's version – a lighter cake with glacé cherries, stem ginger, pineapple and golden syrup – a change from the usual darker fruit cake. They dined with plates on their knees around the fire, and after coffee and mints and another glass of sherry it was half-past eleven.

'We'll ring before midnight,' said Janice. 'They may well have friends round, like we have.'

The telephone was in the living room, and when Janice had dialled it was Cissie who answered. The others could hear her cry of delight.

'Janice! Oh, how lovely to hear from you . . .'

'Val and Sam are with us. We wish you were here, too.'

'Oh, so do I! We've got our parents here, Walter's and mine, just imagine that!' Cissie lowered her voice. 'Actually, it's all going well. The season of goodwill an' all that. Walter and me were both only children, you know, so it's all up to us. Thanks for the pressies; Holly loved her diamond tiara! And Paul's enjoying his new Enid Blyton book; he can read quite a bit on his own now. They'll both be sending you thank-you letters . . . You said Val's there? Can I speak to her an' all?'

New Year greetings were exchanged all round before the six of them promised to meet up early in 1962.

They enjoyed a last drink as the hands of the clock moved round to twelve, and in the distance they could hear the ringing of church bells. After hugs and kisses and seasonal greetings, Val and Sam set off to walk the short distance home.

'I expect Mother and Father will have gone to bed,' said Sam, 'but I didn't want to be too late, just in case either of the children wake up.' They stopped by their gate and exchanged a loving kiss.

'A new year in our new home,' said Sam. 'Happy New Year, darling . . .'

TWENTY-FOUR

'That was a really lovely meal, Valerie,' said Beatrice on New Year's Day. 'Congratulations, my dear. I really believe that was the best meal you've ever cooked for us.'

'Thank you,' said Val, pleased at her mother-in-law's remark but smiling to herself at the slight sting in the tail. Had her previous efforts not come up to scratch? 'I'm glad you enjoyed it.'

They had had their dinner at midday so that the children could take part as well. Val, too, was pleased at the way the pork had turned out, sweet and succulent but crispy and nicely browned on the outside. And her pear and apple crumble had proved to be a winner.

Now there was a mountain of washing up to do, but Sam persuaded her to leave it until later in the day when they would tackle it together. Val knew that Beatrice would not offer to help, neither would she expect her to.

No meal was complete to Joshua without a cup of tea to follow. Then it was he who suggested that they take a walk to work off the excesses of a hearty meal.

'No, you're not staying behind to wash up,' said Sam to Val. 'I've told you, it will keep. It's a cold day, though, so you must wrap up warmly.'

'I think Lucy would be better in the big pram,' said Val, 'rather than her pushchair. She can sit up and see what's going on.'

'I won't come with you,' said Beatrice, although no one had really thought that she would. 'I have a slight touch of indigestion.'

'Oh dear! I hope it wasn't the pork,' said Val.

'No, of course it wasn't,' said Beatrice. 'I've had this pain a few times lately but a couple of Rennies usually takes it off.'

'I've told you to see the doctor,' said Joshua.

'I will if it gets any worse, but I keep telling you it's only indigestion.'

'All right, if you say so . . .'

'I'm not too sure about Russell going out today,' said Val. 'He's got a real sniffle and he keeps coughing.'

'Don't pamper him, Val,' said Sam. 'He'll come to no harm. You want to come for a walk with us, don't you, Russell?'

Russell looked up from the hearth rug where he was playing with the farm set he had been given for Christmas, sorting out the sheep, cows and pigs, horses and tiny ducks and hens, and arranging them in their various homes. There were barns and stables and pigsties, and stretches of green fields. It kept him happily occupied for hours on end.

'No, don't want to,' he said briefly before turning back to his game.

Sam laughed. 'Well, that was straight from the horse's mouth! Perhaps it would be better to leave him, seeing that he's playing happily, and I suppose he is a little off-colour, Val.'

'Yes; I'll give him some junior aspirin later with a drink of hot lemon and honey. But it's best to be occupied when you've got a cold; it takes your mind off it.'

Sam looked at Russell and then at his mother. 'Mum . . .' he began tentatively, '. . . we think it would be better to leave Russell here, if it's all right with you? He won't be any trouble because he's engrossed with his farm. Is that OK? We won't be very long, but I agree with Dad that we all need some fresh air.'

'Yes . . . yes, of course that's all right,' Beatrice answered a trifle unsurely but she couldn't very well say no. 'You'll stay with Grandma, won't you, Russell, while Mummy and Daddy and Grandpa go for a walk?' Her voice was a little strained as she tried to speak cheerfully to her grandson.

He glanced up and nodded. 'Yes, all right,' he said, then turned back to his animals.

'You'll be OK will you, Mother?' said Sam. 'Has your pain gone off?'

'Yes, it's receding,' said Beatrice. 'I shall read the paper and Valerie's magazine . . . and keep an eye on Russell.'

The all departed a few moments later when Lucy had been wrapped in her warm fleecy coat and bonnet with a blanket to cover her legs.

'Bye-bye, Russell,' she called, waving her hand.

'Bye,' he said, scarcely looking up.

'Now be a good boy for Grandma,' said Val.

He nodded. 'I'm a good boy now,' he murmured to himself.

It seemed very quiet when they had all gone. Beatrice leaned back in the comfortable armchair, feeling glad of a bit of peace and quiet. She looked down at Russell playing so contentedly with his farm. He really was a bonny little lad with his mop of golden gingery hair and his chubby, rosy-cheeked face, although he did look a little peaky today. He didn't look like either Samuel or Valerie, but then it wasn't likely that he would. She recalled that she had been very much against the idea of his adoption, to her slight feeling of remorse now. She had never been able to take to him as she had done to darling Rosemary and lovely little Lucy. He had been so very troublesome, too, and she knew that Valerie had despaired of him at times. But now she found herself looking more fondly at him. He turned round as if aware of her glance and smiled at her.

'Good boy, Russell,' she said quietly.

She was still aware of the pain in the region of her chest and abdomen. Heartburn, she supposed. The pork that Valerie had cooked was delicious but maybe a little rich. She rummaged in her bag and took a couple more Rennies. She chewed them up then kept very still. But it was getting worse; a real stabbing pain now that seemed to be travelling all around. She gave an involuntary gasp and Russell looked up at her.

'What's a matter, Gran?' he said. 'Have you got a pain?'

'Yes, just a little one, dear,' she said, 'but it'll go soon.'

But it didn't go away and she cried out again, clutching at her stomach and rocking back and forth.

'Grandma poorly,' said Russell. He got up, went over to her and touched her hand. She had her eyes closed now but she had stopped making a noise. A sudden thought came into his head.

'Get the doctor,' he said more to himself than to her. 'Ring nine-nine-nine.'

He ran into the hall where the big black telephone stood on a little table. He climbed up on to a chair at the side and lifted up the phone. It was heavier than the one at playgroup but Mummy had shown him how to use it. He had rung his gran's number – not this gran, though, the other one. Very carefully

now, he put it to his ear, then he put his finger into the hole
where the number nine was and turned it round three times. He
heard it ringing, then a lady's voice said something he didn't
understand.

Then, 'Who is there?' she asked.

'It's me, Russell James Walker,' he said, 'and my gran's
poorly. She's got a pain.'

'Oh, I see, and where are you, Russell?' asked the lady.

'I'm at my house . . .'

'And where is that? Do you know your address . . . where
you live?'

'Number four, Sycamore Avenue, Harrogate,' he replied.
Mummy had told him he must remember his address in case
he ever got lost.

'And are you on your own with Grandma?'

'Yes, Mummy and Daddy and Grandpa and Lucy went for
a walk. Then Grandma had a pain.'

'Now don't worry, Russell. We'll send an ambulance as fast
as we can. Will you be able to open the door?'

'Don't know . . .'

'Well, I'm sure they'll get in somehow . . . How old are you,
Russell?'

'I'm three and a bit.'

'Well, you're a very clever little boy. What is Grandma doing
now?'

'I think she's asleep. She's got her eyes closed. She's not
crying now.'

'OK, Russell. Somebody will be there soon. Bye-bye, dear.'

'Bye-bye, lady . . .'

He went back to his gran, who still had her eyes closed.
'Ambulance coming, Gran,' he said. He touched her hand but
she didn't answer.

He went over to the window, where he climbed on to the
settee and looked out.

'Snowing,' he said as the first flakes began to fall from
the leaden sky.

'I do believe it's snowing,' said Sam when they had walked
along the Stray, almost to the town. 'It's certainly been cold

enough but I thought it might keep off for a while. Do you want to turn back?'

'No, a bit of snow won't hurt us,' said Joshua. 'I want to see your window display before you change it.'

But the snow was falling fast now, large, feathery flakes that stuck to their clothing and were already starting to lie on the ground.

'I really think we should go back,' said Val.

'OK, happen you're right,' said Joshua. 'Back to a nice warm house, eh?'

They retraced their steps, walking quickly, and Val pulled up the pram hood to protect Lucy.

'There's an ambulance in your avenue, Sam,' said Joshua as they drew nearer. 'I wonder who it is?' Then, 'Good God!' he exclaimed. 'It's at your house. What's going on?'

They dashed up the path to see an ambulance man knocking at the door. 'We had a call,' he said. 'A little boy said his gran was poorly but we can't get in. My mate's just gone round to the back.'

'My God, Beatrice!' said Joshua as Sam quickly opened the door and they all went inside.

Russell rushed to meet them. 'Grandma poorly,' he said. 'I rang nine-nine-nine but I can't open the door.'

Val hugged him. 'Never mind, Russell. The men are here now. You're a very clever boy.'

Joshua hurried over to his wife. He knelt at her side and held her hand. 'Beattie,' he said. 'Come on, Beattie, speak to me.'

'Just a minute, sir,' said the ambulance man. He took hold of her wrist. 'There's a pulse,' he said as her eyelids started to flutter. 'Looks like a heart attack. Come on, Bill. Let's get moving.'

Beatrice was barely conscious as she was lifted on to a stretcher, an oxygen mask fitted on her face, then the ambulance men carried her out.

'I'll go with her, of course,' said Joshua, 'and I'll let you know when there's any news . . . Say a little prayer for her, won't you? I don't know if it does any good, but we have to trust that He's listening.'

'Grandma poorly,' said Russell, sounding a little frightened.

'She'll soon be better,' said Joshua, giving the little boy a hug. 'And what a clever boy you were, ringing for an ambulance.' He ruffled his hair. 'You're a grand little lad.'

The ambulance drove away and Val and Sam looked at one another.

'What a shock,' said Val. 'Perhaps we shouldn't have gone and left her. She was complaining of a pain.'

Sam shook his head. 'I was sure it was indigestion like she said. She's been having twinges for a while but it always goes off. And Mother loves her food, you know. She certainly enjoyed the dinner you made.'

'I hope it wasn't the pork that caused it.'

'Not if it's a heart attack, and I rather think it is. We have our little boy to thank that they got here in time.'

Russell was looking a little woebegone. 'Grandma get better?' he asked.

'Yes, of course she will,' said Sam. 'Now, Mummy and I are going to do the washing up . . . it'll take our minds off it all,' he said to Val. 'You play with your farm set and we'll see if there's a nice programme for you to watch before you have your tea.'

Russell rubbed his tummy. 'Full up,' he said.

Val laughed. 'Well, perhaps you'll be able to eat some ice cream; you deserve it for helping Grandma.'

Lucy was staring around wide-eyed, wondering what was going on. 'And I'm sure Lucy's ready for a nap,' said Val. 'Come along, little lady; it's all very confusing, isn't it?'

They did not speak much as they washed and put away the mountain of pots. Val could tell that Sam was very concerned.

'Your mother's a strong lady,' she said, 'in every way. A strong personality . . .'

'That we know only too well!' said Sam with a wry smile.

'That's true,' agreed Val, 'but she has a strong constitution as well; she's not always complaining of feeling ill as some women do. I'm sure she'll be all right.'

Joshua rang from the hospital a few hours later. 'Your mother's fully conscious now,' he said to Sam.

'Thank God!' breathed Sam.

'Yes, it was a heart attack but luckily only a minor one.

That's what the pains were that she was having but we never suspected that it was her heart. Anyway, she'll be OK as far as they can tell, but she'll have to stay in hospital for a day or two. There's just one problem, Sam. She's in Harrogate, not in Halifax, and they don't want to move her. Can you put me up – or, I should say put up with me! – for a day or two?'

'Of course we can, Dad, for as long as you like, although I hope for Mother's sake that it won't be too long. When are visiting hours?'

'Two till four, then six till eight in the evening. Don't come today, though, Sam; I don't want her to get too excited. But perhaps you could all go tomorrow afternoon; I know she's anxious to see Russell.'

'Yes, we'll be there,' said Sam. 'Will you be coming back here tonight?'

'Yes, I'll stay for visiting hours then I'll get a taxi back. So I'll see you later. You've got a grand little family there, you know.'

Val was relieved at the news. She hadn't realized she had become so fond of her mother-in-law.

'Grandma's getting better,' she told Russell, 'and we'll be going to see her tomorrow.'

It had been an exhausting day, and it was an early bedtime for all of them when Joshua had returned from the hospital.

Fortunately the store was closed the following day. Sam and Colin had agreed to have a two-day break before the New Year sales commenced. They had a quick lunch then set off in Sam's car for the hospital.

'What shall we take for Grandma?' Val had asked Joshua.

'Nothing,' he replied. 'Just ourselves. She has everything she needs and she's in very good hands.'

'We must take her nightdress, though, and her slippers and dressing gown,' said Val. 'She was taken off in a hurry and I know she won't like those awful hospital gowns. And there's that bed jacket we bought for her at Christmas. That's turned out to be a useful present, hasn't it?'

Beatrice was sitting up in bed, propped up by two pillows. She was in a private room. Joshua had known that this was what she would prefer and had made the necessary arrangements.

Understandably, she looked a little pale and her eyes looked tired, but Val had never seen her smile so radiantly or sincerely.

They all kissed her and she said how pleased she was to see them, but it was Russell she really wanted to see.

'Where's my grand little boy?' she said as he stood back rather unsurely.

He was aware that this grandma was not always as friendly towards him as his other gran was. He went and stood closer to her. 'Are you better now, Grandma?' he asked.

'Much better, dear,' she said, 'and that's because you were such a clever boy, phoning for an ambulance.'

Val lifted him up and sat him on the bed, then Beatrice hugged him and kissed his cheek. Everybody kept saying he was a clever boy. He had remembered what they did at playgroup when they were playing at doctors, only this time it was a real doctor and ambulance, not a pretend one.

'We are all very proud of you,' said his gran, 'and somebody is coming to take your photograph. I've told the nurses all about you.'

Val and Sam looked surprised. Then Joshua said, 'Yes, that's right. I didn't tell you last night because it wasn't certain then. There's someone coming from the local newspaper. The doctor and nurses thought it was such a lovely story about a little boy saving his grandma's life . . . She wouldn't have died,' he added quietly, 'at least, we hope not, but they'll make a good story of it, you can be sure.'

In a few moments, sure enough, a photographer and a reporter came. First of all a photo was taken of Beatrice and Russell, her arm around him as she looked at him affectionately. Then a photo of the whole family, the six of them grouped closely around the bed. Val had made sure that Beatrice was wearing her new fleecy bed jacket to cover the austere hospital nightdress.

The story made headlines in the local paper the following day. *Little Boy Saves Grandma's Life*.

Russell was thrilled to see his photo, and Lucy's as well, and all of them. But he wasn't sure what all the fuss was about. It was just something they had been told about at playgroup and he had remembered what to do.

The story told how three-year-old Russell Walker had had the presence of mind to dial 999 when his grandma became ill. There was some family information as well; that Joshua, Beatrice's husband, was the owner of Walker's mill in Halifax, and their son, Samuel, was co-owner of a sports shop in Harrogate.

'We are very proud of our little Russell,' said Beatrice in the report. 'He's a clever boy and a great blessing to our family. He's a little champion!'

'What a lovely thing your mother said, about Russell being a blessing to all our family,' Val commented as she and Sam reread the report in the newspaper later that evening, The children were in bed and Joshua was visiting his wife again. Val's eyes were moist with tears. 'She didn't always think like that, did she?'

'No, she certainly didn't,' agreed Sam. 'She thought we were making a big mistake in adopting him. But it was our decision and there was no way she was going to dissuade us.'

'No . . .' said Val, '. . . but I must admit that I wondered at first if we might have been too hasty. Russell was such a difficult child, so naughty and disobedient and . . . I don't like saying this, but I sometimes felt that I couldn't love him the way that I knew I should. And I wondered if it might have been different if I'd actually given birth to him. There had never been that . . . bonding, you know, that you get with your own child. I felt that with Lucy straight away.'

'Yes, and I know it was more difficult with Russell when Lucy arrived, and so unexpectedly, too,' said Sam. 'But she was a different kettle of fish right from the start, wasn't she? Such a good little child. I'm not surprised you felt that way about Russell. But don't feel guilty about it now, darling. I had my moments, too, of wondering if we'd done the right thing. But he's turned out to be a grand little lad. You don't have any doubts now, do you?'

'No, of course not! I can't imagine life without our Russell. As your mother says, he's a little champion!'